It began as rumors, dread whisperings
on the autumn wind.

Now, as the Companions fight to save
a beautiful princess, all their fears have
come true.

The forces of darkness roam the land,
monsters haunt the roads, and stars fall
from the sky.

But the worst is yet to come, and it's set
to strike at the very heart of the
Companions in . . .

Night of the Dragons

CHRONICLES

BY MARGARET WEIS & TRACY HICKMAN

A RUMOR OF DRAGONS

NIGHT OF THE DRAGONS

THE NIGHTMARE LANDS
(AVAILABLE OCTOBER 2003)

TO THE GATES OF PALANTHAS
(AVAILABLE DECEMBER 2003)

HOPE'S FLAME
(AVAILABLE JANUARY 2004)

A DAWN OF DRAGONS
(AVAILABLE MARCH 2004)

CHRONICLES

PART
2

NIGHT OF THE DRAGONS

MARGARET WEIS & TRACY HICKMAN

COVER ART
Glen Angus

INTERIOR ART
Vinod Rams

NIGHT OF THE DRAGONS

©2003 Wizards of the Coast, Inc.

All characters in this book are fictitious. Any resemblance to actual persons, living or dead, is purely coincidental.

This book is protected under the copyright laws of the United States of America. Any reproduction or unauthorized use of the material or artwork contained herein is prohibited without the express written permission of Wizards of the Coast, Inc.

Distributed in the United States by Holtzbrinck Publishing. Distributed in Canada by Fenn Ltd.

Distributed to the hobby, toy, and comic trade in the United States and Canada by regional distributors.

Distributed worldwide by Wizards of the Coast, Inc. and regional distributors.

DRAGONLANCE and the Wizards of the Coast logo are registered trademarks of Wizards of the Coast, Inc., a subsidiary of Hasbro, Inc.

All Wizards of the Coast characters, character names, and the distinctive likenesses thereof are trademarks of Wizards of the Coast, Inc.

Printed in the U.S.A.

The sale of this book without its cover has not been authorized by the publisher. If you purchased this book without a cover, you should be aware that neither the author nor the publisher has received payment for this "stripped book."

Cover art by Glen Angus
First Printing: June 2003
Library of Congress Catalog Card Number: 2002114093

9 8 7 6 5 4 3 2 1

US ISBN: 0-7869-3090-X
UK ISBN: 0-7869-3091-8
620-86020-001-EN

U.S., CANADA,
ASIA, PACIFIC, & LATIN AMERICA
Wizards of the Coast, Inc.
P.O. Box 707
Renton, WA 98057-0707
+1-800-324-6496

EUROPEAN HEADQUARTERS
Wizards of the Coast, Belgium
T. Hosfveld 6d
1702 Groot-Bijgaarden
Belgium
+322 457 3350

Visit our web site at **www.wizards.com**

To Laura, the true Laurana
—Tracy Raye Hickman

To my children, David and Elizabeth Baldwin, for their
courage and support
—Margaret Weis

The Lands of Abanasinia

TABLE OF CONTENTS

The sacrifice.
The twice-dead city.

1

Despair blacker than the darkness blinded Tanis. It was my plan, the only way we had a chance to get out of here alive, he thought. It was sound, it should have worked! What went wrong? Raistlin—could he have betrayed us? No! Tanis clenched his fist. No! The mage was distant, unlikable, impossible to understand, yes, but he was loyal to them, Tanis would swear it. Where was Raistlin? Dead, perhaps. Not that it mattered. They would all be dead.

"Tanis"—the half-elf felt a firm grasp on his arm and recognized Sturm's deep voice—"I know what you're thinking. We have no choice. We're running out of time. This is our only chance to get the Disks. We won't get another."

"I'm going to look," Tanis said. He climbed past the kender and peered through the grate. It was dark, magically dark. Tanis put his head in his hand and tried to think. Sturm was right: time was running out. Yet how could he trust the knight's judgement? Sturm wanted to fight the dragon! Tanis crawled back down the ladder. "We're going," he said. Suddenly all he wanted to do was get this over with, then they could go home. Home to Solace. "No, Tas." He grabbed hold of the kender and dragged him back down the ladder. "The fighters go first— Sturm and Caramon. Then the rest."

But the knight was already shoving past him eagerly, his sword clanking against his thigh.

"We're always last!" Tasslehoff sniffed, shoving the dwarf along. Flint climbed the ladder slowly, his knees creaking. "Hurry up!" Tas said. "I hope nothing happens before we get there. I've never talked to a dragon."

"I'll bet the dragon's never talked to a kender either!" The dwarf snorted. "You realize, you hare-brain, that we're probably going to die. Tanis knows, I could tell by his voice."

Tas paused, clinging to the ladder while Sturm slowly pushed on the grating. "You know, Flint," the kender said seriously, "my people don't fear death. In a way, we look forward to it, the last big adventure. But I think I'd feel badly about leaving this life. I'd miss my things"—he patted his pouches—"and my maps, and you and Tanis. Unless," he added brightly, "we all go to the same place when we die."

Flint had a sudden vision of the happy-go-lucky kender lying cold and dead. He felt a lump of pain in his chest and was thankful for the concealing darkness. Clearing his throat, he said huskily, "If you think I'm going to share my afterlife with a bunch of kender, you're crazier than Raistlin. Come on!"

Sturm carefully lifted the grating and shoved it to one side. It scraped over the floor, causing him to grit his teeth. He heaved himself up easily. Turning, he bent down to help Caramon who was having trouble squeezing his body and his clanking arsenal through the shaft.

"In the name of Istar, be quiet!" Sturm hissed.

"I'm trying," Caramon muttered, finally climbing over the edge. Sturm gave his hand to Goldmoon. Last came Tas, delighted that nobody had done anything exciting in his absence.

"We've got to have light," Sturm said.

"Light?" replied a voice as cold and dark as winter midnight. "Yes, let us have light."

The darkness fled instantly. The companions saw they were in a huge domed chamber that soared hundreds of feet into the air. Cold gray light filtered into the room through a crack in the ceiling, shining on a large altar in the center of the circular room. On the floor surrounding the altar were masses of jewels, coins, and other treasures of the dead city. The jewels did not gleam. The gold did not glitter. The dim light illuminated nothing, nothing except a black dragon perched on top of the pedestal like some huge beast of prey.

"Feeling betrayed?" the dragon asked in conversational tones.

"The mage betrayed us! Where is he? Serving you?" Sturm cried fiercely, drawing his sword and taking a step forward.

"Stand back, foul Knight of Solamnia. Stand back or your magic-user will use his magic no more!" The dragon snaked her great neck down and stared at them with gleaming red eyes. Then, slowly and delicately, she lifted one clawed foot. Lying beneath it, on the pedestal, was Raistlin.

"Raist!" Caramon roared and lunged for the altar.

"Stop, fool!" the dragon hissed. She rested one pointed claw lightly on the mage's abdomen. With a great effort, Raistlin moved his head to look at his brother with his strange golden eyes. He made a weak gesture and Caramon halted. Tanis saw something move on the floor beneath the altar. It was Bupu, huddled among the riches, too afraid even to whimper. The Staff of Magius lay next to her.

"Move one step closer and I will impale this shriveled human upon the altar with my claw."

Caramon's face flushed a deep, ugly red. "Let him go!" he shouted. "Your fight is with me."

"My fight is with none of you," the dragon said, lazily moving its wings. Raistlin flinched as the dragon's clawed foot shifted slightly, teasingly, digging her claw into his flesh. The mage's metallic skin glistened with sweat. He drew a deep, ragged breath. "Don't even twitch, mage," the dragon sneered. "We speak the same language, remember? One word of a spell and your friends' carcasses will be used to feed the gully dwarves!"

Raistlin's eyes closed as in exhaustion. But Tanis could see the mage's hands clench and unclench, and he knew Raistlin was preparing one final spell. It would be his last—by the time he cast it the dragon would kill him. But it might give Riverwind a chance to reach the Disks and get out alive with Goldmoon. Tanis edged toward the Plainsman.

"As I was saying," the dragon continued smoothly. "I do not choose to fight any of you. How you have escaped my wrath so far, I do not understand. Still, you are here. And you return to me that which was stolen. Yes, Lady of Que-shu, I see you hold the blue crystal staff. Bring it to me."

Tanis hissed one word to Goldmoon—"Stall!" But, looking at her cool marble face, he wondered if she heard him or if she even heard the dragon. She seemed to be listening to other words, other voices.

"Obey me." The dragon lowered her head menacingly. "Obey me or the mage dies. And after him—the knight. And then the half-elf. And so on—one after the other, until you, Lady of Que-shu, are the last survivor. Then you will bring me the staff and you will beg me to be merciful."

Goldmoon bowed her head in submission. Gently pushing Riverwind away with her hand, she turned to Tanis and clasped the half-elf in a loving embrace. "Farewell, my friend," she said loudly, laying her cheek against his. Her voice dropped to a whisper. "I know what I must do. I am going to take the staff to the dragon and—"

"No!" Tanis said fiercely. "It won't matter. The dragon intends to kill us anyway."

"Listen to me!" Goldmoon's nails dug into Tanis's arm. "Stay with Riverwind, Tanis. Do not let him try to stop me."

"And if *I* tried to stop you?" Tanis asked gently, holding Goldmoon close in his arms.

"You won't," she said with a sweet, sad smile. "You know that each of us has a destiny to fulfill, as the Forestmaster said. Riverwind will need you. Farewell, my friend."

Goldmoon stepped back, her clear blue eyes on River-wind as though she would memorize every detail to keep with her throughout eternity. Realizing she was saying good-bye, he started to go to her.

"Riverwind," Tanis said softly. "Trust her. She trusted you, all those years. She waited while you fought the battles. Now it is you who must wait. This is her battle."

Riverwind trembled, then stood still. Tanis could see the veins swell in his neck, his jaw muscles clench. The half-elf gripped the Plainsman's arm. The tall man didn't even look at him. His eyes were on Goldmoon.

"What is this delay?" the dragon asked. "I grow bored. Come forward."

Goldmoon turned away from Riverwind. She walked past Flint and Tasslehoff. The dwarf bowed his head. Tas watched wide-eyed and solemn. Somehow this wasn't as exciting as he had imagined. For the first time in his life, the kender felt small and helpless and alone. It was a horrible, unpleasant feeling, and he thought death might be preferable.

Goldmoon stopped near Caramon, put her hand on his arm. "Don't worry," she said to the big warrior, who was staring at his brother in agony, "he'll be all right." Caramon choked and nodded. And then Goldmoon neared Sturm. Suddenly, as if the horror of the dragon was too overwhelming, she slumped forward. The knight caught her and held her.

"Come with me, Sturm," Goldmoon whispered as he put his arm around her. "You must vow to do as I command, no matter what happens. Vow on your honor as a knight of Solamnia."

Sturm hesitated. Goldmoon's eyes, calm and clear, met his. "Vow," she demanded, "or I go alone."

"I vow, lady," he said reverently. "I will obey."

Goldmoon sighed thankfully. "Walk with me. Make no threatening gesture."

Together the barbarian woman of the Plains and the knight walked toward the dragon.

Raistlin lay beneath the dragon's claw, his eyes closed, preparing himself mentally for the spell that would be his last. But the words to the spell would not form out of the turmoil in his mind. He fought to regain control.

I am wasting myself—and for what? Raistlin wondered bitterly. To get these fools out of the mess they got themselves into. They will not attack for fear of hurting me—even though they fear and despise me. It makes no sense—just as my sacrifice makes no sense. Why am I dying for them when I deserve to live more than they?

It is not for them you do this, a voice answered him. Raistlin started, trying to concentrate, to catch hold of the voice. It was a real voice, a familiar voice, but he couldn't remember whose it was or where he had heard it. All he knew was that it spoke to him in moments of great stress. The closer to death he came, the louder was the voice.

It is not for them that you make this sacrifice, the voice repeated. *It is because you cannot bear defeat! Nothing has ever defeated you, not even death itself. . . .*

Raistlin drew a deep breath and relaxed. He did not understand the words completely, just as he could not remember the voice. But now the spell came easily to his mind. *"Astol arakhkh um—"* he murmured, feeling the magic begin to course through his frail body. Then another voice broke his concentration and this voice was a living voice speaking to his mind. He opened his eyes, turned his head slowly, and stared into the chamber at his companions.

The voice came from the woman—barbarian princess of a dead tribe. Raistlin looked at Goldmoon as she walked toward him, leaning on Sturm's arm. The words in her mind had touched Raistlin's mind. He regarded the woman coldly, detachedly. His distorted vision had forever killed any physical desire the mage might have felt when he looked upon human flesh. He could not see the beauty that so captivated Tanis and his brother. His hourglass eyes saw her withering and dying. He felt no closeness, no compassion for her. He knew she pitied him—and he hated her for that—but she feared him as well. So why, then, was she speaking to him?

She was telling him to wait.

Raistlin understood. She knew what he intended and she was telling him it wasn't necessary. She had been chosen. She was the one who was going to make the sacrifice.

He watched Goldmoon with his strange golden eyes as she drew nearer and nearer, her own eyes on the dragon. He saw Sturm moving solemnly beside her, looking as ancient and noble as old Huma himself. What a perfect cat's paw Sturm made, the ideal participant in Goldmoon's sacrifice. But why had Riverwind allowed her to go? Couldn't he see this coming? Raistlin glanced quickly at Riverwind. Ah, of course! The half-elf stood by his side, looking pained and grieved, dropping words of wisdom like blood, no doubt. The barbarian was becoming as gullible as Caramon. Raistlin flicked his eyes back to Goldmoon.

She stood before the dragon now, her face pale with resolve. Next to her, Sturm appeared grave and tortured, gnawed by inner conflict. Goldmoon had probably extracted some vow of strict obedience which the knight was honor-bound to fulfill. Raistlin's lip curled in a sneer.

The dragon spoke and the mage tensed, ready for action. "Lay the staff down with the other remnants of mankind's folly," the dragon commanded Goldmoon, inclining her shining, scaled head toward the pile of treasure below the altar.

Goldmoon, overcome with dragonfear, did not move. She could do nothing but stare at the monstrous creature, trembling. Sturm, next to her, searched the treasure trove with his eyes, looking for the Disks of Mishakal, fighting to control his fear of the dragon. Sturm had not known he could be this frightened of anything. He repeated the code, "Honor is Life," over and over, and he knew it was pride alone that kept him from running away.

Goldmoon saw Sturm's hand shake, she saw the knight's face glistening with sweat. Dear goddess, she cried in her soul, grant me courage! Then Sturm nudged her. She had to say something, she realized. She had been silent too long.

"What will you give us in return for the miraculous staff?" Goldmoon asked, forcing herself to speak calmly, though her throat was parched and her tongue felt swollen.

The dragon laughed—shrill, ugly laughter. "What will I give you?" The dragon snaked her head to stare at Goldmoon. "Nothing! Nothing at all. I do not deal with thieves. Still—" The dragon reared its head back, its red eyes closed to slits. Playfully she dug her claw into Raistlin's flesh; the mage flinched, but he bore the pain without a murmur. The dragon removed the claw and held it just high enough so that they could all see the blood drip from it. "It is not inconceivable that Lord Verminaard—the Dragon Highmaster—may view favorably the fact that you surrender the staff. He may even be inclined to mercy—he is a cleric and they have strange values. But know this, Lady of Que-shu, Lord Verminaard does not need your friends. Give up the staff now and they will be spared. Force me to take it—and they will die. The mage first of all!"

Goldmoon, her spirit seemingly broken, slumped in defeat. Sturm moved close to her, appearing to console her.

"I have found the Disks," he whispered harshly. He grasped her arm, feeling her shivering with fear. "Are you resolved on this course of action, my lady?" he asked softly.

Goldmoon bowed her head. She was deathly pale but composed and calm. Tendrils of her fine silver-golden hair had escaped from the binding and fell around her face, hiding her expression from the dragon. Though she appeared defeated, she looked up at Sturm and smiled. There was both peace and sorrow in her smile, much like the smile on the marble goddess. She did not speak but Sturm had his answer. He bowed in submission.

"May my courage be equal to yours, lady," he said. "I will not fail you."

"Farewell, knight. Tell Riverwind—" Goldmoon faltered, blinking her eyes as tears filled them. Fearing her resolve might yet break, she swallowed her words and turned to face the dragon as the voice of Mishakal filled her being, answering her prayer. *Present the staff boldly!* Goldmoon, imbued with an inner strength, raised the blue crystal staff.

"We do not choose to surrender!" Goldmoon shouted, her voice echoing throughout the chamber. Moving swiftly, before the startled dragon could react, Chieftain's Daughter swung her staff one last time, striking the clawed foot poised above Raistlin.

The staff made a low ringing sound as it struck the dragon—then it shattered. A burst of pure, radiant blue light beamed from the broken staff. The light grew brighter, spreading out in concentric waves, engulfing the dragon.

Khisanth screamed in rage. The dragon was injured, terribly, mortally. She lashed out with her tail, flung her head about, and fought to escape the burning blue flame. She wanted nothing except to kill those that dared inflict such pain, but the intense blue fire relentlessly consumed her—as it consumed Goldmoon.

The Chieftain's Daughter had not dropped the staff when it shattered. She held on to the fragmented end, watching as the light grew, keeping it as close to the dragon as she could. When the blue light touched her hands she felt intense, burning pain. Staggering, she fell to her knees, still clutching the staff. She heard the dragon shrieking and roaring above her, then she could hear nothing but the ringing of the staff. The pain grew so horrible it was no longer a part of her, and she was overcome with a great weariness. I will sleep, she thought. I will sleep and when I waken, I will be where I truly belong. . . .

Sturm saw the blue light slowly destroy the dragon, then it spread along the staff to Goldmoon. He heard the ringing sound grow louder and louder until it drowned out even the screams of the dying dragon. Sturm took a step toward Goldmoon, thinking to wrench the splintered staff from her hand and drag her clear of the deadly blue flame . . . but even as he approached, he knew he could not save her.

Half-blinded by the light and deafened by the sound, the knight realized that it would take all his strength and courage to fulfill his oath—to retrieve the Disks. He tore his gaze from Goldmoon, whose face was twisted in agony and whose flesh was withering in the fire. Gritting his teeth against the pain in his head, he staggered toward the treasure pile where he had seen the Disks—hundreds of thin sheets of platinum bound together by a single ring through the top. Reaching down, he lifted them, amazed at their lightness. Then his heart almost stopped beating when a bloody hand reached up from the pile of treasure and grasped his wrist.

"Help me!"

He could not hear the voice so much as sense the thought. Grasping Raistlin's hand, he pulled the mage to his feet. Blood was visible through the red of Raistlin's robe, but he did not appear to be seriously injured—at least he could stand. But could he walk? Sturm needed help. He wondered where the others were; he couldn't see them in the brilliance. Suddenly Caramon loomed up by his side, his armor gleaming in the blue flame.

Raistlin clutched at him. "Help me find the spellbook!" he hissed.

"Who cares about that?" Caramon roared, reaching for his brother. "I'll get you out of here!"

Raistlin's mouth twisted so in fury and frustration that he could not speak. He dropped to his knees and began to search frantically through the pile of treasure. Caramon tried to draw him away, but Raistlin shoved him back with his frail hand.

And still the ringing sound pierced their ears. Sturm felt tears of pain trickle down his cheeks. Suddenly something crashed to the floor in front of the knight. The chamber ceiling was collapsing! The entire building shook around them, the ringing sound causing the pillars to tremble and the walls to crack.

Then the ringing died—and with it the dragon. Khisanth had vanished, leaving behind nothing but a pile of smoldering ash.

Sturm gasped in relief but not for long. As soon as the ringing sound ended, he could hear the sounds of the palace caving in, the cracking of the ceiling and the thuds and explosive crashes as huge stone slabs struck the floor. Then, out of the dust and noise, Tanis appeared before him. Blood trickled from a cut on the half-elf's cheek. Sturm grabbed his friend and pulled him to the altar as another chunk of ceiling plummeted near them.

"The whole city is collapsing!" Sturm yelled. "How do we get out?"

Tanis shook his head. "The only way I know is back the way we came, through that tunnel," he shouted. He ducked as another piece of ceiling crashed onto the empty altar.

"That'll be a death trap! There must be another way!"

"We'll find it," Tanis said firmly. He peered through the billowing dust. "Where are the others?" he asked. Then, turning, he saw Raistlin and Caramon. Tanis stared in horror and disgust at the mage scavenging among the treasure. Then he saw a small figure tugging Raistlin's sleeve. Bupu! Tanis made a lunge for her, nearly scaring the gully dwarf witless. She shrank back against Raistlin with a startled scream.

"We've got to get out of here!" Tanis roared. He grabbed hold of Raistlin's robes and dragged the slender young man to his feet. "Stop looting and get that gully dwarf of yours to show us the way out, or so help me, you'll die by my hands!"

Raistlin's thin lips parted in a ghastly smile as Tanis flung him back against the altar. Bupu shrieked. "Come! We go! I know way!"

"Raist," Caramon begged, "you can't find it! You'll die if we don't get out of here!"

"Very well," the mage snarled. He lifted the Staff of Magius from the altar and stood up, reaching out his arm for his brother's aid. "Bupu, show us the way," he commanded.

"Raistlin, light your staff so we can follow you." Tanis ordered. "I'm going to find the others."

"Over there," Caramon said grimly. "You're going to need help with the Plainsman."

Tanis flung his arm over his face as more stone fell, then jumped across the rubble. He found Riverwind collapsed where Goldmoon had been standing, Flint and Tasslehoff trying to get the Plainsman to his feet. There was nothing there now except a large area of blackened stone. Goldmoon had been totally consumed in the flames.

"Is he alive?" Tanis shouted.

"Yes!" Tas answered, his voice carrying shrilly above the noise. "But he won't move!"

"I'll talk to him," Tanis said. "Follow the others. We'll be there in a moment. Go on!"

Tasslehoff hesitated, but Flint, after a glance at Tanis's face, put his hand on the kender's arm. Snuffling, Tas turned and began running through the rubble with the dwarf.

Tanis knelt beside Riverwind, then the half-elf glanced up as Sturm appeared out of the gloom. "Go on," Tanis said. "You're in command now."

Sturm hesitated. A column toppled over near them, showering them in rock dust. Tanis flung his body across Riverwind's. "Go on!" he yelled at Sturm. "I'm holding you responsible!" Sturm drew a breath, laid a hand on Tanis's shoulder, then ran toward the light from Raistlin's staff.

The knight found the others huddled in a narrow hallway. The arched ceiling above them seemed to be holding together, but Sturm could hear thudding sounds above. The ground shook beneath their feet and little rivulets of water were beginning to seep through new cracks in the walls.

"Where's Tanis?" Caramon asked.

"He'll be along," Sturm said harshly. "We'll wait . . . a few moments at least." He did not mention that he would wait until waiting had dissolved into death.

There was a shattering crack. Water began to gush through the wall, flooding the floor. Sturm was about to order the others out when a figure emerged from the collapsing doorway. It was Riverwind, carrying Tanis's inert body in his arms.

"What happened? " Sturm leaped forward, his throat constricting. "He's not—"

"He stayed with me," Riverwind said softly. "I told him to leave me. I wanted to die—there with her. Then—a slab of stone. He never saw it—"

"I'll carry him," Caramon said.

"No!" Riverwind glared at the big warrior. His arms gripped Tanis's body tighter. "I will carry him. We must go."

"Yes! This way! We go now!" urged the gully dwarf. She led them out of the city that was dying a second time. They emerged from the dragon's lair into the plaza, which was rapidly being submerged as Newsea poured into the crumbling cavern. The companions waded across, holding onto each other to keep from being swept away in the vicious current. Howling gully dwarves swarmed everywhere in a state of wild confusion, some getting caught in the current, others climbing up into the top stories of shaking buildings, still others dashing down the streets.

Sturm could think of only one way out. "Go east!" he shouted, gesturing down the broad street that led to the waterfall. He looked anxiously at Riverwind. The dazed Plainsman seemed oblivious to the commotion around him. Tanis was unconscious—maybe dead. Fear chilled Sturm's blood, but he forcibly suppressed all emotions. The knight ran ahead, catching up with the twins.

"Our only chance is the lift!" he yelled.

Caramon nodded slowly. "It will mean a fight."

"Yes, damn it!" said Sturm in exasperation, envisioning all of the draconians trying to leave this stricken city. "It *will* mean a fight! You got any better ideas?"

Caramon shook his head.

At a corner, Sturm waited to herd his limping, exhausted band in the right direction. Peering through the dust and mist, he could see the lift ahead of them. It was, as he had foreseen, surrounded by a dark, writhing mass of draconians. Fortunately, they were all intent on escape. They had to strike quickly, Sturm knew, to catch the creatures off guard. Timing was critical. He caught hold of the kender as Tas scurried past.

"Tas!" he yelled. "We're going up the lift!"

Tasslehoff nodded to show he understood, then made a face to imitate a draconian and slashed his hand across his throat.

"When we get near," Sturm shouted—"sneak around to where you can see the pot descending. When it starts to come down, signal me. We'll attack when it reaches the ground."

Tasslehoff's topknot bobbed.

"Tell Flint!" Sturm finished, his voice nearly gone from shouting. Tas nodded again and raced off to find the dwarf. Sturm straightened his aching back with a sigh and continued on down the street. He could see about twenty or twenty-five draconians gathered in the courtyard, watching for the pot that would carry them to safety to begin its descent. Sturm imagined the confusion up on the top—draconians whipping and bullying the panic-stricken gully dwarves, forcing them into the lift. He hoped the confusion would last.

Sturm saw the brothers in the shadows at the edge of the courtyard. He joined them, glancing up nervously as a stone slab crashed down behind him. As Riverwind staggered out of the mist and dust, Sturm started to help him, but the Plainsman looked at the knight as if he had never seen him before in his life.

"Bring Tanis over here," Sturm said. "You can lay him down and rest a moment. We're going up in the lift and we'll have a fight on our hands. Wait here. When we signal—"

"Do what you must," Riverwind interrupted coldly. He laid Tanis's body gently on the ground and slumped down beside him, burying his face in his hands.

Sturm hesitated. He started to kneel down by Tanis as Flint came to stand by his side.

"Go on. I'll check on him," the dwarf offered.

Sturm nodded thankfully. He saw Tasslehoff skitter across the courtyard and into a doorway. Looking toward the lift, he saw the draconians yelling and cursing into the mist as if they could hurry the pot's descent.

Flint poked Sturm in the ribs. "How are we going to fight all of them?" he shouted.

"We're not. You're going to stay here with Riverwind and Tanis," Sturm said. "Caramon and I can handle this," he added, wishing he believed it himself.

"And I," whispered the mage. "I still have my spells." The knight did not answer. He distrusted magic and he distrusted Raistlin. Still, he had no choice—Caramon would not go into battle without his brother by his side. Tugging at his moustaches, Sturm restlessly loosened his sword. Caramon flexed his arms, clenching and unclenching his huge hands. Raistlin, his eyes closed, was lost in concentration. Bupu, hidden in a niche in the wall behind him, watched everything with wide, frightened eyes.

The pot swung into view, gully dwarves hanging from its sides. As Sturm hoped, the draconians on the ground began to fight among themselves, none wanting to be left behind. Their panic increased as great cracks ran through the pavement toward them. Water rose through the cracks. The city of Xak Tsaroth would soon be lying at the bottom of Newsea.

As the pot touched ground, the gully dwarves scurried over the sides and fled. The draconians clambered in, hitting and shoving each other.

"Now!" the knight yelled.

"Get out of my way!" the mage hissed. Pulling a handful of sand from one of his pouches, he sprinkled it on the ground and whispered, *"Ast tasark sinuralan krynaw,"* moving his right hand in an arc in the direction of the draconians. First one, then a few more blinked their eyes and slumped to the ground in sleep, but others remained standing, glancing around in alarm. The mage ducked back into the doorway and, seeing nothing, the draconians turned back to the lift, stepping on the bodies of their sleeping comrades in their frantic rush. Raistlin leaned against the wall, closing his eyes wearily.

"How many?" he asked.

"Only about six." Caramon drew his sword from its sheath.

"Just get in the damn pot!" Sturm yelled. "We'll come back for Tanis when the fight's ended."

Under cover of the mist, the two warriors—swords drawn—covered the distance to the draconians within a few heartbeats, Raistlin stumbling behind. Sturm shouted his battle cry. At the sound, the draconians spun around in alarm.

And Riverwind raised his head.

The sound of battle penetrated Riverwind's fog of despair. The Plainsman saw Goldmoon before him, dying in the blue flame. The dead expression left his face, replaced by a ferocity so bestial and terrifying that Bupu, still hiding in the doorway, screamed in alarm. Riverwind leaped to his feet. He didn't even draw his sword but charged forward, emptyhanded. He tore into the ranks of the scrambling draconians like a starving panther and began to kill. He killed with his bare hands, twisting, choking, gouging. Draconians stabbed at him with their swords; soon his leather tunic was soaked with blood. Yet he never stopped moving among them, never stopped killing. His face was that of a madman. The draconians in Riverwind's path saw death in his eyes, and they also saw that their weapons had no effect. One broke and ran and, soon, another.

Sturm, finishing an opponent, looked up grimly, prepared to find six more coming at him. Instead he saw the enemy fleeing for their lives into the mist. Riverwind, covered with blood, collapsed onto the ground.

"The lift!" The mage pointed. It was hovering about two feet off the ground and starting to move upward. There were gully dwarves in the top pot coming down.

"Stop it!" Sturm yelled. Tasslehoff raced from his hiding place and leaped for the edge. He clung, his feet dangling, trying desperately to keep the empty pot from rising. "Caramon! Hang onto it!" Sturm ordered the warrior. "I'll get Tanis!"

"I can hold it, but not for long."The big man grunted, grasping onto the edge and digging his feet into the ground. He dragged the lift to a halt.Tasslehoff climbed inside, hoping his small body might add ballast.

Sturm ran back swiftly to Tanis. Flint was beside him, his axe in his hands.

"He's alive!" the dwarf called as the knight approached.

Sturm paused a moment to thank some god, somewhere, then he and Flint lifted the unconscious half-elf and carried him to the pot. They placed him inside, then returned for Riverwind. It took four of them to get Riverwind's bloody body into the lift. Tas tried without much success to stanch the wounds with one of his handkerchiefs.

"Hurry!" Caramon gasped. Despite all his efforts, the pot was rising slowly.

"Get in!" Sturm ordered Raistlin.

The mage glanced at him coldly and ran back into the mist. Within moments, he reappeared, carrying Bupu in his arms. The knight grabbed the trembling gully dwarf and flung her into the lift. Bupu, whimpering, crouched on the bottom, still clutching her bag to her chest. Raistlin climbed over the side. The pot continued to rise; Caramon's arms were nearly pulled out of their sockets.

"Go on," Sturm ordered Caramon, the knight being the last to leave the field of battle as usual. Caramon knew better than to argue. He heaved himself up, nearly tipping the pot over. Flint and Raistlin dragged him in. Without Caramon holding it, the pot lunged upward rapidly. Sturm caught hold of it with both hands and clung to the side as it rose into the air. After two or three tries, he managed to swing a leg over the edge and climbed in with Caramon's help.

The knight knelt down beside Tanis and was relieved beyond expression to see the half-elf stir and moan. Sturm grasped the half-elf and held him close. "You have no idea how glad I am you're back!" the knight said, his voice husky.

"Riverwind—" Tanis murmured groggily.

"He's here. He saved your life. He saved all our lives." Sturm talked rapidly, almost incoherently. "We're in the lift, going up. The city's destroyed. Where are you hurt?"

"Broken ribs, feels like." Wincing in pain, Tanis looked over at Riverwind, still conscious, despite his wounds. "Poor man," Tanis said softly. "Goldmoon. I saw her die, Sturm. There was nothing I could do."

Sturm helped the half-elf rise to his feet. "We have the Disks," the knight said firmly. "It was what she wanted, what she fought for. They're in my pack. Are you sure you can stand?"

"Yes," Tanis said. He drew a ragged, painful breath. "We have the Disks, whatever good that will do us."

They were interrupted by the shrill screams as the second pot, gully dwarves flying like banners, went past them. The gully dwarves shook their fists and cursed the companions. Bupu laughed, then she stood up, looking at Raistlin in concern. The mage leaned wearily against the side of the pot, his lips moving silently, calling to mind another spell.

Sturm peered up through the mist. "I wonder how many will be at the top?" he asked.

Tanis, too, glanced up. "Most have fled, I hope," he said. He caught his breath sharply and clutched at his ribs.

There was a sudden lurch. The pot fell about a foot, stopped with a jolt, then slowly started to rise again. The companions looked at each other in alarm.

"The mechanism—"

"It's either starting to collapse or the draconians have recognized us and are trying to destroy it," Tanis said.

"There's nothing we can do," Sturm said in bitter frustration. He stared down at the pack containing the Disks, which lay at his feet. "Except pray to these gods—"

The pot lurched and dropped again. For a moment it hung, suspended, swaying in the mist-shrouded air. Then it started up, moving slowly, shuddering. The companions could see the edge of the rock ledge and the opening above them. The pot rose inch by creaking inch, each of those inside mentally supporting every link of the chain that was carrying them up to—

"Draconians!" cried Tas shrilly, pointing up.

Two draconians stared down at them. As the pot crept closer and closer, Tanis saw the draconians crouch, ready to jump.

"They're going to leap down here! The pot won't hold!" Flint rumbled. "We'll crash!"

"That may be their intent," Tanis said. "They have wings."

"Stand back," Raistlin said, staggering to his feet.

"Raist, don't!" His brother caught hold of him. "You're too weak."

"I have strength for one more spell," the mage whispered. "But it may not work. If they see I am magi, they may be able to resist my magic."

"Hide behind Caramon's shield," Tanis said swiftly. The big man thrust his body and his shield in front of his brother.

The mist swirled around them, concealing them from draconian eyes but also preventing them from seeing the draconians. The pot rose, inch by inch, the chain creaking and lurching upward. Raistlin stood poised behind Caramon's shield, his strange eyes staring, waiting for the mists to part.

Cool air touched Tanis's cheek. A breeze swirled the mists apart, just for an instant. The draconians were so close they could have almost touched them! The draconians saw them at the same time. One spread its wings and floated down toward the pot, sword in hand, shrieking in triumph.

Raistlin spoke. Caramon moved his shield and the mage spread his thin fingers. A ball of white shot from his hands, hitting the draconian squarely in the chest. The ball exploded, covering the creature in sticky webbing. Its cry of triumph changed to a horrifying shriek as the webbing tangled its wings. It plummeted into the mist, its body striking the edge of the iron pot as it fell. The pot began to rock and sway.

"There's still one more!" Raistlin gasped, sinking to his knees. "Hold me up, Caramon, help me stand. The mage began to cough violently, blood trickling from his mouth.

"Raist!" his brother pleaded, dropping his shield and catching his fainting twin. "Stop! There's nothing you can do. You'll kill yourself!"

A look of command was enough. The warrior supported his brother as the mage began to speak again the eerie-sounding language of magic.

The remaining draconian hesitated, still hearing the yells of its fallen companion. It knew the human was a magic-user. It also knew that it could probably resist the magic. But this human facing it was like no human magic-user it had ever encountered. The human's body seemed weak practically to the point of death, but a strong aura of power surrounded him.

The mage raised his hand, pointing at the creature. The draconian cast one last, vicious glance at the companions, then turned and fled. Raistlin, unconscious, sank into his brother's arms as the pot completed its journey to the surface.

2

Just as they pulled Riverwind out of the lift, a sharp tremor shook the floor of the Hall of the Ancestors. The companions, dragging Riverwind with them, scrambled back as the floor cracked. The floor gave way and tumbled down, carrying the great wheel and the iron pots down into the mist below.

"This whole place is caving in!" Caramon shouted in alarm, holding his brother in his arms.

"Run! Back to the Temple of Mishakal." Tanis gasped with pain.

"Trusting in the gods again, huh?" Flint said. Tanis could not answer.

Sturm took hold of Riverwind's arms and started to lift him, but the Plainsman shook his head and shoved him away. "My wounds are not serious. I can manage. Leave me." He remained slumped on the shattered floor. Tanis glanced questioningly at Sturm. The knight shrugged. The Solamnic Knights considered suicide noble and honorable. The elves considered it blasphemy.

The half-elf took hold of the Plainsman's long dark hair and jerked his head back so that the startled man was forced to look into Tanis's eyes. "Go ahead. Lie down and die!" Tanis said through clenched teeth. "Shame your chieftain! She at least had the courage to fight!"

Riverwind's eyes smoldered. He caught hold of Tanis's wrist and flung the half-elf away from him with such force that Tanis staggered into the wall, groaning in agony. The Plainsman stood up, staring at Tanis with hatred. Then he turned and stumbled down the shaking corridor, his head bent.

Sturm helped Tanis to his feet, the half-elf dizzy from the pain. They followed the others as fast as they could. The floor tilted crazily. When Sturm slipped, they crashed against a wall. A sarcophagus slid out into the hallway, spilling its grisly contents. A skull rolled over by Tanis's feet, startling the half-elf who fell to his knees. He feared he might faint from the pain.

"Go," he tried to say to Sturm, but he couldn't talk. The knight picked him up and together they staggered on through the dust-choked corridor. At the foot of the stairs called the Paths of the Dead, they found Tasslehoff waiting.

"The others?" Sturm gasped, coughing in the dust.

"They've already gone up to the temple," Tasslehoff said. "Caramon told me to wait here for you. Flint says the temple's safe, dwarven stonework, you know. Raistlin's conscious. He said it was safe, too. Something about being held in the palm of the goddess. Riverwind's there. He glared at me. I think he could have killed me! But he made it up the stairs—"

"All right!" Tanis said to stop the prattling. "Enough! Put me down, Sturm. I've got to rest a minute or I'll pass out. Take Tas and I'll meet you upstairs. Go on!"

Sturm grabbed Tasslehoff by the collar and dragged him upstairs. Tanis sank back. Sweat chilled his body; every breath was agony. Suddenly the remainder of the floor in the Hall of the Ancestors collapsed with a loud snapping noise. The Temple of Mishakal trembled and shook. Tanis staggered to his feet, then he paused a moment. Faintly, behind him, he could now hear the low, thundering rumble of water surging. Newsea had claimed Xak Tsaroth. The city that was dead was now buried.

MARGARET WEIS & TRACY HICKMAN

Tanis emerged slowly from the stairwell into the circular room at the top. The climb had been a nightmare, each new step a miracle. The chamber was blessedly quiet, the only sound the harsh breathing of his friends who had made it that far and collapsed. He, too, could go no farther.

The half-elf glanced around to make certain the others were all right. Sturm had set down the pack containing the Disks and was slumped against a wall. Raistlin lay on a bench, his eyes closed, his breathing quick and shallow. Of course, Caramon sat beside him, his face dark with anxiety. Tasslehoff sat at the bottom of the pedestal, staring up at the top. Flint leaned against the doors, too tired to grumble.

"Where's Riverwind?" Tanis asked. He saw Caramon and Sturm exchange glances, then lower their eyes. Tanis staggered up, anger defeating his pain. Sturm rose and blocked his path.

"It's his decision, Tanis. It is the way of his people as it is the way of mine."

Tanis shoved the knight aside and walked toward the double doors. Flint did not move.

"Get out of my way," the half-elf said, his voice shaking. Flint looked up; the lines of grief and sorrow etched by a hundred years softened the dwarf's scowling expression. Tanis saw in Flint's eyes the accumulated wisdom that had drawn an unhappy half-human, half-elven boy into a strange and lasting friendship with a dwarf.

"Sit down, lad," Flint said in a gentle voice, as if he, too, remembered their origins. "If your elven head cannot understand, then listen to your human heart for once."

Tanis shut his eyes, tears stinging his lids. Then he heard a great cry from inside the temple—Riverwind. Tanis thrust the dwarf aside and pushed open the huge golden doors. Striding rapidly, ignoring his pain, he threw open the second set of doors and entered the chamber of Mishakal. Once again he felt peace and tranquillity flood over him, but now the feelings only added to his anger over what had happened.

"I cannot believe in you!" Tanis cried. "What kind of gods are you, that you demand a human sacrifice? You are the same gods who brought the Cataclysm down on man. All right—so you're powerful! Now leave us alone! We don't need you!" The half-elf wept. Through his tears, he could see that Riverwind, sword in hand, knelt before the statue. Tanis stumbled forward, hoping to prevent the act of self-destruction. Tanis rounded the base of the statue and stopped, stunned. For a minute he refused to believe his own sense of sight; perhaps grief and pain were playing tricks on his mind. He lifted his eyes to the statue's beautiful, calm face and steadied his reeling, confused senses. Then he looked again.

Goldmoon lay there, sound asleep, her breast rising and falling with the rhythm of her quiet breathing. Her silver-gold hair had come loose from its braid and drifted around her face in the gentle wind that filled the chamber with the fragrance of spring. The staff was once again part of the marble statue, but Tanis saw that Goldmoon wore around her throat the necklace that had once adorned the statue.

"I am a true cleric now," Goldmoon said softly. "I am a disciple of Mishakal and, though I have much to learn, I have the power of my faith. Above all else, I am a healer. I bring the gift of healing back into the land."

Reaching out her hand, Goldmoon touched Tanis on the forehead, whispering a prayer to Mishakal. The half-elf felt peace and strength flow through his body, cleansing his spirit and healing his wounds.

"We've got a cleric, now," Flint said, "and that'll come in handy. But from what we hear, this Lord Verminaard's a cleric, too, and a powerful one at that. We may have found the ancient gods of good, but he found the ancient gods of evil a lot sooner. I don't see how these Disks are going to help much against hordes of dragons."

"You are right," Goldmoon said softly. "I am not a warrior. I am a healer. I do not have the power to unite the peoples of our world to fight this evil and restore the balance. My duty is to *find* the person who has the strength and the wisdom for this task. I am to give the Disks of Mishakal to that person."

The companions were silent for long moments. Then . . .

"We must leave here, Tanis," Raistlin hissed from out of the shadows of the Temple where he stood, staring out the door into the courtyard. "Listen."

Horns. They could all hear the shrill braying of many, many horns, carried on the north wind.

"The armies," said Tanis softly. "War has begun."

The companions fled Xak Tsaroth into the twilight. They traveled west, toward the mountains. The air was cold with the bite of early winter. Dead leaves, blown by chill winds, flew past their faces. They decided to head for Solace, planning to stock up on supplies and gather what information they could before determining where to go in their search for a leader. Tanis could foresee arguments along those lines. Already Sturm was talking of Solamnia. Goldmoon mentioned Haven, while Tanis himself was thinking the Disks of Mishakal would be safest in the elven kingdom.

Discussing vague plans, they traveled on well into the night. They saw no draconians and supposed that those escaping Xak Tsaroth had traveled north to join up with the armies of this Lord Verminaard, Dragon Highmaster. The silver moon rose, then the red. The companions climbed high, the sound of the horns driving them on past the point of exhaustion. They made camp on the summit of the mountain. After eating a cheerless supper, not daring to light a fire, they set the watch, then slept.

Raistlin woke in the cold gray hour before dawn. He had heard something. Had he been dreaming? No, there it was again—the sound of someone crying. Goldmoon, the mage thought irritably, and started to lie back down. Then he saw Bupu, curled in a ball of misery, blubbering into a blanket.

Raistlin glanced around. The others were asleep except for Flint standing watch on the other side of camp. The dwarf had apparently heard nothing, and he wasn't looking in Raistlin's direction. The mage stood up and padded softly over. Kneeling down beside the gully dwarf, he laid his hand on her shoulder.

"What is it, little one?"

Bupu rolled over to face him. Her eyes were red, her nose swollen. Tears streaked down her dirty face. She snuffled and wiped her hand across her nose. "I don't want to leave you. I want to go with you," she said brokenly, "but—oh—I will miss my people!" Sobbing, she buried her face in her hands.

A look of infinite tenderness touched Raistlin's face, a look no one in his world would ever see. He reached out and stroked Bupu's coarse hair, knowing what it felt like to be weak and miserable, an object of ridicule and pity.

"Bupu," he said, "you have been a good and true friend to me. You saved my life and the lives of those I care about. Now you will do one last thing for me, little one. Go back. I must travel roads that will be dark and dangerous before the end of my long journey. I cannot ask you to go with me."

Bupu lifted her head, her eyes brightening. Then a shadow fell across her face. "But you will be unhappy without me."

"No," Raistlin said, smiling, "my happiness will lie in knowing you are back with your people."

"You sure?" Bupu asked anxiously.

"I am sure," Raistlin answered.

"Then I go." Bupu stood up. "But first, you take gift." She began to rummage around in her bag.

"No, little one," Raistlin began, remembering the dead lizard, "that's not necessary—" The words caught in his throat as he watched Bupu pull from her bag—a book! He stared in amazement, seeing the pale light of the chill morning illuminate silver runes on a night-blue leather binding.

Raistlin reached out a trembling hand. "The spellbook of Fistandantilus!" he breathed.

"You like?" Bupu said shyly.

"Yes, little one!" Raistlin took the precious object in his hands and held it lovingly, stroking the leather. "Where—"

"I take from dragon," Bupu said, "when blue light shine. I glad you like. Now, I go. Find Highbulp Phudge I, the great." She slung her bag over her shoulder. Then she stopped and turned. "That cough, you sure you not want lizard cure?"

"No, thank you, little one," Raistlin said, rising.

Bupu looked at him sadly, then—greatly daring—she caught his hand in hers and kissed it swiftly. She turned away, her head bowed, sobbing bitterly.

Raistlin stepped forward. He laid his hand on her head. If I have any power at all, Great One, he said inside himself, power that has not yet been revealed to me, grant that this little one goes through her life in safety and happiness.

"Farewell, Bupu," he said softly.

She stared at him with wide, adoring eyes, then turned and ran off as fast as her floppy shoes would carry her.

"What was all that about?" Flint said, stumping over from the other side of the camp. "Oh," he added, seeing Bupu running off. "So you got rid of your pet gully dwarf."

Raistlin did not answer, but simply stared at Flint with a malevolence that made the dwarf shiver and walk hurriedly away.

The mage held the spellbook in his hands, admiring it. He longed to open it and revel in its treasures, but he knew that long weeks of study lay ahead of him before he could even read the new spells, much less acquire them. And with the spells would come more power! He sighed in ecstasy and hugged the book to his thin chest. Then he slipped it swiftly into his pack with his own spellbook. The others would be waking soon—let them wonder how he got the book.

Raistlin stood up, glancing out to the west, to his homeland, where the sky was brightening with the early morning sun. Suddenly he stiffened. Then, dropping his pack, he ran across the camp and knelt down beside the half-elf.

"Tanis!" Raistlin hissed. "Wake up!"

Tanis woke and grabbed his dagger. "What—"

Raistlin pointed to the west.

Tanis blinked, trying to focus his sleep-scummed eyes. The view from the top of the mountain where they were camped was magnificent. He could see the tall trees give way to the grassy Plains. And beyond the Plains, snaking up into the sky—

"No!" Tanis choked. He gripped the mage. "No, it can't be!"

"Yes," Raistlin whispered. "Solace is burning."

3

Tika wrung the rag out in the pail and watched, dully, as the water turned black. She threw the rag down on the bar and started to lift the bucket to carry it back to the kitchen to draw more water. Then she thought, why bother! Picking up the rag, she began to mop the tables again. When she thought Otik wasn't watching, she wiped her eyes with her apron.

But Otik was watching. His pudgy hands took hold of Tika's shoulders and gently turned her around. Tika gave a choking sob and laid her head on his shoulder.

"I'm sorry," Tika sobbed, "but I can't get this clean!"

Otik knew, of course, that this wasn't the real reason the girl was weeping, but it came close. He patted her back gently. "I know, I know, child. Don't cry. I understand."

"It's this soot!" Tika wailed. "It covers everything with black and every day I scrub it up and the next day it's back. They keep burning and burning!"

"Don't worry about it, Tika," Otik said, stroking her hair. "Be thankful the Inn's in one piece—"

"Be thankful!" Tika pushed away from him, her face flushed. "No! I wish it had burned like everything else in Solace, then *they* wouldn't come in here! I wish it had burned! I wish it had burned!" Tika sank down at the table, sobbing uncontrollably. Otik hovered around her.

"I know, my dear, I know," he repeated, smoothing the puffy sleeves of the blouse Tika had taken such pride in keeping clean and white. Now it was dingy and covered with soot, like everything in the ravaged town.

The attack on Solace had come without warning. Even when the first pitiable refugees began to trickle into the town from the north, telling horror stories of huge, winged monsters, Hederick, the High Theocrat, assured the people of Solace that they were safe, their town would be spared. And the people believed him because they wanted to believe him.

And then came the night of the dragons.

The Inn was crowded that night, one of the few places people could go and not be reminded of the storm clouds hanging low in the northern skies. The fire burned brightly, the ale was rich, the spiced potatoes were delicious. Yet, even here, the outside world intruded: everyone talked loudly and fearfully of war.

Hederick's words soothed their fearful hearts.

"We are not like these reckless fools to the north who made the mistake of defying the might of the Dragon Highlords," he called out, standing on a chair to be heard. "Lord Verminaard has personally assured the Council of Highseekers in Haven that he wants only peace. He seeks permission to move his armies through our town so that he may conquer the elflands to the south. And I say more power to him!"

Hederick paused for scattered cheering and applause.

"We have tolerated the elves in Qualinesti too long. I say, let this Verminaard drive them back to Silvanost or wherever they came from! In fact"—Hederick warmed to his subject—"some of you young men might consider joining the armies of this great lord. And he is a great lord! I have met him! He is a true cleric! I have seen the miracles he has performed! We will enter a new age under his leadership! We will drive the elves, dwarves, and other foreigners from our land and—"

There came a low, dull, roaring sound, like the gathering of the waters of a mighty ocean. Silence fell abruptly. Everyone listened, puzzled, trying to figure out what might make such a noise. Hederick, aware that he had lost his audience, glanced around in irritation. The roaring sound grew louder and louder, coming closer. Suddenly the Inn was plunged into thick, smothering darkness. A few people screamed. Most ran for the windows, trying to peer out the few clear panes scattered among the colored glass.

"Go down and find out what's going on," someone said.

"It's so blasted dark I can't see the stairs," someone else muttered.

And then it was no longer dark.

Flames exploded outside the Inn. A wave of heat hit the building with force enough to shatter windows, showering those inside with glass. The mighty vallenwood tree—which no storm on Krynn had ever stirred—began to sway and rock from the blast. The Inn tilted. Tables scooted sideways; benches slid down the floor to slam up against the wall. Hederick lost his balance and tumbled off his chair. Hot coals spewed from the fireplace as oil lamps from the ceiling and candles from the tables started small fires.

A high-pitched shriek rose above the noise and confusion—the scream of some living creature—a scream filled with hatred and cruelty. The roaring noise passed over the Inn. There was a rush of wind, then the darkness lifted as a wall of flame sprang up to the south.

Tika dropped a tray of mugs to the floor as she grabbed desperately at the bar for support. People around her shouted and screamed, some in pain, some with terror.

Solace was burning.

A lurid orange glow lit the room. Clouds of black smoke rolled in through the broken windows. Smells of blazing wood filled Tika's nostrils, along with a more horrible smell, the smell of burned flesh. Tika choked and looked up to see small flames licking the great limbs of the vallenwood that held up the ceiling. Sounds of varnish sizzling and popping in the heat mingled with the screams of the injured.

"Douse those fires!" Otik was yelling wildly.

"The kitchen!" The cook screamed as she flew out of the swinging doors, her clothes smoldering, a solid wall of flame behind her. Tika grabbed a pitcher of ale from the bar and tossed it on the cook's dress and held her still to drench her clothes. Rhea sank into a chair, weeping hysterically.

"Get out! The whole place'll go up!" someone shouted.

Hederick, pushing past the injured, was one of the first to reach the door. He ran onto the Inn's front landing, then stopped, stunned, and gripped the rail for support. Staring northward, he saw the woods blazing and, by the ghastly light of the flames, he could see hundreds of marching creatures, the lurid firelight reflecting off their leathery wings. Draconian ground troops. He watched, horrified, as the front ranks poured into the city of Solace, knowing there must be thousands more behind them. And above them flew creatures out of the stories of children.

Dragons.

Five red dragons wheeled overhead in the flame-lit sky. First one, then another, dove down, incinerating parts of the small town with its fiery breath, casting the thick, magical darkness. It was impossible to fight them—warriors could not see well enough to aim their arrows or strike with their swords.

The rest of the night blurred in Tika's memory. She kept telling herself she must leave the burning Inn, yet the Inn was her home, she felt safe there, and so she stayed though the heat from the flaming kitchen grew so intense it hurt her lungs to breathe. Just when the flames spread to the common room, the kitchen crashed to the ground. Otik and the barmaids flung buckets of ale on the flames in the common room until, finally, the fire was extinguished.

Once the fire was out, Tika turned her attention to the wounded. Otik collapsed in a corner, shaking and sobbing. Tika sent one of the other barmaids to tend to him, while she began treating the injured. She worked for hours, resolutely refusing to look out of the windows, blocking from her mind the awful sounds of death and destruction outside.

Suddenly it occurred to her that there was no end to the wounded, that more people were lying on the floor than had been in the Inn when it was attacked. Dazed, she looked up to see people straggling in. Wives helped their husbands. Husbands carried their wives. Mothers carried dying children.

"What's going on?" Tika asked a Seeker guard who staggered in, clutching his arm where an arrow had penetrated it. Others pushed behind him. "What's happening? Why are these people coming here?"

The guard looked at her with dull, pain-filled eyes. "This is the only building," he mumbled. "All burning. All . . ."

"No!" Tika went limp with shock and her knees trembled. At that moment, the guard fainted in her arms and she was forced to pull herself together. The last thing she saw as she dragged him inside was Hederick, standing on the porch, staring out over the flaming town with glazed eyes. Tears streamed unheeded down his soot-streaked face.

"There's been a mistake," he whimpered, wringing his hands. "There's been a mistake made somewhere."

That had been a week ago. As it turned out, the Inn was not the only building left standing. The draconians knew which buildings were essential to their needs and destroyed all those that were not. The Inn, Theros Ironfeld's blacksmith shop, and the general store were saved. The blacksmith shop had always been on the ground—because of the inadvisability of having the hot forge located in a tree—but the others had to be lowered to the ground because the draconians found it difficult to get into the trees.

Lord Verminaard ordered the dragons to lower the buildings. After a space had been scorched clear, one of the huge red monsters stuck his claws into the Inn and lifted it. The draconians cheered as the dragon dropped it, not gently, onto the blackened grass. Fewmaster Toede, in charge of the town, ordered Otik to repair the Inn immediately. The draconians had one great weakness, a thirst for strong drink. Three days after the town was taken, the Inn reopened.

"I'm all right now," Tika told Otik. She sat up and dried her eyes, wiping her nose with her apron. "I haven't cried once, since that night," she said, more to herself than to him. Her lips tightened into a thin line. "And I'll never cry again!" she swore, rising from the table.

Otik, not understanding but thankful that Tika had regained her composure before the patrons arrived, bustled back behind the bar. "Nearly opening time," he said, trying to sound cheerful. "Maybe we'll have a good crowd today."

"How can you take their money!" Tika flared.

Otik, fearing another outburst, looked at her pleadingly. "Their money is as good as anyone else's. Better than most these days," he said.

"Humpf!" Tika snorted. Her thick red curls quivered as she stalked angrily across the floor. Otik, knowing her temper, stepped backward. It didn't help. He was caught. She jabbed her finger into his fat stomach. "How can you laugh at their crude jokes and cater to their whims?" she demanded. "I hate the stench of them! I hate their leers and their cold, scaly hands touching mine! Someday I'll—"

"Tika, please!" Otik begged. "Have some regard for me. I'm too old to be carried off to the slave mines! And you, they'd take you tomorrow if you didn't work here. Please behave— there's a good girl!"

Tika bit her lip in anger and frustration. She knew Otik was right. She risked more than being sent off in the slave caravans that passed through town almost daily—an angered draconian killed swiftly and without mercy. Just as she was thinking this, the door banged open and six draconian guards swaggered in. One of the them pulled the CLOSED sign off the door and tossed it into a corner.

"You're open," the creature said, dropping into a chair.

"Yes, certainly." Otik grinned weakly. "Tika . . ."

"I see them," Tika said dully.

The stranger. Captured!

4

The crowd at the Inn that night was sparse. The patrons were now draconians, though occasionally Solace residents came in for a drink. They generally did not stay long, finding the company unpleasant and memories of former times hard to bear.

Tonight there was a group of hobgoblins who kept wary eyes on the draconians and three crudely dressed humans from the north. Originally impressed into Lord Verminaard's service, they now fought for the sheer pleasure of killing and looting. A few Solace citizens sat huddled in a corner. Hederick, the Theocrat, was not in his nightly spot. Lord Verminaard had rewarded the High Theocrat's service by placing him among the first to be sent to the slave mines.

Near dusk, a stranger entered the Inn, taking a table in a dark corner near the door. Tika couldn't tell much about him—he was heavily cloaked and wore a hood pulled low over his head. He seemed fatigued, sinking down into his chair as though his legs would not support him.

"What will you have?" Tika asked the stranger.

The man lowered his head, pulling down one side of his hood with a slender hand. "Nothing, thank you," he said in a soft, accented voice. "Is it permissible to sit here and rest? I'm supposed to meet someone."

"How about a glass of ale while you wait?" Tika smiled.

The man glanced up, and she saw brown eyes flash from the depths of his hood. "Very well," the stranger said. "I am thirsty. Bring me your ale."

Tika headed for the bar. As she drew the ale, she heard more customers entering the Inn.

"Just a half second," she called out, unable to turn around. "Sit anywhere you've a mind. I'll be with you soon as I can!" She glanced over her shoulder at the newcomers and nearly dropped the mug. Tika gasped, then got a grip on herself. Don't give them away!

"Sit down anywhere, *strangers*," she said loudly.

One of the men, a big fellow, seemed about to speak. Tika frowned fiercely at him and shook her head. Her eyes shifted to the draconians seated in the center of the room. A bearded man led the group past the draconians, who examined the strangers with a great deal of interest.

They saw four men and a woman, a dwarf, and a kender. The men were dressed in mud-stained cloaks and boots. One was unusually tall, another unusually big. The woman was cloaked in furs and walked with her hand through the arm of the tall man. All of them seemed downcast and tired. One of the men coughed and leaned heavily upon a strange-looking staff. They crossed the room and sat down at a table in the far corner.

"More refugee scum," sneered a draconian. "The humans look healthy, though, and all know dwarves are hard workers. Wonder why they haven't been shipped out?"

"They will be, soon as the Fewmaster sees them."

"Perhaps we should take care of the matter now," said a third, scowling in the direction of the eight strangers.

"Naw, I'm off duty. They won't go far."

The others laughed and returned to their drinking. A number of empty glasses already sat before each of them.

Tika carried the ale to the brown-eyed stranger, set it before him hurriedly, then bustled back to the newcomers.

"What'll you have?" she asked coldly.

The tall, bearded man answered in a low, husky voice. "Ale and food," he said. "And wine for him," he nodded at the man who was coughing almost continually.

The frail man shook his head. "Hot water," he whispered.

Tika nodded and left. Out of habit, she started back toward where the old kitchen had been. Then, remembering it was gone, she whipped around and headed for the makeshift kitchen that had been built by goblins under draconian supervision. Once inside, she astounded the cook by grabbing the entire skillet of fried spiced potatoes and carrying it back out into the common room.

"Ale all around and a mug of hot water!" she called to Dezra behind the bar. Tika blessed her stars that Otik had gone home early. "Itrum, take that table." She motioned to the hobgoblins as she hurried back to the newcomers. She slammed the skillet down, glancing at the draconians. Seeing them absorbed in their drinking, she suddenly flung her arms around the big man and gave him a kiss that made him flush.

"Oh, Caramon," she whispered swiftly. "I knew you'd come back for me! Take me with you! Please, please!"

"Now, there, there," Caramon said, patting her awkwardly on the back and looking pleadingly at Tanis. The half-elf swiftly intervened, his eyes on the draconians.

"Tika, calm down," he told her. "We've got an audience."

"Right," she said briskly and stood up, smoothing her apron. Handing plates around, she began to ladle out the spiced potatoes as Dezra brought the ale and hot water.

"Tell us what happened to Solace," Tanis said, his voice choked.

Quickly Tika whispered the story as she filled everyone's plate, giving Caramon a double portion. The companions listened in grim silence.

"And so," Tika concluded, "every week, the slave caravans leave for Pax Tharkas, except now they've taken almost everyone—leaving only the skilled, like Theros Ironfeld, behind. I fear for him." She lowered her voice. "He swore to me last night that he would work for them no more. It all started with that captive party of elves—"

"Elves? What are elves doing here?" Tanis asked, speaking too loudly in his astonishment. The draconians turned to stare at him; the hooded stranger in the corner raised his head. Tanis hunched down and waited until the draconians turned their attention to their drinks. Then he started to ask Tika more about the elves. At that moment, a draconian yelled for ale.

Tika sighed. "I better go." She set the skillet down. "I'll leave that here. Finish them off."

The companions ate listlessly, the food tasting like ashes. Raistlin mixed his strange herbal brew and drank it down; his cough improved almost immediately. Caramon watched Tika as he ate, his expression thoughtful. He could still feel the warmth of her body as she had embraced him and the softness of her lips. Pleasant sensations flowed through him, and he wondered if the stories he had heard about Tika were true. The thought both saddened him and made him angry.

One of the draconians raised its voice. "We may not be men like you're accustomed to, sweetie," it said drunkenly, flinging its scaled arm around Tika's waist. "But that doesn't mean we can't find ways of making you happy."

Caramon rumbled, deep in his chest. Sturm, overhearing, glowered and put his hand on his sword. Catching hold of the knight's arm, Tanis said urgently, "Both of you, stop it! We're in an occupied town! Be sensible. This is no time for chivalry! You, too, Caramon! Tika can handle herself."

Sure enough, Tika slipped deftly out of the draconian's grip and flounced angrily into the kitchen.

"Well, what do we do now?" Flint grumbled. "We came back to Solace for supplies and find nothing but draconians. My house is little more than a cinder. Tanis doesn't even have a vallenwood tree, much less a home. All we've got are platinum Disks of some ancient goddess and a sick mage with a few new spells." He ignored Raistlin's glower. "We can't eat the Disks and the magician hasn't learned to conjure up food, so even if we knew where to go, we'd starve before we got there!"

"Should we still go to Haven?" Goldmoon asked, looking up at Tanis. "What if it is as bad as this? How do we know the Highseeker Council is even in existence?"

"I don't have the answers," Tanis said, sighing. He rubbed his eyes with his hand. "But I think we should try to reach Qualinesti."

Tasslehoff, bored by the conversation, yawned and leaned back in his chair. It didn't matter to him where they went. Examining the Inn with intense interest, he wanted to get up and look at where the kitchen had burned, but Tanis had warned him before they entered to stay out of trouble. The kender contented himself with studying the other customers.

He immediately noticed the hooded and cloaked stranger in the front of the Inn watching them intently as the conversation among the companions grew heated. Tanis raised his voice, and the word "Qualinesti" rang out again. The stranger set down his mug of ale with a thud. Tas was just about to call Tanis's attention to this when Tika came out of the kitchen and slammed food down in front of the draconians, skillfully avoiding their clawed hands. Then she walked back over to the group.

"Could I have some more potatoes?" Caramon asked.

"Of course." Tika smiled at him and picked up the skillet to return to the kitchen. Caramon felt Raistlin's eyes on him. He flushed and began to play with his fork.

"In Qualinesti—" Tanis reiterated, his voice rising as he contested a point with Sturm who wanted to go north.

Tas saw the stranger in the corner rise and start walking toward them. "Tanis, company," the kender said softly.

The conversation ceased. Their eyes on their tankards, all of them could feel and hear the approach of the stranger. Tanis cursed himself for not noticing him sooner.

The draconians, however, had noticed the stranger. Just as he reached the creatures' table, one of the draconians stuck out its clawed foot. The stranger tripped over it, stumbling headlong into a nearby table. The creatures laughed loudly. Then a draconian caught a glimpse of the stranger's face.

"Elf!" the draconian hissed, pulling off the hood to reveal the almond-shaped eyes, slanted ears, and delicate, masculine features of an elflord.

"Let me pass," the elf said, backing up, his hands raised. "I was only going to exchange a word of greeting with these travelers."

"You'll exchange a word of greeting with the Fewmaster, elf," the draconian snarled. Jumping up and grabbing the stranger's cloak collar, the creature shoved the elf back up against the bar. The other two draconians laughed loudly.

Tika, on her way back to the kitchen with the skillet, stalked over toward the draconians. "Stop this!" she cried, taking hold of one of the draconians by the arm. "Leave him alone. He's a paying customer. Same as you."

"Go about your business, girl!" The draconian shoved Tika aside, then grabbed the elf with a clawed hand and hit him, twice, across the face. The blows drew blood. When the draconian let go, the elf staggered, shook his head groggily.

"Ah, kill him," shouted one of the humans from the north. "Make him screech, like the others!"

"I'll cut his slanty eyes out of his head, that's what I'll do!" The draconian drew his sword.

"This has gone far enough!" Sturm rushed forward, the others behind him, though all feared there was little hope of saving the elf—they were too far from him. But help was closer. With a shrill cry of rage, Tika Waylan brought her heavy iron skillet down on the draconian's head.

There was a loud clunking sound. The draconian stared stupidly at Tika for an instant, then slithered to the floor. The elf jumped forward, drawing a knife as the other two draconians leaped for Tika. Sturm reached her side and clubbed one of the draconians with his sword. Caramon caught the other up in his great arms and tossed it over the bar.

"Riverwind! Don't let them out the door!" Tanis cried, seeing the hobgoblins leap up. The Plainsman caught one hobgoblin as it put its hand on the doorknob, but another escaped his grasp. They could hear it shouting for the guard.

Tika, still wielding her skillet, thunked a hobgoblin over the head. But another hobgoblin, seeing Caramon charge over, leaped out of the window.

Goldmoon rose to her feet. "Use your magic!" she said to Raistlin, grabbing him by the arm. "Do something!"

The mage looked at the woman coldly. "It is hopeless," he whispered. "I will not waste my strength."

Goldmoon glared at him in fury, but he had returned to his drink. Biting her lip, she ran over to Riverwind, the pouch with the precious Disks of Mishakal in her arms. She could hear horns blowing wildly in the streets.

"We've got to get out of here!" Tanis said, but at that moment one of the human fighters wrapped his arms around Tanis's neck, dragging him to the floor. Tasslehoff, with a wild shout, leaped onto the bar and began flinging mugs at the half-elf's attacker, narrowly missing Tanis in the process.

Flint stood in the midst of the chaos, staring at the elven stranger. "I know you!" he yelled suddenly. "Tanis, isn't this—"

A mug hit the dwarf in the head, knocking him cold.

"Oops," said Tas.

Tanis throttled the northerner and left him unconscious under a table. He grabbed Tas off the bar, set the kender on the floor, and knelt down beside Flint who was groaning and trying to sit up.

"Tanis, that elf—" Flint blinked groggily, then asked "What hit me?"

"That big guy, under the table!" Tas said pointing.

Tanis stood up and looked at the elf Flint indicated. "Gilthanas?"

The elf stared at him. "Tanthalas," he said coldly. "I would never have recognized you. That beard—"

Horns blew again, this time closer.

"Great Reorx!" The dwarf groaned, staggering to his feet. "We've got to get out of here! Come on! Out the back!"

"There is no back!" Tika cried wildly, still hanging onto the skillet.

"No," said a voice at the door. "There is no back. You are my prisoners."

A blaze of torchlight flared into the room. The companions shielded their eyes, making out the forms of hobgoblins behind a squat figure in the doorway. The companions could hear the sounds of flapping feet outside, then what seemed like a hundred goblins stared into the windows and peered in through the door. The hobgoblins inside the bar that were still alive or conscious picked themselves up and drew their weapons, regarding the companions hungrily.

"Sturm, don't be a fool!" Tanis cried, catching hold of the knight as he prepared to charge into the seething mass of goblins slowly forming a ring of steel around them. "We surrender," the half-elf called out.

Sturm glared at the half-elf in anger, and for a moment Tanis thought he might disobey.

"Please, Sturm," Tanis said quietly. "Trust me. This is not our time to die."

Sturm hesitated, glanced around at the goblins crowding inside the Inn. They stood back, fearful of his sword and his skill, but he knew they would charge in a rush if he made the slightest move. "It is not our time to die." What odd words. Why had Tanis said them? Did a man ever have a "time to die"? If so, Sturm realized, this wasn't it—not if he could help it. There was no glory dying in an inn, trampled by stinking, flapping goblin feet.

Seeing the knight put his weapon away, the figure at the door decided it was safe to enter, surrounded as he was by a

MARGARET WEIS & TRACY HICKMAN

hundred or so loyal troops. The companions saw the gray, mottled skin and red, squinting pig eyes of Fewmaster Toede.

Tasslehoff gulped and moved quickly to stand beside Tanis. "Surely he won't recognize us," Tas whispered. "It was dusk when they stopped us, asking about the staff."

Apparently Toede did not recognize them. A lot had happened in a week's time and the Fewmaster had important things stuffed in a mind already overloaded. His red eyes focused on the knight's emblems beneath Sturm's cloak. "More refugee scum from Solamnia," Toede remarked.

"Yes," Tanis lied quickly. He doubted if Toede knew of the destruction of Xak Tsaroth. He thought it highly unlikely that this fewmaster would know anything about the Disks of Mishakal. But Lord Verminaard knew of the Disks and he would soon learn of the dragon's death. Even a gully dwarf could add that one up. No one must know they came out of the east. "We have journeyed long days from the north. We did not intend to cause trouble. These draconians started it—"

"Yes, yes," Toede said impatiently. "I've heard this before." His squinty eyes suddenly narrowed. "Hey, you!" he shouted, pointing at Raistlin. "What are you doing, skulking back there? Fetch him, lads!" The Fewmaster took a nervous step behind the door, watching Raistlin warily. Several goblins charged back, overturning benches and tables to reach the frail young man. Caramon rumbled deep in his chest. Tanis gestured to the warrior, warning him to remain calm.

"On yer feet!" one of the goblins snarled, prodding at Raistlin with a spear.

Raistlin stood slowly and carefully gathered his pouches. As he reached for his staff, the goblin grabbed hold of the mage's thin shoulder.

"Touch me not!" Raistlin hissed, drawing back. "I am magi!"

The goblin hesitated and glanced back at Toede.

"Take him!" yelled the Fewmaster, moving behind a very large goblin. "Bring him here with the others. If every man wearing red robes was a magician, this country'd be overrun with rabbits! If he won't come peaceably, stick him!"

"Maybe I'll stick him anyway," the goblin croaked. The creature held the tip of its spear up to the mage's throat, gurgling with laughter.

Again Tanis held back Caramon. "Your brother can take care of himself," he whispered swiftly.

Raistlin raised his hands, fingers spread, as though to surrender. Suddenly he spoke the words, "*Kalith karan, tobanis-kar!*" and pointed his fingers at the goblin. Small, brightly glowing darts made of pure white light beamed from the mage's fingertips, streaked through the air, and embedded themselves deep in the goblin's chest. The creature fell over with a shriek and lay writhing on the floor.

As the smell of burning flesh and hair filled the room, other goblins sprang forward, howling in rage.

"Don't kill him, you fools!" Toede yelled. The Fewmaster had backed clear out the door, keeping the big goblin in front of him as cover. "Lord Verminaard pays a handsome bounty for magic-users. But"—Toede was inspired—"the Lord does not pay a bounty for live kenders, only their tongues! Do that again, magician, and the kender dies!"

"What is the kender to me?" Raistlin snarled.

There was a long heartbeat of silence in the room. Tanis felt cold sweat chill him. Raistlin could certainly take care of himself! Damn the mage!

That was certainly not the answer Toede had expected either, and it left him not quite knowing what to do—especially since these big warriors still had their weapons. He looked almost pleadingly at Raistlin. The magician appeared to shrug.

"I will come peaceably," Raistlin whispered, his golden eyes gleaming. "Just do not touch me."

"No, of course not," Toede muttered. "Bring him."

The goblins, casting uneasy glances in the direction of the Fewmaster, allowed the mage to stand beside his brother.

"Is that everyone?" demanded Toede irritably. "Then take their weapons and their packs."

Tanis, hoping to avoid more trouble, pulled his bow from his shoulder and laid it and his quiver on the soot-blackened floor of the Inn. Tasslehoff quickly laid down his hoopak; the dwarf—grumbling—added his battle-axe. The others followed Tanis's lead, except Sturm, who stood, his arms folded across his chest, and—

"Please, let me keep my pack," Goldmoon said. "I have no weapons in it, nothing of value to you. I swear!"

The companions turned to face her—each remembering the precious Disks she carried. A strained, tense silence fell. Riverwind stepped in front of Goldmoon. He had laid his bow down, but he still wore his sword, as did the knight.

Suddenly Raistlin intervened. The mage had laid down his staff, his pouches of spell components, and the precious bag that contained his spellbooks. He was not worried about these—spells of protection had been laid on the books; anyone other than their owner attempting to read them would go insane; and the Staff of Magius was quite capable of taking care of itself. Raistlin held out his hands toward Goldmoon.

"Give them the pack," he said gently. "Otherwise they will kill us."

"Listen to him, my dear," called out Toede hastily. "He's an intelligent man."

"He's a traitor!" cried Goldmoon, clutching the pack.

"Give them the pack," Raistlin repeated hypnotically.

Goldmoon felt herself weakening, felt his strange power breaking her. "No!" She choked. "This is our hope—"

"It will be all right," Raistlin whispered, staring intently into her clear blue eyes. "Remember the staff? Remember when I touched it?"

Goldmoon blinked. "Yes," she murmured. "It shocked you—"

"Hush," Raistlin warned swiftly. "Give them the pouch. Do not worry. All will be well. The gods protect their own."

Goldmoon stared at the mage, then nodded reluctantly. Raistlin reached out his thin hands to take the pouch from her. Fewmaster Toede stared at it greedily, wondering what was in it. He would find out, but not in front of all these goblins.

Finally there was only one person left who had not obeyed the command. Sturm stood unmoving, his face pale, his eyes glittering feverishly. He held his father's ancient, two-handed sword tightly. Suddenly Sturm turned, shocked to feel Raistlin's burning fingers on his arm.

"I will insure its safety," the mage whispered.

"How?" the knight asked, withdrawing from Raistlin's touch as from a poisonous snake.

"I do not explain my ways to you," Raistlin hissed. "Trust me or not, as you choose."

Sturm hesitated.

"This is ridiculous!" shrieked Toede. "Kill the knight! Kill them if they cause more trouble. I'm losing sleep!"

"Very well!" Sturm said in a strangled voice. Walking over, he reverently laid the sword down on the pile of weapons. Its ancient silver scabbard, decorated with the kingfisher and rose, gleamed in the light.

"Ah, truly a beautiful weapon," Toede said. He had a sudden vision of himself walking into audience with Lord Verminaard, the sword of a Solamnic knight hanging at his side. "Perhaps I should take that into custody myself. Bring it—"

Before he could finish, Raistlin stepped forward swiftly and knelt beside the pile of weapons. A bright flash of light sprang from the mage's hand. Raistlin closed his eyes and began to murmur strange words, holding his outstretched hands above the weapons and packs.

"Stop him!" yelled Toede. But none dared.

Finally Raistlin ceased speaking and his head slumped forward. His brother hurried to help.

Raistlin stood. "Know this!" the mage said, his golden eyes staring around the common room. "I have cast a spell upon our belongings. Anyone who touches them will be slowly devoured by the great worm, Catyrpelius, who will rise from the Abyss and suck the blood from your veins until you are nothing more than a dried husk."

"The great worm Catyrpelius!" breathed Tasslehoff, his eyes shining. "That's incredible. I've never heard of—"

Tanis clapped his hand over the kender's mouth.

The goblins backed away from the pile of weapons, which seemed to almost glow with a green aura.

"Get those weapons, somebody!" ordered Toede in a rage.

"You get 'em," muttered a goblin.

No one moved. Toede was at a loss. Although he was not particularly imaginative, a vivid picture of the great worm, Catyrpelius, reared up in his mind. "Very well," he muttered, "take the prisoners away! Load them into the cages. And bring those weapons, too, or you'll wish that worm what's-its-name was sucking your blood!" Toede stomped off angrily.

The goblins began to shove their prisoners toward the door, prodding them in the back with their swords. None, however, touched Raistlin.

"That's a wonderful spell, Raist," Caramon said in a low voice. "How effective is it? Could it—"

"It's about as effective as your wit!" Raistlin whispered and held up his right hand. As Caramon saw the tell-tale black marks of flashpowder, he smiled grimly in sudden understanding.

Tanis was the last to leave the Inn. He cast a final look around. A single light swung from the ceiling. Tables were over-turned, chairs broken. The beams of the ceiling were blackened from the fires, in some cases burned through completely. The windows were covered with greasy black soot.

"I almost wish I had died before I saw this."

The last thing he heard as he left were two hobgoblin captains arguing heatedly about who was going to move the enchanted weapons.

THE SLAVE CARAVAN.
A STRANGE OLD MAGICIAN.

5

The companions spent a chill, sleepless night, penned up in an iron-barred cage on wheels in the Solace Town Square. Three cages were chained to one of the posts driven into the ground around the clearing. The wooden posts were black from flame and heat, the bases scorched and splintered. No living thing grew in the clearing; even the rocks were black and melted.

When day dawned, they could see other prisoners in the other cages. The last slave caravan leaving Solace for Pax Tharkas, it was to be personally led by the Fewmaster himself, Toede having decided to take this opportunity to impress Lord Verminaard who was in residence at Pax Tharkas.

Caramon tried once, during the cover of night, to bend the bars of the cage and had to give up.

A cold mist arose in the early morning hours, hiding the ravaged town from the companions. Tanis glanced over at Goldmoon and Riverwind. Now I understand them, Tanis thought. Now I know the cold emptiness inside that hurts worse than any sword thrust. My home is gone.

He glanced over at Gilthanas, huddled in a corner. The elf had spoken to no one that night, excusing himself by begging that his head hurt and he was tired. But Tanis, who had kept watch all through the night, saw that Gilthanas did not sleep or even make a pretense of sleeping. He gnawed his lower lip and stared out into the darkness. The sight reminded Tanis that he had—if he chose to claim it—another place he could call home: Qualinesti.

No, Tanis thought, leaning against the bars, Qualinesti was never home. It was simply a place I lived. . . .

Fewmaster Toede emerged from the mist, rubbing his fat hands together and grinning widely as he regarded the slave caravan with pride. There may be a promotion here. A fine catch, considering pickings were drying up in this burned-out shell of a town. Lord Verminaard should be pleased, especially with this last batch. That large warrior, particularly—an excellent specimen. He could probably do the work of three men in the mines. The tall barbarian would do nicely, too. Probably have to kill the knight, though, the Solamnics were notoriously uncooperative. But Lord Verminaard will certainly enjoy the two females—very different, but both lovely. Toede himself had always been attracted to the red-haired barmaid, with her alluring green eyes, the low-cut white blouse purposefully revealing just enough of her lightly freckled skin to tantalize a man with thoughts of what lay beyond.

The Fewmaster's reveries were interrupted by the sound of clashing steel and hoarse shouts floating eerily through the mist. The shouts grew louder and louder. Soon almost everyone in the slave caravan was awake and peering through the fog, trying to see.

Toede cast an uneasy glance at the prisoners and wished he'd kept a few more guards handy. The goblins, seeing the prisoners stir, jumped to their feet and trained their bows and arrows on the wagons.

"What is this?" Toede grumbled aloud. "Can't those fools even take one prisoner without all this turmoil?"

Suddenly a cry bellowed above the noise. It was the cry of a man in torment and pain, but whose rage surpassed all else.

Gilthanas stood up, his face pale.

"I know that voice," he said. "Theros Ironfeld. I feared this. He's been helping elves escape ever since the slaughter. This Lord Verminaard has sworn to exterminate the elves"—Gilthanas watched Tanis's reaction—"or didn't you know?"

"No!" Tanis said, shocked. "I didn't know. How could I?"

Gilthanas fell silent, studying Tanis for long moments. "Forgive me," he said at last. "It appears I have misjudged you. I thought perhaps that was why you had grown the beard."

"Never!" Tanis leaped up. "How dare you accuse me—"

"Tanis," cautioned Sturm.

The half-elf turned to see the goblin guards crowding forward, their arrows trained at his heart. Raising his hands, he stepped back to his place just as a squadron of hobgoblins dragged a tall, powerfully built man into sight.

"I heard Theros had been betrayed," Gilthanas said softly. "I returned to warn him. But for him, I never would have escaped Solace alive. I was supposed to meet him in the Inn last night. When he did not come, I was afraid—"

Fewmaster Toede threw open the door to the companions' cage, yelling and gesturing for the hobgoblins to hurry their prisoner forward. The goblins kept the other prisoners covered while the hobgoblins threw Theros into the cage.

Fewmaster Toede slammed the door shut quickly. "That's it!" he yelled. "Hitch up the beasts. We're moving out."

Squads of goblins drove huge elk into the clearing and began hitching them to wagons. Their yelling and the confusion registered only in the back of Tanis's mind. For the moment, his shocked attention was on the smith.

Theros Ironfeld lay unconscious on the straw-covered floor of the cage. Where his strong right arm should have been was a mangled stump. His arm had been hacked off, apparently by some blunt weapon, just below the shoulder. Blood poured from the terrible wound and pooled on the floor of the cage.

"Let that be a lesson to all those who help elves!" The Fewmaster peered in the cage, his red pig eyes squinching in their pouches of fat. "He won't be forging anything ever again, unless it be a new arm! I, eh—" A huge elk lumbered into the Fewmaster, forcing him to scramble for his life.

Toede turned on the creature leading the elk. "Sestun! You oaf!" Toede knocked the smaller creature to the ground.

Tasslehoff stared down at the creature, thinking it was a very short goblin. Then he saw it was a gully dwarf dressed in a goblin's armor. The gully dwarf picked himself up, shoved his oversized helm back, and glared after the Fewmaster, who was waddling up to the front of the caravan. Scowling, the gully dwarf began kicking mud in his direction. This apparently relieved his soul, for he soon quit and returned to prodding the slow elk into line.

"My faithful friend," Gilthanas murmured, bending over Theros and taking the smith's strong, black hand in his. "You have paid for your loyalty with your life."

Theros looked at him with vacant eyes, clearly not hearing the elf's voice. Gilthanas tried to stanch the dreadful wound, but blood continued to pump onto the floor of the cart. The smithy's life was emptying before their eyes.

"No," said Goldmoon, coming to kneel beside the smith. "He need not die. I am a healer."

"Lady," Gilthanas said impatiently, "there exists no healer on Krynn who could help this man. He has lost more blood than the dwarf has in his whole body! His lifebeat is so faint I can barely feel it. The kindest thing to do is let him die in peace without any of your barbarian rituals!"

Goldmoon ignored him. Placing her hand upon Theros's forehead, she closed her eyes.

"Mishakal," she prayed, "beloved goddess of healing, grace this man with your blessing. If his destiny be not fulfilled, heal him, that he may live and serve the cause of truth."

Gilthanas began to remonstrate once more, reaching out to pull Goldmoon away. Then he stopped and stared in amazement. Blood ceased to drain from the smith's wound and, even as the elf watched, the flesh began to close over it.

Warmth returned to the smith's dusky black skin, his breathing grew peaceful and easy, and he appeared to drift into a healthful, relaxed sleep. There were gasps and murmurs of astonishment from the other prisoners in the nearby cages. Tanis glanced around fearfully to see if any of the goblins or draconians had noticed, but apparently they were all preoccupied with hitching the recalcitrant elk to the wagons. Gilthanas subsided back into his corner, his eyes on Goldmoon, his expression thoughtful.

"Tasslehoff, pile up some of that straw," Tanis instructed. "Caramon, you and Sturm help me move him to a corner."

"Here." Riverwind offered his cloak. "Take this to cover him from the chill."

Goldmoon made certain Theros was comfortable, then returned to her place beside Riverwind. Her face radiated a peace and calm serenity that made it seem as if the reptilian creatures on the outside of the cage were the true prisoners.

It was nearly noon before the caravan got under way. Goblins came by and threw some food into the cages, hunks of meat and bread. No one, not even Caramon, could eat the rancid, stinking meat and they threw it back out. But they devoured the bread hungrily, having eaten nothing since last nightfall. Soon Toede had everything in order and, riding by on his shaggy pony, gave the orders to move out. The gully dwarf, Sestun, trotted after Toede. Seeing the hunk of meat lying in the mud and filth outside the cage, the gully dwarf stopped, grabbed it eagerly, and crammed it into his mouth.

Each wheeled cage was pulled by four elk. Two hobgoblins sat high on crude wooden platforms, one holding the reins of the elk, the other a whip and a sword. Toede took his place at the front of the line, followed by about fifty draconians dressed in armor and heavily armed. Another troop of about twice as many hobgoblins fell into line behind the cages.

After a great deal of confusion and swearing, the caravan finally lurched forward. Some of the remaining residents of

Solace stared at them as they drove off. If they knew anyone among the prisoners, they made no sound or gesture of farewell. The faces, both inside and outside the cages, were the faces of those who no longer can feel pain. Like Tika, they had vowed never to cry again.

The caravan traveled south from Solace, down the old road through Gateway Pass. The hobgoblins and draconians grumbled about traveling in the heat of the day, but they cheered up and moved faster once they marched into the shade of the Pass's high canyon walls. Although the prisoners were chilled in the canyon, they had their own reasons for being grateful—they no longer had to look upon their ravaged homeland.

It was evening by the time they left the canyon's winding roads and reached Gateway. The prisoners strained against the bars for some glimpse of the thriving market town. But now only two low stone walls, melted and blackened, marked where the town might have once stood. No living creature stirred. The prisoners sank back in misery.

Once more out in the open country, the draconians announced their preference for traveling by night, out of the sun's light. Consequently, the caravan made only brief stops until dawn. Sleep was impossible in the filthy cages jolting and jouncing over every rut in the road. The prisoners suffered from thirst and hunger. Those who managed to gag down the food the draconians tossed them soon vomited it back up. They were given only small cups of water two or three times a day.

Goldmoon remained near the injured smithy. Although Theros Ironfeld was no longer at the point of death, he was still very ill. He developed a high fever and, in his delirium, he raved about the sacking of Solace. Theros spoke of draconians whose bodies, when dead, turned into pools of acid, burning the flesh of their victims; and of draconians whose bones exploded after death, destroying everything within a wide radius. Tanis listened to the smith relive horror after horror until he felt sick. For the first time, Tanis realized the enormity of the situation. How could they hope to fight dragons whose breath could kill, whose magic exceeded that of all but the most powerful magic-users who had ever lived? How could they defeat vast armies of these draconians when even the corpses of the creatures had the power to kill?

All we have, Tanis thought bitterly, are the Disks of Mishakal—and what good are they? He had examined the Disks during their journey from Xak Tsaroth to Solace. He had been able to read little of what was written, however. Although Goldmoon had been able to understand those words that pertained to the healing arts, she could decipher little more.

"All will be made clear to the leader of the people," she said with steadfast faith. "My calling now is to find him."

Tanis wished he could share her faith, but as they traveled through the ravaged countryside, he began to doubt that any leader could defeat the might of this Lord Verminaard.

These doubts merely compounded the half-elf's other problems. Raistlin, bereft of his medicine, coughed until he was nearly in as bad a state as Theros, and Goldmoon had two patients on her hands. Fortunately, Tika helped the Plainswoman tend the mage. Tika, whose father had been a magician of sorts, held anyone who could work magic in awe.

In fact, it had been Tika's father who inadvertently introduced Raistlin to his calling. Raistlin's father took the twin boys and his stepdaughter, Kitiara, to the local Summer's End festival where the children watched the Wonderful Waylan perform his illusions. Eight-year-old Caramon was soon bored and readily agreed to accompany his teenage half-sister to the event that attracted her—the swordplay. Raistlin, thin and frail even then, had no use for such active sports. He spent the entire day watching Waylan the Illusionist. When the family returned home that evening, Raistlin astounded them by being able to duplicate flawlessly every trick. The next day, his father took the boy to study with one of the great masters of the magic arts.

Tika had always admired Raistlin and she had been impressed by the stories she heard about his mysterious journey to the fabled Towers of High Sorcery. Now she helped care for the mage out of respect and her own innate need to help those weaker than herself. She also tended him (she admitted privately to herself) because her deeds won a smile of gratitude and approval from Raistlin's handsome twin brother.

Tanis wasn't certain which to worry about most, the worsening condition of the mage or the growing romance between the older, experienced soldier and the young and—Tanis believed, despite gossip to the contrary—inexperienced, vulnerable barmaid.

He had another problem as well. Sturm, humiliated at being taken prisoner and hauled through the countryside like an animal to slaughter, lapsed into a deep depression from which Tanis thought he might never escape. Sturm either sat all day, staring out between the bars, or—perhaps worse—he lapsed into periods of deep sleep from which he could not be wakened.

Finally Tanis had to cope with his own inner turmoil, physically manifested by the elf sitting in the corner of the cage. Every time he looked at Gilthanas, Tanis's memories of his home in Qualinesti haunted him. As they neared his homeland, the memories he had thought long buried and forgotten crept into his mind, their touch every bit as chilling as the touch of the undead in Darken Wood.

Gilthanas, childhood friend—more than friend, brother. Raised in the same household and close to the same age, the two had played and fought and laughed together. When Gilthanas's little sister grew old enough, the boys allowed the captivating blonde child to join them. One of the threesome's greatest delights was teasing the older brother, Porthios, a strong and serious youth who took on the responsibilities and sorrows of his people at an early age. Gilthanas, Laurana, and Porthios were the children of the Speaker of the Suns, the ruler of the elves of Qualinesti, a position Porthios would inherit at his father's death.

Some in the elven kingdom thought it odd that the Speaker would take into his house the bastard son of his dead brother's wife after she had been raped by a human warrior. She had died of grief only months after the birth of her half-breed child. But the Speaker, who had strong views on responsibility, took in the child without hesitation. It was only in later years, as he watched with growing unease the developing relationship between his beloved daughter and the bastard half-elf, that he began to regret his decision. The situation confused Tanis as well. Being half-human, the young man acquired a maturity the slower developing elfmaid could not understand. Tanis saw the unhappiness their union must bring down upon the family he loved. He also was beset by the inner turmoil that would torment him in later life: the constant battle between the elvish and the human within him. At the age of eighty—about twenty in human years—Tanis left Qualinost. The Speaker was not sorry to see Tanis leave. He tried to hide his feelings from the young half-elf, but both of them knew it.

Gilthanas had not been so tactful. He and Tanis had exchanged bitter words over Laurana. It was years before the sting of those words faded, and Tanis wondered if he had ever truly forgotten or forgiven. Clearly, Gilthanas had done neither.

The journey for these two was very long. Tanis made a few attempts at desultory conversation and became immediately aware that Gilthanas had changed. The young elflord had always been open and honest, fun-loving and light-hearted. He did not envy his older brother the responsibilities inherent in his role as heir to the throne. Gilthanas was a scholar, a dabbler in the magic arts, though he never took them as seriously as Raistlin. He was an excellent warrior, though he disliked fighting, as do all elves. He was deeply devoted to his family, especially his sister. But now he sat silent and moody, an unusual characteristic in elves. The only time he showed any interest in anything was when Caramon had begun plotting an escape. Gilthanas told him sharply to forget it, he would ruin everything. When pressed to elaborate, the elf fell silent, muttering only something about "overwhelming odds."

By sunrise of the third day, the draconian army was flagging from the night's long march and looking forward to a rest. The companions had spent another sleepless night and looked forward to nothing but another chill and dismal day. But the cages suddenly rolled to a stop. Tanis glanced up, puzzled at the change in routine. The other prisoners roused themselves and looked out the cage bars. They saw an old man, dressed in long robes that once might have been white and a battered, pointed hat. He appeared to be talking to a tree.

"I say, did you hear me?" The old man shook a worn walking stick at the oak. "I said move and I meant it! I was sitting on that rock"—he pointed to a boulder—"enjoying the rising sun on my old bones when you had the nerve to cast a shadow over it and chill me! Move this instant, I say!"

The tree did not respond. It also did not move.

"I won't take any more of your insolence!" The old man began to beat on the tree with his stick. "Move or I'll, I'll—"

"Someone shut that loony in a cage!" Fewmaster Toede shouted, galloping back from the front of the caravan.

"Get your hands off me!" the old man shrieked at the draconians who ran up and accosted him. He beat on them feebly with his staff until they took it away from him. "Arrest the tree!" he insisted. "Obstructing sunlight! That's the charge!"

The draconians threw the old man roughly into the companions' cage. Tripping over his robes, he fell to the floor.

"Are you all right, Old One?" Riverwind asked as he assisted the old man to a seat.

Goldmoon left Theros's side. "Yes, Old One," she said softly. "Are you hurt? I am a cleric of—"

"Mishakal!" he said, peering at the amulet around her neck. "How very interesting. My, my." He stared at her in astonishment. "You don't look three hundred years old!"

Goldmoon blinked, uncertain how to react. "How did you know? Did you recognize—? I'm not three hundred—" She was growing confused.

"Of course, you're not. I'm sorry, my dear." The old man patted her hand. "Never bring up a lady's age in public. Forgive me. It won't happen again. Our little secret," he said in a piercing whisper. Tas and Tika started to giggle. The old man looked around. "Kind of you to stop and offer me a lift. The road to Qualinost is long."

"We're not going to Qualinost," Gilthanas said sharply. "We're prisoners, going to the slave mines of Pax Tharkas."

"Oh?" the old man glanced around vaguely. "Is there another group due by here soon, then? I could have sworn this was the one."

"What is your name, Old One?" Tika asked.

"My name?" The old man hesitated, frowning. "Fizban? Yes, that's it. Fizban."

"Fizban!" Tasslehoff repeated as the cage lurched to a start again. "That's not a name!"

"Isn't it?" the old man asked wistfully. "That's too bad. I was rather fond of it."

"I think it's a splendid name," Tika said, glaring at Tas. The kender subsided into a corner, his eyes on the pouches slung over the old man's shoulder.

Suddenly Raistlin began to cough and they all turned their attention to him. His coughing spasms had been growing worse and worse. He was exhausted and in obvious pain; his skin burned to the touch. Goldmoon was unable to help him. Whatever was burning the mage up inside, the cleric could not heal. Caramon knelt beside him, wiping away the bloody saliva that flecked his brother's lips.

"He's got to have that stuff he drinks!" Caramon looked up in anguish. "I've never seen him this bad. If they won't listen to reason"—the big man scowled—"I'll break their heads! I don't care how many there are!"

"We'll talk to them when we stop for the night," Tanis promised, though he could guess the Fewmaster's answer.

"Excuse me," the old man said. "May I?" Fizban sat down beside Raistlin. He laid his hand on the mage's head and sternly spoke a few words.

Caramon, listening closely, heard "Fistandan . . ." and "not the time . . ." Certainly it wasn't a healing prayer, such as Goldmoon had tried, but the big man saw that his brother responded! The response was astonishing, however. Raistlin's eyes fluttered and opened. He looked up at the old man with a wild expression of terror and grasped Fizban's wrist in his thin, frail hand. For an instant it seemed Raistlin knew the old man, then Fizban passed his hand over the mage's eyes. The look of terror subsided, replaced by confusion.

"Hullo," Fizban beamed at him. "Name's—uh—Fizban." He shot a stern glance at Tasslehoff, daring the kender to laugh.

"You are . . . magi!" Raistlin whispered. His cough was gone.

"Why, yes, I suppose I am."

"I am magi!" Raistlin said, struggling to sit up.

"No kidding!" Fizban seemed immensely tickled. "Small world, Krynn. I'll have to teach you a few of my spells. I have one . . . a fireball . . . let's see, how did that go?"

The old man rambled on long past the time the caravan stopped at the rising of the sun.

Rescued! Fizban's magic.

6

Raistlin suffered in body, Sturm suffered in mind, but perhaps the one who experienced the keenest suffering during the companions' four-day imprisonment was Tasslehoff.

The cruelest form of torture one can inflict on a kender is to lock him up. Of course, it is also widely believed that the cruelest form of torture one can inflict on any other species is to lock them up with a kender. After three days of Tasslehoff's incessant chatter, pranks, and practical jokes, the companions would have willingly traded the kender for a peaceful hour of being stretched on the rack—at least that's what Flint said. Finally, after even Goldmoon lost her temper and nearly slapped him, Tanis sent Tasslehoff to the back of the cart. His legs hanging over the edge, the kender pressed his face against the iron bars and thought he would die of misery. He had never been so bored in his entire life.

Things got interesting with the discovery of Fizban, but the old man's amusement value wore thin when Tanis made Tas return the old magician's pouches. And so, driven to the point of desperation, Tasslehoff latched onto a new diversion.

Sestun, the gully dwarf.

The companions generally regarded Sestun with amused pity. The gully dwarf was the object of Toede's ridicule and mistreatment. He ran the Fewmaster's errands all night long, carrying messages from Toede at the front of the caravan to the hobgoblin captain at the rear, lugging food up to the Fewmaster from the supply cart, feeding and watering the Fewmaster's pony, and any other nasty jobs the Fewmaster could devise. Toede knocked him flat at least three times a day, the draconians tormented him, and the hobgoblins stole his food. Even the elk kicked at him whenever he trotted past. The gully dwarf bore it all with such a grimly defiant spirit that it won him the sympathy of the companions.

Sestun began to stay near the companions when not busy. Tanis, eager for information about Pax Tharkas, asked him about his homeland and how he came to work for the Fewmaster. The story took over a day for Sestun to relate and another day for the companions to piece together, since he started in the middle and plunged headlong into the beginning.

What it amounted to, eventually, wasn't much help. Sestun was among a large group of gully dwarves living in the hills around Pax Tharkas when Lord Verminaard and his draconians captured the iron mines which he needed to make steel weapons for his troops.

"Big fire—all day, all night. Bad smell." Sestun wrinkled his nose. "Pound rock. All day, all night. I get good job in kitchen"—his face brightened a moment—"fix hot soup. Very hot." His face fell. "Spill soup. Hot soup heat up armor real fast. Lord Verminaard sleep on back for week." He sighed. "I go with Fewmaster. Me volunteer."

"Maybe we can shut the mines down," Caramon suggested.

"That's a thought," Tanis mused. "How many draconians does Lord Verminaard have guarding the mines?"

"Two!" Sestun said, holding up ten grubby fingers.

Tanis sighed, remembering where they had heard that before.

Sestun looked at him hopefully. "There be only two dragons, too."

"Two dragons!" Tanis said incredulously.

"Not more than two."

Caramon groaned and settled back. The warrior had been giving dragon fighting serious thought ever since Xak Tsaroth. He and Sturm had reviewed every tale about Huma, the only known dragon fighter the knight could remember. Unfortunately, no one had ever taken the legends of Huma seriously before (except the Solamnic Knights, for which they were ridiculed), so much of Huma's tale had been distorted by time or forgotten.

"A knight of truth and power, who called down the gods themselves and forged the mighty Dragonlance," Caramon murmured now, glancing at Sturm, who lay asleep on the straw-covered floor of their prison.

"Dragonlance?" muttered Fizban, waking with a snort. "Dragonlance? Who said anything about the Dragonlance?"

"My brother," Raistlin whispered, smiling bitterly. "Quoting the Canticle. It seems he and the knight have taken a fancy to children's stories that have come to haunt them."

"Good story, Huma and the Dragonlance," said the old man, stroking his beard.

"Story—that's all it is." Caramon yawned and scratched his chest. "Who knows if it's real or if the Dragonlance was real or if even Huma was real?"

"We know the dragons are real," Raistlin murmured.

"Huma was real," Fizban said softly. "And so was the Dragonlance." The old man's face grew sad.

"Was it?" Caramon sat up. "Can you describe it?"

"Of course!" Fizban sniffed disdainfully.

Everyone was listening now. Fizban was, in fact, a bit disconcerted by his audience for his stories.

"It was a weapon similar to—no, it wasn't. Actually it was—no, it wasn't that either. It was closer to . . . almost a . . . rather it was, sort of a—lance, that's it! A lance!" He nodded earnestly. "And it was quite good against dragons."

"I'm taking a nap," Caramon grumbled.

Tanis smiled and shook his head. Sitting back against the bars, he wearily closed his eyes. Soon everyone except Raistlin and Tasslehoff fell into a fitful sleep. The kender, wide awake and bored, looked at Raistlin hopefully. Sometimes, if Raistlin was in a good mood, he would tell stories about magic-users of old. But the mage, wrapped in his red robes, was staring curiously at Fizban. The old man sat on a bench, snoring gently, his head bobbing up and down as the cart jounced over the road. Raistlin's golden eyes narrowed to gleaming slits as though he had been struck by a new and disturbing thought. After a moment, he pulled his hood up over his head and leaned back, his face lost in the shadows.

Tasslehoff sighed. Then, glancing around, he saw Sestun walking near the cage. The kender brightened. Here, he knew, was an appreciative audience for his stories.

Tasslehoff, calling him over, began to relate one of his own personal favorites. The two moons sank. The prisoners slept. The hobgoblins trailed along behind, half-asleep, talking about making camp soon. Fewmaster Toede rode up ahead, dreaming about promotion. Behind the Fewmaster, the draconians muttered among themselves in their harsh language, casting baleful glances at Toede when he wasn't looking.

Tasslehoff sat, swinging his legs over the side of the cage, talking to Sestun. The kender noticed without seeming to that Gilthanas was only pretending to sleep. Tas saw the elf's eyes open and glance quickly around when he thought no one was watching. This intrigued Tas immensely. It seemed almost as if Gilthanas was watching or waiting for something. The kender lost the thread of his story.

"And so I . . . uh . . . grabbed a rock from my pouch, threw it and—thunk—hit the wizard right on the head," Tas finished hurriedly. "The demon grabbed the wizard by the foot and dragged him down into the depths of the Abyss."

"But first demon thank you," prompted Sestun who had heard this story—with variations—twice before. "You forgot."

"Did I?" Tas asked, keeping an eye on Gilthanas. "Well, yes, the demon thanked me and took away the magic ring he'd given me. If it wasn't dark, you could see the outline the ring burned on my finger."

"Sun uping. Morning soon. I see then," the gully dwarf said eagerly.

It was still dark, but a faint light in the east hinted that soon the sun would be rising on the fourth day of their journey.

Suddenly Tas heard a bird call in the woods. Several answered it. What odd-sounding birds, Tas thought. Never heard their like before. But then he'd never been this far south before. He knew where they were from one of his many maps. They had passed over the only bridge across the Whiterage River and were heading south toward Pax Tharkas, which was marked on the kender's map as the site of the famed Thadarkan iron mines. The land began to rise, and thick forests of aspens appeared to the west. The draconians and hobgoblins kept eyeing the forests, and their pace picked up. Concealed within these woods was Qualinesti, the ancient elvenhome.

Another bird called, much nearer now. Then the hair rose on Tasslehoff's neck as the same bird call sounded from right behind him. The kender turned to see Gilthanas on his feet, his fingers to his lips, an eerie whistle splitting the air.

"Tanis!" Tas yelled, but the half-elf was already awake. So was everyone in the cart.

Fizban sat up, yawned, and glanced around. "Oh, good," he said mildly, "the elves are here."

"What elves, where?" Tanis sat up.

There was a sudden whirring sound like a covey of quail taking flight. A cry rang out from the supply wagon in front of them, then there was a splintering sound as the wagon, now driverless, lurched into a rut and tipped over. The driver of their cage wagon pulled sharply on the reins, stopping the elk before they ran into the wrecked supply wagon.

The cage tipped precariously, sending the prisoners sprawling. The driver got the elk going again and guided them around the wreckage.

Suddenly the driver of the cage screamed and clutched at his neck where the companions saw the feathered shaft of an arrow silhouetted against the dimly lit morning sky. The driver's body tumbled from the seat. The other guard stood up, sword raised, then he, too, toppled forward with an arrow in his chest. The elk, feeling the reins go slack, slowed until the cage rolled to a halt. Cries and screams echoed up and down the caravan as arrows whizzed through the air.

The companions fell for cover face first on the floor of the cage.

"What is it? What's going on?" Tanis asked Gilthanas.

But the elf, ignoring him, peered through the dawn gloom into the forest. "Porthios!" he called.

"Tanis, what's happening?" Sturm sat up, speaking his first words in four days.

"Porthios is Gilthanas's brother. I take it this is a rescue," Tanis said. An arrow zipped past and lodged in the wooden side of the cart, narrowly missing the knight.

"It won't be much of a rescue if we end up dead!" Sturm dropped to the floor. "I thought elves were expert marksmen!"

"Keep low." Gilthanas ordered. "The arrows are only to cover our escape. This is a strike-and-run raid. My people are not capable of attacking a large body directly. We must be ready to run for the woods."

"And how do we get out of these cages?" Sturm demanded.

"We cannot do everything for you!" Gilthanas replied coldly. "There are magic-users—"

"I cannot work without my spell components!" Raistlin hissed from beneath a bench. "Keep down, Old One," he said to Fizban who, head raised, was looking around with interest.

"Perhaps I can help," the old magician said, his eyes brightening. "Now, let me think—"

"What in the name of the Abyss is going on?" roared a voice out of the darkness. Fewmaster Toede appeared, galloping on his pony. "Why have we stopped?"

"We under attack!" Sestun cried, crawling out from under the cage where he'd taken cover.

"Attack? Blyxtshok! Get this cart moving!" Toede shouted. An arrow thunked into the Fewmaster's saddle. Toede's red eyes flew open and he stared fearfully into the woods. "We're under attack! Elves! Trying to free the prisoners!"

"Driver and guard dead!" Sestun shouted, flattening himself against the cage as another arrow just missed him. "What me do?"

An arrow zipped over Toede's head. Ducking, he had to clutch his pony's neck to keep himself from falling off. "I'll get another driver," he said hastily. "You stay here. Guard these prisoners with your life! I'll hold you responsible if they escape."

The Fewmaster stuck his spurs into his pony and the fear-crazed animal leaped forward. "My guard! Hobgoblins! To me!" the Fewmaster yelled as he galloped to the rear of the line. His shouts echoed back. "Hundreds of elves! We're surrounded. Charge to the north! I must report this to Lord Verminaard." Toede reined in at the sight of a draconian captain. "You draconians tend to the prisoners!" He spurred his horse on, still shouting, and one hundred hobgoblins charged after their valiant leader away from the battle. Soon, they were completely out of sight.

"Well, that takes care of the hobgoblins," Sturm said, his face relaxing in a smile. "Now all we have left to worry about is fifty or so draconians. I don't suppose, by the way, that there are hundreds of elves out there?"

Gilthanas shook his head. "More like twenty."

Tika, lying flat on the floor, cautiously raised her head and looked south. In the pale morning light, she could see the hulking forms of the draconians about a mile ahead, leaping into the cover on either side of the road as the elven

69

archers moved down to fire into their ranks. She touched Tanis's arm, pointing.

"We've got to get out of this cage," Tanis said, looking back. "The draconians won't bother taking us to Pax Tharkas now that the Fewmaster's gone. They'll just butcher us in these cages. Caramon?"

"I'll try," the fighter rumbled. He stood and gripped the bars of the cage in his huge hands. Closing his eyes, he took a deep breath and tried to force the bars apart. His face reddened, the muscles in his arms bunched, the knuckles on his big hands turned white. It was useless. Gasping for breath, Caramon flattened himself on the floor.

"Sestun!" Tasslehoff cried. "Your axe! Break the lock!"

The gully dwarf's eyes opened wide. He stared at the companions, then he glanced down the trail the Fewmaster had taken. His face twisted in an agony of indecision.

"Sestun—" Tasslehoff began. An arrow zinged past the kender. The draconians behind them were moving forward, firing into the cages. Tas flattened himself on the floor. "Sestun," he began again, "help free us and you can come with us!"

A look of firm resolve hardened Sestun's features. He reached for his axe, which he wore strapped onto his back. The companions watched in nail-biting frustration as Sestun felt all around his shoulders for the axe, which was located squarely in the middle of his back. Finally, one hand discovered the handle and he pulled the axe out. The blade glinted in the gray light of dawn.

Flint saw it and groaned. "That axe is older than I am! It must date back to the Cataclysm! He probably couldn't cut through a kender's brain, let alone that lock!"

"Hush!" Tanis instructed, although his own hopes sank at the sight of the gully dwarf's weapon. It wasn't even a battle-axe, just a small, battered, rusty wood-cutting axe the gully dwarf had apparently picked up somewhere, thinking it was a weapon. Sestun tucked the axe between his knees and spat on his hands.

Arrows thunked and clattered around the bars of the cage. One struck Caramon's shield. Another pinned Tika's blouse to the side of the cage, grazing her arm. Tika couldn't remember being more terrified in her life—not even the night dragons struck Solace. She wanted to scream, she wanted Caramon to put his arm around her. But Caramon didn't dare move.

Tika caught sight of Goldmoon, shielding the injured Theros with her body, her face pale but calm. Tika pressed her lips together and drew a deep breath. Grimly she yanked the arrow out of the wood and tossed it to the floor, ignoring the stinging pain in her arm. Looking south, she saw that the draconians, momentarily confused by the sudden attack and the disappearance of Toede, were organized now, on their feet and running toward the cages. Their arrows filled the air. Their chest armor gleamed in the dim gray light of morning, so did the bright steel of their longswords, which they carried clamped in their jaws as they ran.

"Draconians, closing in," she reported to Tanis, trying to keep her voice from shaking.

"Hurry, Sestun!" Tanis shouted.

The gully dwarf gripped the axe, swung it with all his might, and missed the lock, striking the iron bars a blow that nearly jarred the axe from his hands. Shrugging apologetically, he swung again. This time he struck the lock.

"He didn't even dent it," Sturm reported.

"Tanis," Tika quavered, pointing. Several draconians were within ten feet of them, pinned down for a few moments by the elven archers, but all hope of rescue seemed lost.

Sestun struck the lock again.

"He chipped it," Sturm said in exasperation. "At this rate we'll be out in about three days! What are those elves doing, anyway? Why don't they quit skulking about and attack!"

"We don't have enough men to attack a force this size!" Gilthanas returned angrily, crouching next to the knight. "They'll get to us when they can! We are at the front of the line. See, others are escaping."

The elf pointed to the two wagons behind them. The elves had broken the locks and the prisoners were dashing madly for the woods as the elves covered them, darting out from the trees to let fly their deadly barrage of arrows. But once the prisoners were safe, the elves retreated into the trees.

The draconians had no intention of going into the elven woods after them. Their eyes were on the last prison cage and the wagon containing the prisoners' possessions. The companions could hear the shouts of the draconian captains. The meaning was clear: "Kill the prisoners. Divide the spoils."

Everyone could see that the draconians would reach them long before the elves did. Tanis swore in frustration. Everything seemed futile. He felt a stirring at his side. The old magician, Fizban, was getting to his feet.

"No, Old One!" Raistlin grasped at Fizban's robes. "Keep under cover!"

An arrow zipped through the air and stuck in the old man's bent and battered hat. Fizban, muttering to himself, did not seem to notice. He presented a wonderful target in the gray light. Draconian arrows flew around him like wasps, and seemed to have as little effect, although he did appear mildly annoyed when one stuck into a pouch he happened to have his hand in at the moment.

"Get down!" Caramon roared. "You're drawing their fire!"

Fizban did kneel down for a moment, but it was only to talk to Raistlin. "Say there, my boy," he said as an arrow flew past right where he'd been standing. "Have you got a bit of bat guano on you? I'm out."

"No, Old One," Raistlin whispered frantically. "Get down!"

"No? Pity. Well, I guess I'll have to wing it." The old magician stood up, planted his feet firmly on the floor, and rolled up the sleeves of his robes. He shut his eyes, pointed at the cage door, and began to mumble strange words.

"What spell is he casting?" Tanis asked Raistlin. "Can you understand?"

The young mage listened intently, his brow furrowed. Suddenly Raistlin's eyes opened wide. "NO!" he shrieked, trying to pull on the old magician's robe to break his concentration. But it was too late. Fizban said the final word and pointed his finger at the lock on the back door of the cage.

"Take cover!" Raistlin threw himself beneath a bench. Sestun, seeing the old magician point at the cage door—and at him on the other side of it—fell flat on his face. Three draconians, reaching the cage door, their weapons dripping with their saliva, skidded to a halt, staring up in alarm.

"What is it?" Tanis yelled.

"Fireball!" Raistlin gasped, and at that moment a gigantic ball of yellow-orange fire shot from the old magician's fingertips and struck the cage door with an explosive boom. Tanis buried his face in his hands as flames billowed and crackled around him. A wave of heat washed over him, searing his lungs. He heard the draconians scream in pain and smelled burning reptile flesh. Then smoke flew down his throat.

"The floor's on fire!" Caramon yelled.

Tanis opened his eyes and staggered to his feet. He expected to see the old magician nothing but a mound of black ash like the bodies of the draconians lying behind the wagon. But Fizban stood staring at the iron door, stroking his singed beard in dismay. The door was still shut.

"That really should have worked," he said.

"What about the lock?" Tanis yelled, trying to see through the smoke. The iron bars of the cell door already glowed red hot.

"It didn't budge!" Sturm shouted. He tried to approach the cage door to kick it open, but the heat radiating from the bars made it impossible. "The lock may be hot enough to break!" He choked in the smoke.

"Sestun!" Tasslehoff's shrill voice rose above the crackling flames. "Try again! Hurry!"

The gully dwarf staggered to his feet, swung the axe, missed, swung again, and hit the lock. The superheated metal shattered, the lock gave way, and the cage door swung open.

"Tanis, help us!" Goldmoon cried as she and Riverwind struggled to pull the injured Theros from his smoking pallet.

"Sturm, the others!" Tanis yelled, then coughed in the smoke. He staggered to the front of the wagon, as the rest jumped out, Sturm grabbing hold of Fizban, who was still staring sadly at the door.

"Come on, Old One!" he yelled, his gentle actions belying his harsh words as he took Fizban's arm. Caramon, Raistlin, and Tika caught Fizban as he jumped from the flaming wreckage. Tanis and Riverwind lifted Theros by the shoulders and dragged him out, Goldmoon stumbled after them. She and Sturm jumped from the cart just as the ceiling collapsed.

"Caramon! Get our weapons from the supply wagon!" Tanis shouted. "Go with him, Sturm. Flint and Tasslehoff, get the packs. Raistlin—"

"I will, get my pack," the mage said, choking in the smoke. "And my staff. No one else may touch them."

"All right," Tanis said, thinking quickly. "Gilthanas—"

"I am not yours to order around, Tanthalas," the elf snapped and ran off into the woods without looking back.

Before Tanis could answer, Sturm and Caramon ran back. Caramon's knuckles were split and bleeding. There had been two draconians looting the supply wagon.

"Get moving!" Sturm shouted. "More coming! Where's your elf friend?" he asked Tanis suspiciously.

"He's gone ahead into the woods," Tanis said. "Just remember, he and his people saved us."

"Did they?" Sturm said, his eyes narrow. "It seems that between the elves and the old man, we came closer to getting killed than with just about anything short of the dragon!"

At that moment, six draconians rushed out from the smoke, skidding to a halt at the sight of the warriors.

"Run for the woods!" Tanis yelled, bending down to help Riverwind lift Theros. They carried the smith to cover while Caramon and Sturm stood, side by side, covering their retreat. Both noticed immediately that the creatures they faced were unlike the draconians they had fought before. Their armor and coloring were different, and they carried bows and longswords, the latter dripping with some sort of awful icor. Both men remembered stories about draconians that turned to acid and those whose bones exploded.

Caramon charged forward, bellowing like an enraged animal, his sword slashing in an arc. Two draconians fell before they knew what was attacking. Sturm saluted the other four with his sword and swept off the head of one in the return stroke. He jumped at the others, but they stopped just out of his range, grinning, apparently waiting for something.

Sturm and Caramon watched uneasily, wondering what was going on. Then they knew. The bodies of the slain draconians near them began to melt into the road. The flesh boiled and ran like lard in a skillet. A yellowish vapor formed over them, mixing with the thinning smoke from the smoldering cage. Both men gagged as the yellow vapor rose around them. They grew dizzy and knew they were being poisoned.

"Come on! Get back!" Tanis yelled from the woods.

The two stumbled back, fleeing through a rainstorm of arrows as a force of forty or fifty draconians swept around the cage, screeching in anger. The draconians started after them, then fell back when a clear voice called out, "Hai! Ulsain!" and ten elves, led by Gilthanas, ran from the woods.

"Quen talas uvenelei!" Gilthanas shouted. Caramon and Sturm staggered past him, the elves covering their retreat, then the elves fell back.

"Follow me," Gilthanas told the companions, switching to High Common. At a sign from Gilthanas, four of the elven warriors picked up Theros and carried him into the woods.

Tanis looked back at the cage. The draconians had come to a halt, eyeing the woods warily.

"Hurry!" Gilthanas urged. "My men will cover you."

Elven voices rose out of the woods, taunting the approaching draconians, trying to lure them into arrow range. The companions looked at each other hesitantly.

"I do not want to enter Elvenwood," Riverwind said harshly.

"It is all right," Tanis said, putting his hand on Riverwind's arm. "You have my pledge." Riverwind stared at him for a moment, then plunged into the woods, the others walking by his side. Last to come were Caramon and Raistlin, helping Fizban. The old man glanced back at the cage, now nothing more than a pile of ashes and twisted iron.

"Wonderful spell. And did anyone say a word of thanks?" he asked wistfully.

The elves led them swiftly through the wilderness. Without their guidance, the party would have been hopelessly lost. Behind them, the sounds of battle turned half-hearted.

"The draconians know better than to follow us into the woods," Gilthanas said, smiling grimly. Tanis, seeing armed elven warriors hidden among the leaves of the trees, had little fear of pursuit. Soon all sounds of fighting were lost.

A thick carpeting of dead leaves covered the ground. Bare tree limbs creaked in the chill wind of early morning. After spending days riding cramped in the cage, the companions moved slowly and stiffly, glad for the exercise that warmed their blood. Gilthanas led them into a wide glade as the morning sun lit the woods with a pale light.

The glade was crowded with freed prisoners. Tasslehoff glanced eagerly around the group, then shook his head sadly.

"I wonder what happened to Sestun," he said to Tanis. "I thought I saw him run off."

"Don't worry." The half-elf patted him on the shoulder.

"He'll be all right. The elves have no love for gully dwarves, but they wouldn't kill him."

Tasslehoff shook his head. It wasn't the elves he was worried about.

Entering the clearing, the companions saw an unusually tall and powerfully built elf speaking to the group of refugees. His voice was cold, his demeanor serious and stern.

"You are free to go, if any are free to go in this land. We have heard rumors that the lands south of Pax Tharkas are not under the control of the Dragon Highlord. I suggest, therefore, that you head southeast. Move as far and as fast as you can this day. We have food and supplies for your journey, all that we can spare. We can do little else for you."

The refugees from Solace, stunned by their sudden freedom, stared around bleakly and helplessly. They had been farmers on the outskirts of Solace, forced to watch while their homes burned and their crops were stolen to feed the Dragon Highlord's army. Most of them had never been farther from Solace than Haven. Dragons and elves were creatures of legend. Now children's stories had come to haunt them.

Goldmoon's clear blue eyes glinted. She knew how they felt. "How can you be so cruel?" she called out angrily to the tall elf. "Look at these people. They have never been out of Solace in their lives and you tell them calmly to walk through a land overrun by enemy forces—"

"What would you have me do, human?" the elf interrupted her. "Lead them south myself? It is enough that we have freed them. My people have their own problems. I cannot be concerned with those of humans." He shifted his eyes to the group of refugees. "I warn you. Time is wasting. Be on your way!"

Goldmoon turned to Tanis, seeking support, but he just shook his head, his face dark and shadowed.

One of the men, giving the elves a haggard glance, stumbled off on the trail that meandered south through the wilderness.

The other men shouldered crude weapons, women caught up their children, and the families straggled off.

Goldmoon strode forward to confront the elf. "How can you care so little for—"

"For humans?" The elf stared at her coldly. "It was humans who brought the Cataclysm upon us. They were the ones who sought the gods, demanding in their pride the power that was granted Huma in humility. It was humans who caused the gods to turn their faces from us—"

"They haven't!" Goldmoon shouted. "The gods are among us!"

Porthios's eyes flared with anger. He started to turn away when Gilthanas stepped up to his brother and spoke to him swiftly in the elven language.

"What do they say?" Riverwind asked Tanis suspiciously.

"Gilthanas is telling how Goldmoon healed Theros," Tanis said slowly. It had been many, many years since he had heard or spoken more than a few words in the elven tongue. He had forgotten how beautiful the language was, so beautiful it seemed to cut his soul and leave him wounded and bleeding inside. He watched as Porthios's eyes widened in disbelief.

Then Gilthanas pointed at Tanis. Both the brothers turned to face him, their expressive elven features hardening. Riverwind flicked a glance at Tanis, saw the half-elf standing pale but composed under this scrutiny.

"You return to the land of your birth, do you not?" Riverwind asked. "It does not seem you are welcome."

"Yes," Tanis said grimly, aware of what the Plainsman was thinking. He knew Riverwind was not prying into personal affairs out of curiosity. In many ways, they were in more danger now than they had been with the Fewmaster.

"They will take us to Qualinost," Tanis said slowly, the words apparently causing him deep pain. "I have not been there for many years. As Flint will tell you, I was not forced out, but few were sorry to see me leave. As you once said to me, Riverwind—to humans I am half-elven. To elves, I was half-man."

78

"Then let us leave and travel south with the others," Riverwind said.

"You would never get out of here alive," Flint murmured.

Tanis nodded. "Look around," he said.

Riverwind glanced around him and saw the elven warriors moving like shadows among the trees, their brown clothing blending in with the wilderness that was their home. As the two elves ended their conversation, Porthios turned his gaze from Tanis back to Goldmoon.

"I have heard strange tales from my brother that bear investigation. I extend to you, therefore, what the elves have extended to no humans in years—our hospitality. You will be our honored guests. Please follow me."

Porthios gestured. Nearly two dozen elven warriors emerged from the woods, surrounding the companions.

"Honored prisoners is more like it. This is going to be rough on you, my lad," Flint said to Tanis in a low, gentle voice.

"I know, old friend." Tanis rested his hand on the dwarf's shoulder. "I know."

The Speaker of the Suns.

7

I have never imagined such beauty existed," Goldmoon said softly. The day's march had been difficult, but the reward at the end was beyond their dreams. The companions stood on a high cliff over the fabled city of Qualinost.

Four slender spires rose from the city's corners like glistening spindles, their brilliant white stone marbled with shining silver. Graceful arches, swooping from spire to spire, soared through the air. Crafted by ancient dwarven metalsmiths, they were strong enough to hold the weight of an army, yet they appeared so delicate that a bird lighting on them might overthrow the balance. These glistening arches were the city's only boundaries; there was no wall around Qualinost. The elven city opened its arms lovingly to the wilderness.

The buildings of Qualinost enhanced nature, rather than concealing it. The houses and shops were carved from rose-colored quartz. Tall and slender as aspen trees, they vaulted upward in impossible spirals from quartz-lined avenues. In the center stood a great tower of burnished gold, catching the sunlight and throwing it back in whirling, sparkling patterns that gave the tower life. Looking down upon the city, it seemed that peace and beauty unchanged from ages past must dwell in Qualinost, if it dwelled anywhere in Krynn.

"Rest here," Gilthanas told them, leaving them in a grove of aspen trees. "The journey has been long, and for that I apologize. I know you are weary and you hunger—"

Caramon looked up hopefully.

"But I must beg your indulgence a few moments longer. Please excuse me." Gilthanas bowed, then walked to stand by his brother. Sighing, Caramon began rummaging through his pack for the fifth time, hoping perhaps he had overlooked a morsel. Raistlin read his spellbook, his lips repeating the difficult words, trying to grasp their meaning, to find the correct inflection and phrasing that would make his blood burn and so tell him the spell was his at last.

The others looked around, marveling at the beauty of the city beneath them and the aura of ancient tranquillity that lay over it. Even Riverwind seemed touched; his face softened and he held Goldmoon close. For a brief instant, their caress and their sorrows eased and they found comfort in each other's nearness. Tika sat apart, watching them wistfully. Tasslehoff was trying to map their way from Gateway into Qualinost, although Tanis had told him four times that the way was secret and the elves would never permit him to carry off a map. The old magician, Fizban, was asleep. Sturm and Flint watched Tanis in concern—Flint because he alone had any idea of what the half-elf was suffering; Sturm because he knew what it was like returning to a home that didn't want you.

The knight laid his hand on Tanis's arm. "Coming home isn't easy, my friend, is it?" he asked.

"No," Tanis answered softly. "I thought I had left this behind long ago, but now I know I never truly left at all. Qualinesti is part of me, no matter how much I want to deny it."

"Hush, Gilthanas," Flint warned.

The elf came over to Tanis. "Runners were sent ahead and now they have returned," he said in elven. "My father has asked to see you—all of you—at once, in the Tower of the Sun. I cannot permit time for refreshment. In this we seem crude and impolite—"

"Gilthanas," Tanis interrupted in Common. "My friends and I have been through unimagined peril. We have traveled roads where—literally—the dead walked. We won't faint from hunger"—he glanced at Caramon—"some of us won't, at any rate."

The warrior, hearing Tanis, sighed and tightened his belt.

"Thank you," Gilthanas said stiffly. "I am glad you understand. Now, please follow as swiftly as you can."

The companions gathered their things hastily and woke Fizban. Rising to his feet, he fell over a tree root. "Big lummox!" he snapped, striking it with his staff. "There—did you see it? Tried to trip me!" he said to Raistlin.

The mage slipped his precious book back into its pouch. "Yes, Old One." Raistlin smiled, assisting Fizban to his feet. The old magician leaned on the young one's shoulder as they walked after the others. Tanis watched them, wondering. The old magician was obviously a dotard. Yet Tanis remembered Raistlin's look of stark terror when he woke and found Fizban leaning over him. What had the mage seen? What did he know about this old man? Tanis reminded himself to ask. Now, however, he had other, more pressing matters on his mind. Walking forward, he caught up with the elf.

"Tell me, Gilthanas," Tanis said in elven, the unfamiliar words haltingly coming back to him. "What's going on? I have a right to know."

"Have you?" Gilthanas asked harshly, glancing at Tanis from the corners of his almond-shaped eyes. "Do you care what happens to elves anymore? You can barely speak our language!"

"Of course, I care," Tanis said angrily. "You are my people, too!"

"Then why do you flaunt your human heritage?" Gilthanas gestured to Tanis's bearded face. "I would think you would be ashamed—" He stopped, biting his lip, his face flushing.

Tanis nodded grimly. "Yes, I was ashamed, and that's why I left. But if I was ashamed—who made me so?"

"Forgive me, Tanthalas," Gilthanas said, shaking his head. "What I said was cruel and, truly, I did not mean it. It's just that . . . if you only understood the danger we face!"

"Tell me!" Tanis practically shouted in his frustration. "I want to understand!"

"We are leaving Qualinesti," Gilthanas said.

Tanis stopped and stared at the elf. "Leaving Qualinesti?" he repeated, switching to Common in his shock. The companions heard him and cast quick glances at each other. The old magician's face darkened as he tugged at his beard.

"You can't mean it!" Tanis said softly. "Leaving Qualinesti! Why? Surely things aren't this bad—"

"They are worse," Gilthanas said sadly. "Look around you, Tanthalas. You see Qualinost in its final days."

They entered the first streets of the city. Tanis, at first glance, saw everything exactly as he had left it fifty years ago. Neither the streets of crushed gleaming rock nor the aspen trees they ran among had changed; the clean streets sparkled brightly in the sunshine; the aspens had grown perhaps, perhaps not. Their leaves glimmered in the late morning light, the gold and silver-inlaid branches rustled and sang. The houses along the streets had not changed. Decorated with quartz, they shimmered in the sunlight, creating small rainbows of color everywhere the eye looked. All seemed as the elves loved it—beautiful, orderly, unchanging. . . .

No, that was wrong, Tanis realized. The song of the trees was now sad and lamenting, not the peaceful, joyful song Tanis remembered. Qualinost *had* changed and the change was change itself. He tried to grasp hold of it, to understand it, even as he felt his soul shrivel with loss. The change was not in the buildings, not in the trees, or the sun shining through the leaves. The change was in the air. It crackled with tension, as before a storm. And, as Tanis walked the streets of Qualinost, he saw things he had never before seen in his homeland. He saw haste. He saw hurry. He saw indecision. He saw panic, desperation, and despair.

Women, meeting friends, embraced and wept, then parted and hurried on separate ways. Children sat forlorn, not understanding, knowing only that play was out of place. Men gathered in groups, hands on their swords, keeping watchful eyes on their families. Here and there, fires burned as the elves destroyed what they loved and could not carry with them, rather than let the coming darkness consume it.

Tanis had grieved over the destruction of Solace, but the sight of what was happening in Qualinost entered his soul like the blade of a dull knife. He had not realized it meant so much to him. He had known, deep in his heart, that even if he never returned, Qualinesti would always be there. But no, he was losing even that. Qualinesti would perish.

Tanis heard a strange sound and turned around to see the old magician weeping.

"What plans have you made? Where will you go? Can you escape?" Tanis asked Gilthanas bleakly.

"You will find out the answers to those questions and more, too soon, too soon," Gilthanas murmured.

The Tower of the Sun rose high above the other buildings in Qualinost. Sunlight reflecting off the golden surface gave the illusion of whirling movement. The companions entered the Tower in silence, awestruck by the beauty and majesty of the ancient building. Only Raistlin glanced around, unimpressed. To his eyes, there existed no beauty, only death.

Gilthanas led the companions to a small alcove. "This room is just off the main chamber," he said. "My father is meeting with the Heads of Household to plan the evacuation. My brother has gone to tell him of our arrival. When the business is finished, we will be summoned." At his gesture, elves entered, bearing pitchers and basins of cool water. "Please, refresh yourselves as time permits."

The companions drank, then washed the dust of the journey from their faces and hands. Sturm removed his cloak and carefully polished his armor as best he could with one of Tasslehoff's handkerchiefs. Goldmoon brushed out her shining hair, kept her cloak fastened around her neck. She and Tanis had decided the medallion she wore should remain hidden until the time seemed proper to reveal it; some would recognize it. Fizban tried, without much success, to straighten his bent and shapeless hat. Caramon looked around for something to eat. Gilthanas stood apart from them all, his face pale and drawn.

Within moments, Porthios appeared in the arched doorway. "You are called," he said sternly.

The companions entered the chamber of the Speaker of the Suns. No human had seen the inside of this building for hundreds of years. No kender had ever seen it. The last dwarves who saw it were the ones present at its construction, hundreds of years before.

"Ah, now this is craftsmanship," Flint said softly, tears misting his eyes.

The chamber was round and seemed immensely larger than the slender Tower could possibly encompass. Built entirely of white marble, there were no support beams, no columns. The room soared upwards hundreds of feet to form a dome at the very top of the tower where a beautiful mosaic made of inlaid, glittering tile portrayed the blue sky and the sun on one half; the silver moon, the red moon, and the stars on the other half, the halves separated by a rainbow.

There were no lights in the chamber. Cunningly built windows and mirrors focused sunlight into the room, no matter where the sun was located in the sky. The streams of sunlight converged in the center of the chamber illuminating a rostrum.

There were no seats in the Tower. The elves stood—men and women together; only those designated as Heads of Household had the right to be in this meeting. There were more women present than Tanis ever remembered seeing; many dressed in deep purple, the color of mourning. Elves marry for life and if the spouse dies do not remarry. Thus the widow has the status of Head of Household until her death.

The companions were led to the front of the chamber. The elves made room for them in respectful silence but gave them strange, forbidding looks—particularly the dwarf, the kender, and the two barbarians, who seemed grotesque in their outlandish furs. There were astonished murmurs at the sight of the proud and noble Knight of Solamnia. And there were scattered mutterings over the appearance of Raistlin in his red robes. Elven magic-users wore the white robes of good, not the red robes proclaiming neutrality. That, the elves believed, was just one step removed from black. As the crowd settled down, the Speaker of the Suns came forward to the rostrum.

It had been many years since Tanis had seen the Speaker, his adopted father, as it were. And here, too, he saw change. The man was still tall, taller even than his son Porthios. He was dressed in the yellow, shimmering robes of his office. His face was stern and unyielding, his manner austere. He was the Speaker of the Suns, called the Speaker; he had been called the Speaker for well over a century. Those who knew his name never pronounced it—including his children. But Tanis saw in his hair touches of silver, which had not been there before, and there were lines of care and sorrow in the face, which had previously seemed untouched by time.

Porthios joined his brother as the companions, led by the elves, entered. The Speaker extended his arms and called them by name. They walked forward into their father's embrace.

"My sons," the Speaker said brokenly, and Tanis was startled at this show of emotion. "I never thought to see either of you in this life again. Tell me of the raid—" he said, turning to Gilthanas.

"In time, Speaker," said Gilthanas. "First, I bid you, greet our guests."

"Yes, I am sorry." The Speaker passed a trembling hand over his face and it seemed to Tanis that he aged even as he stood before them. "Forgive me, guests. I bid you welcome, you who have entered this kingdom no one has entered for many years."

Gilthanas spoke a few words and the Speaker stared shrewdly at Tanis, then beckoned the half-elf forward. His words were cool, his manner polite, if strained. "Is it indeed you, Tanthalas, son of my brother's wife? The years have been long, and all have wondered about your fate. We welcome you back to your homeland, though I fear you come only to see its final days. My daughter, in particular, will be glad to see you. She has missed her childhood playmate."

Gilthanas stiffened at this, his face darkening as he looked at Tanis. The half-elf felt his own face flush. He bowed low before the Speaker, unable to say a word.

"I welcome the rest of you and hope to learn more of you later. We shall not keep you long, but it is right that you learn in this room what is happening in the world. Then you will be allowed to rest and refresh yourselves. Now, my son—" The Speaker turned to Gilthanas, obviously thankful to end the formalities. "The raid on Pax Tharkas?"

Gilthanas stepped forward, his head bowed. "I have failed, Speaker of the Suns."

A murmur passed among the elves like the wind among the aspens. The Speaker's face bore no expression. He simply sighed and stared unseeing out a tall window. "Tell your story," he said quietly.

Gilthanas swallowed, then spoke, his voice so low many in the back of the room leaned forward to hear.

"I traveled south with my warriors in secrecy, as was planned. All went well. We found a group of human resistance fighters, refugees from Gateway, who joined us, adding to our numbers. Then, by the cruelest mischance, we stumbled into the advance patrols of the dragonarmy. We fought valiantly, elves and humans together, but for naught. I was struck on the head and remember nothing more. When I awoke, I was lying in a ravine, surrounded by the bodies of my comrades. Apparently, the foul dragonmen shoved the wounded over the cliff, leaving us for dead." Gilthanas paused, clearing his throat. "Druids in the woods tended my injuries. From them, I learned that many of my warriors were still alive and had been taken prisoner. Leaving the druids to bury the dead, I followed the tracks of the dragonarmy and eventually came to Solace."

Gilthanas stopped. His face glistened with sweat and his hands twitched nervously. He cleared his throat again, tried to speak and failed. His father watched him with growing concern.

Gilthanas spoke. "Solace is destroyed."

There was a gasp from the audience.

"The mighty vallenwoods have been cut and burned, few now stand."

The elves wailed and cried out in dismay and anger. The Speaker held up his hand for order. "This is grievous news," he said sternly. "We mourn the passing of trees old even to us. But continue—what of our people?"

"I found my men tied to stakes in the center of the town square along with the humans who had helped us," Gilthanas said, his voice breaking. "They were surrounded by draconian guards. I hoped to be able to free them at night. Then—" His voice failed completely and he bowed his head as his older brother came over and laid a hand on his shoulder. Gilthanas straightened. "A red dragon appeared in the sky—"

Sounds of shock and dismay came from the assembled elves. The Speaker shook his head in sorrow.

"Yes, Speaker," Gilthanas said and his voice was loud, unnaturally loud and jarring. "It is true. These monsters have returned to Krynn. The red dragon circled above Solace and all who saw him fled in terror. He flew lower and lower and then landed in the town square. His great gleaming red reptile body filled the clearing, his wings spread destruction, his tail toppled trees. Yellow fangs glistened, green saliva dripped from his massive jaws, his huge talons tore the ground . . . and riding upon his back was a human male.

"Powerfully built, he was dressed in the black robes of a cleric of the Queen of Darkness. A black and gold cape fluttered around him. His face was hidden by a hideous horned mask fashioned in black and gold to resemble the face of a dragon. The dragonmen fell to their knees in worship as the dragon landed. The goblins and hobgoblins and foul humans who fight with the dragonmen cowered in terror; many ran away. Only the example of my people gave me the courage to stay."

Now that he was speaking, Gilthanas seemed eager to tell the story. "Some of the humans tied to stakes went into a frenzy of terror, screaming piteously. But my warriors remained calm and defiant, although all were affected alike by the dragonfear the monster generates. The dragonrider did not seem to find this pleasing. He glared at them, and then spoke in a voice that came from the depths of the Abyss. His words still burn in my mind.

"'I am Verminaard, Dragon Highlord of the North. I have fought to free this land and these people from the false beliefs spread by those who call themselves Seekers. Many have come to work for me, pleased to further the great cause of the Dragon Highlords. I have shown them mercy and graced them with the blessings my goddess has granted me. Spells of healing I possess, as do no others in this land, and therefore you know that I am the representative of the true gods. But you humans who stand before me now have defied me. You chose to fight me and therefore your punishment will serve as an example to any others who choose folly over wisdom.'

"Then he turned to the elves and said, 'Be it known by this act that I, Verminaard, will destroy your race utterly as decreed by my goddess. Humans can be taught to see the errors of their ways, but elves—never!' The man's voice rose until it raged louder than the winds. 'Let this be your final warning—all who watch! Ember, destroy!'

"And, with that, the great dragon breathed out fire upon all those tied to the stakes. They writhed helplessly, burning to death in terrible agony. . . ."

There was no sound at all in the chamber. The shock and horror were too great for words.

"A madness swept over me," Gilthanas continued, his eyes burning feverishly, almost a reflection of what he had seen. "I started to rush forward, to die with my people, when a great hand grasped me and dragged me backward. It was Theros Ironfeld, 'Now is not the time to die, elf,' he told me. "Now is the time for revenge.' I . . . I collapsed then, and he took me back to his house, in peril of his own life. And he would have paid for his kindness to elves with his life, had not this woman healed him!"

Gilthanas pointed to Goldmoon, who stood at the back of the group, her face shrouded by her fur cape. The Speaker turned to stare at her, as did the other elves in the chamber, their murmurings dark and ominous.

"Theros is the man brought here today, Speaker," Porthios said. "The man with but one arm. Our healers say he will live. But they say it is only by a miracle that his life was spared, so dreadful were his wounds."

"Come forward, woman of the Plains," the Speaker commanded sternly. Goldmoon took a step toward the rostrum, Riverwind at her side. Two elven guards moved swiftly to block him. He glared at them but stood where he was.

The Chieftain's Daughter moved forward, holding her head proudly. As she removed her hood, the sun shone on the silver-gold hair cascading down her back. The elves marveled at her beauty.

"You claim to have healed this man—Theros Ironfeld?" The Speaker asked her with disdain.

"I claim nothing," Goldmoon answered coolly. "Your son saw me heal him. Do you doubt his words?"

"No, but he was overwrought, sick and confused. He may have mistaken witchcraft for healing."

"Look on this," Goldmoon said gently and untied her cape, letting it fall away from her neck. The medallion sparkled in the sunlight.

The Speaker left the rostrum and came forward, his eyes widening in disbelief. Then his face became distorted with rage. "Blasphemy!" he shouted. Reaching out, he started to rip the medallion from Goldmoon's throat.

There was a flash of blue light. The Speaker crumbled to the floor with a cry of pain. As the elves shouted out in alarm, drawing their swords, the companions drew theirs. Elven warriors rushed to surround them.

"Stop this nonsense!" said the old magician in a strong, stern voice. Fizban tottered up to the rostrum, calmly pushing aside the sword blades as if they were slender branches of an aspen tree. The elves stared in astonishment, seemingly unable to stop him. Muttering to himself, Fizban came up to the Speaker, who was lying stunned on the floor. The old man helped the elf to his feet.

"Now then, you asked for that, you know," Fizban scolded, brushing the Speaker's robes as the elf gaped at him.

"Who are you?" the Speaker gasped.

"Mmmm. What was that name?" The old magician glanced around at Tasslehoff.

"Fizban," the kender said helpfully.

"Yes, Fizban. That's who I am." The magician stroked his white beard. "Now, Solostaran, I suggest you call off your guards and tell everyone to settle down. I, for one, would like to hear the story of this young woman's adventures, and you, for one, would do well to listen. It wouldn't hurt you to apologize, either."

As Fizban shook his finger at the Speaker, his battered hat tilted forward, covering his eyes. "Help! I've gone blind!" Raistlin, with a distrustful glance at the elven guards, hurried forward. He took the old man's arm and straightened his hat.

"Ah, thank the true gods," the magician said, blinking and shuffling across the floor. The Speaker watched the old magician, a puzzled expression on his face. Then, as if in a dream, he turned to face Goldmoon.

"I do apologize, lady of the Plains," he said softly. "It has been over three hundred years since the elven clerics vanished, three hundred years since the symbol of Mishakal was seen in this land. My heart bled to see the amulet profaned, as I thought. Forgive me. We have been in despair so long I failed to see the arrival of hope. Please, if you are not weary, tell us your story."

Goldmoon related the story of the medallion, telling of Riverwind and the stoning, the meeting of the companions at the Inn, and their journey to Xak Tsaroth. She told of the destruction of the dragon and of how she received the medallion of Mishakal. But she didn't mention the Disks.

The sun's rays lengthened as she spoke, changing color as twilight approached. When her story ended, the Speaker was silent for long moments.

"I must consider all of this and what it means to us," he said finally. He turned to the companions. "You are exhausted. I see some of you stand by courage alone. Indeed"—he smiled, looking at Fizban who leaned against a pillar, snoring softly— "some of you are asleep on your feet. My daughter, Laurana, will guide you to a place where you can forget your fears. We will hold a banquet in your honor tonight, for you bring us hope. May the peace of the true gods go with you."

The elves parted, and out of their midst came an elf-maiden who walked forward to stand beside the Speaker. At sight of her, Caramon's mouth sagged open. Riverwind's eyes widened. Even Raistlin stared, his eyes seeing beauty at last, for no hint of decay touched the young elfmaiden.

Her hair was honey pouring from a pitcher; it spilled over her arms and down her back, past her waist, touching her wrists as she stood with her arms at her sides. Her skin was smooth and woodland brown. She had the delicate, refined features of the elves, but these were combined with full, pouting lips and large liquid eyes that changed color like leaves in flickering sunshine.

"On my honor as a knight," Sturm said with a catch in his voice, "I've never seen any woman so lovely."

"Nor will you in this world," Tanis murmured.

All the companions glanced at Tanis sharply as he spoke, but the half-elf did not notice. His eyes were on the elfmaid. Sturm raised his eyebrows, exchanged looks with Caramon who nudged his brother. Flint shook his head and sighed a sigh that seemed to come from his toes.

"Now much is made clear," Goldmoon said to Riverwind.

"It hasn't been made clear to me," Tasslehoff said. "Do you know what's going on, Tika?"

All Tika knew was that, looking at Laurana, she felt suddenly dumpy and half-dressed, freckled and red-headed. She tugged her blouse up higher over her full bosom, wishing it didn't reveal quite so much or that she had less to reveal.

"Tell me what's going on,"Tasslehoff whispered, seeing the knowing looks exchanged by the others.

"I don't know!" Tika snapped. "Just that Caramon's making a fool of himself. Look at the big ox. You'd think he'd never seen a woman before."

"She is pretty," Tas said. "Different from you, Tika. She's slender and she walks like a tree bending in the wind and—"

"Oh, shut up!" Tika snapped furiously, giving Tas a shove that nearly knocked him down.

Tasslehoff gave her a wounded glance, then walked over to stand beside Tanis, determined to keep near the half-elf until he figured out what was going on.

"I welcome you to Qualinost, honored guests," Laurana said shyly, in a voice that was like a clear stream rippling among the trees. "Please follow me. The way is not far, and there is food and drink and rest at the end."

Moving with childlike grace, she walked among the companions who parted for her as the elves had done, all of them staring at her admiringly. Laurana lowered her eyes in maidenly modesty and self-consciousness, her cheeks flushing. She looked up only once, and that was as she passed Tanis— a fleeting glance, that only Tanis saw. His face grew troubled, his eyes darkened.

The companions left the Tower of the Sun, waking Fizban as they departed.

TANIS AND LAURANA.

8

Laurana led them to a sun-dappled grove of aspens in the very center of the city. Here, though surrounded by buildings and streets, they seemed to be in the heart of a forest. Only the murmurings of a nearby brook broke the stillness. Laurana, gesturing toward fruit trees among the aspens, told the companions to pick and eat their fill. Elfmaids brought in baskets of fresh, fragrant bread. The companions washed in the brook, then returned to relax on soft moss beds to revel in the silent peacefulness around them.

All except Tanis. Refusing food, the half-elf wandered around the grove, absorbed in his own thoughts. Tasslehoff watched him closely, eaten alive by curiosity.

Laurana was a perfect, charming hostess. She made certain everyone was seated and comfortable, speaking a few words to each of them.

"Flint Fireforge, isn't it?" she said. The dwarf flushed with pleasure. "I still have some of the wonderful toys you made me. We have missed you, these many years."

So flustered he couldn't talk, Flint plopped down on the grass and gulped down a huge mug of water.

"You are Tika?" Laurana asked, stopping by the barmaid.

"Tika Waylan," the girl said huskily.

"Tika, what a pretty name. And what beautiful hair you have," Laurana said, reaching out to touch the bouncy red curls admiringly.

"Do you think so?" Tika said, blushing, seeing Caramon's eyes on her.

"Of course! It is the color of flame. You must have a spirit to match. I heard how you saved my brother's life in the Inn, Tika. I am deeply indebted to you."

"Thank you," Tika answered softly. "Your hair is real pretty, too."

Laurana smiled and moved on. Tasslehoff noticed, however, that her eyes constantly strayed to Tanis. When the half-elf suddenly threw down an apple and disappeared into the trees, Laurana excused herself hurriedly and followed.

"Ah, now I'll find out what's going on!" Tas said to himself. Glancing around, he slipped after Tanis.

Tas crept along the winding trail among the trees and suddenly came upon the half-elf standing beside the foaming stream alone, tossing dead leaves into the water. Seeing movement to his left, Tas quickly crouched down into a clump of bushes as Laurana emerged from another trail.

"Tanthalas Quisif nan-Pah!" she called.

As Tanis turned at the sound of his elven name, she flung her arms around his neck, kissing him. "Ugh," she said teasingly, pulling back. "Shave off that horrible beard. It itches! And you don't look like Tanthalas anymore."

Tanis put his hands to her waist and gently pushed her away. "Laurana—" he began.

"No, don't be mad about the beard. I'll learn to like it, if you insist," Laurana pleaded, pouting. "Kiss me back. No? Then I'll kiss you until you cannot help yourself." She kissed him again until finally Tanis broke free of her grip.

"Stop it, Laurana," he said harshly, turning away.

"Why, what's the matter?" she asked, catching hold of his hand. "You've been gone so many years. And now you're back.

Don't be cold and gloomy. You are my betrothed, remember? It is proper for a girl to kiss her betrothed."

"That was a long time ago," Tanis said. "We were children, then, playing a game, nothing more. It was romantic, a secret to share. You know what would have happened if your father had found out. Gilthanas did find out, didn't he?"

"Of course! I told him," Laurana said, hanging her head, looking up at Tanis through her long eyelashes. "I tell Gilthanas everything, you know that. I didn't think he'd react like that! I know what he said to you. He told me later. He felt badly."

"I'll bet he did." Tanis gripped her wrists, holding her hands still. "What he said was true, Laurana! I am a bastard half-breed. Your father would have every right to kill me! How could I bring disgrace down on him, after what he did for my mother and me? That was one reason I left—that and to find out who I am and where I belong."

"You are Tanthalas, my beloved, and you belong here!" Laurana cried. She broke free of his grip and caught his hands in her own. "Look! You wear my ring still. I know why you left. It was because you were afraid to love me, but you don't need to be, not anymore. Everything's changed. Father has so much to worry about, he won't mind. Besides, you're a hero now. Please, let us be married. Isn't that why you came back?"

"Laurana," Tanis spoke gently but firmly—"my returning was an accident—"

"No!" she cried, pushing him away. "I don't believe you."

"You must have heard Gilthanas's story. If Porthios had not rescued us, we would have been in Pax Tharkas now!"

"He made it up! He didn't want to tell me the truth. You came back because you love me. I won't listen to anything else."

"I didn't want to tell you, but I see that I must," Tanis said, exasperated. "Laurana, I'm in love with someone else—a human woman. Her name is Kitiara. That doesn't mean I don't love you, too. I do—" Tanis faltered.

Laurana stared at him, all color drained from her face.

"I do love you, Laurana. But, you see, I can't marry you, because I love her, too. My heart is divided, just like my blood." He took off the ring of golden ivy leaves and handed it to her. "I release you from any promises you made to me, Laurana. And I ask you to release me."

Laurana took the ring, unable to speak. She looked at Tanis pleadingly, then, seeing only pity in his face, shrieked and flung the ring away from her. It fell at Tas's feet. He picked it up and slipped it into a pouch.

"Laurana," Tanis said sorrowfully, taking her in his arms as she sobbed wildly. "I'm so sorry. I never meant—"

At this point, Tasslehoff slipped out of the brush and made his way back up the trail.

"Well," said the kender to himself, sighing in satisfaction— "now at least I know what's going on."

Tanis awoke suddenly to find Gilthanas standing over him. "Laurana?" he asked, getting to his feet.

"She is all right," Gilthanas said quietly. "Her maidens brought her home. She told me what you said. I just want you to know I understand. It was what I feared all along. The human half of you cries to other humans. I tried to tell her, hoping she wouldn't get hurt. She will listen to me now. Thank you, Tanthalas. I know it cannot have been easy."

"It wasn't," Tanis said, swallowing. "I'm going to be honest, Gilthanas—I love her, I really do. It's just that—"

"Please, say no more. Let us leave it as it is and perhaps, if we cannot be friends, we can at least respect each other." Gilthanas's face was drawn and pale in the setting sun. "You and your friends must prepare yourselves. When the silver moon rises, there will be a feast, and then the High Council meeting. Now is the time when decisions must be made."

He left. Tanis stared after him a moment, then, sighing, went to wake the others.

MARGARET WEIS & TRACY HICKMAN

FAREWELL.
THE COMPANIONS' DECISION.

9

The feast held in Qualinost reminded Goldmoon of her mother's funeral banquet. Like the feast, the funeral was supposed to be a joyous occasion—after all, Tearsong had become a goddess. But the people found it difficult to accept the death of this beautiful woman. And so the Que-shu mourned her passing with a grief that approached blasphemy.

Tearsong's funeral banquet was the most elaborate to be given in the memory of the Que-shu. Her grieving husband had spared no expense. Like the banquet in Qualinost on this night, there was a great deal of food which few could eat. There were half-hearted attempts at conversation when no one wanted to talk. Occasionally someone, overcome with sorrow, was forced to leave the table.

So vivid was this memory that Goldmoon could eat little; the food was ash in her mouth. Riverwind regarded her with concern. His hand found hers beneath the table and she gripped it hard, smiling as his strength flowed into her body.

The elven feast was held in the courtyard just south of the great golden tower. There were no walls about the platform of crystal and marble which sat atop the highest hill in Qualinost, offering an unobstructed view of the glittering city below, the dark forest beyond, and even the deep purple edge of the Tharkadan Mountains far to the south. But the beauty was lost on those in attendance, or made more poignant by the knowledge that soon it would be gone forever. Goldmoon sat at the right hand of the Speaker. He tried to make polite conversation, but eventually his worries and concerns overwhelmed him and he fell silent.

To the Speaker's left sat his daughter, Laurana. She made no pretense at eating, just sat with her head bowed, her long hair flowing around her face. When she did look up, it was to gaze at Tanis, her heart in her eyes.

The half-elf, very much aware of the heart-broken stare as well as of Gilthanas eyeing him coldly, ate his food without appetite, his eyes fixed on his plate. Sturm, next to him, was drawing up in his mind plans for the defense of Qualinesti.

Flint felt strange and out of place as dwarves always feel among elves. He didn't like elven food anyway and refused everything. Raistlin nibbled at his food absently, his golden eyes studying Fizban. Tika, feeling awkward and out of place among the graceful elven women, couldn't eat a morsel. Caramon decided he knew why elves were so slender: the food consisted of fruits and vegetables, cooked in delicate sauces, served with bread and cheeses and a very light, spicy wine. After starving for four days in the cage, the food did nothing to satisfy the big warrior's hunger.

The only two in the entire city of Qualinost to enjoy the feast were Tasslehoff and Fizban. The old magician carried on a one-sided argument with an aspen, while Tasslehoff simply enjoyed everything, discovering later—to his surprise—that two golden spoons, a silver knife, and a butter dish made of a seashell had wandered into one of his pouches.

The red moon was not visible. Solinari, a slim band of silver in the sky, began to wane. As the first stars appeared, the Speaker of the Suns nodded sadly at his son. Gilthanas rose and moved to stand next to his father's chair.

Gilthanas began to sing. The elven words flowed into a melody delicate and beautiful. As he sang, Gilthanas held a small crystal lamp in both hands, the candlelight within illuminating his marble features. Tanis, listening to the song, closed his eyes; his head sank into his hands.

"What is it? What do the words mean?" Sturm asked softly.

Tanis raised his head. His voice breaking, he whispered:

The Sun
The splendid eye
Of all our heavens
Dives from the day,

And leaves
The dozing sky,
Spangled with fireflies,
Deepening in gray.

The elves about the table stood quietly now, taking up their own lamps as they joined in the song. Their voices blended, weaving a haunting song of infinite sadness.

Now Sleep,
Our oldest friend,
Lulls in the trees
And calls
Us in.

The Leaves
Give off cold fire,
They blaze into ash
At the end of the year.

And birds
Coast on the winds,
And wheel to the North
When Autumn ends.

The day grows dark,
The seasons bare,
But we
Await the sun's
Green fire upon
The trees.

Points of flickering lantern light spread from the court-yard like ripples in a still, calm pond, through the streets, into the forests and beyond. And, with each lamp lit, another voice was raised in song, until the surrounding forest itself seemed to sing with despair.

The wind
Dives through the days.
By season, by moon
Great kingdoms arise.

The breath
Of firefly, of bird,
Of trees, of mankind
Fades in a word.

Now Sleep,
Our oldest friend,
Lulls in the trees
And calls
Us in.

The Age,
The thousand lives
Of men and their stories
Go to their graves.

But We,
The people long

In poem and glory
Fade from the song.

Gilthanas's voice died away. With a gentle breath, he blew out the flame of his lamp. One by one, as they had started, the others around the table ended the song and blew out their candles. All through Qualinost, the voices hushed and the flames were extinguished until it seemed that silence and darkness swept over the land. At the very end, only the distant mountains returned the final chords of the song, like the whispering of leaves falling to the ground.

The Speaker stood.

"And now," he said heavily, "it is time for the meeting of the High Council. It will be held in the Hall of the Sky. Tanthalas, if you will lead your companions there."

The Hall of the Sky, they discovered, was a huge square, lit by torches. The giant dome of the heavens, glittering with stars, arched above it. But it was dark to the north where lightning played on the horizon. The Speaker motioned to Tanis to bring the companions to stand near him, then the entire population of Qualinost gathered around them. There was no need to call for silence. Even the wind hushed as the Speaker began.

"Here you see our situation." He gestured at something on the ground. The companions saw a gigantic map beneath their feet. Tasslehoff, standing in the middle of the Plains of Abanasinia, drew in a deep breath. He couldn't remember ever seeing anything so wonderful.

"There's Solace!" he cried in excitement, pointing.

"Yes, Kenderkin," the Speaker replied. "And that is where the dragonarmies mass. In Solace"—he touched the spot on the map with a staff—"and in Haven. Lord Verminaard has made no secret of his plans to invade Qualinesti. He waits only to gather his forces and secure his supply routes. We cannot hope to stand against such a horde."

"Surely Qualinost is easily defended," Sturm spoke up. "There is no direct route overland. We crossed bridges over ravines that no army in existence could get through if the bridges were cut. Why do you not stand up to them?"

"If it were only an army, we could defend Qualinesti," the Speaker answered. "But what can we do against dragons?" The Speaker spread his hands helplessly. "Nothing! According to legends, it was only with the Dragonlance that the mighty Huma defeated them. There are none now—at least that we know of—who remember the secret of that great weapon."

Fizban started to speak, but Raistlin hushed him.

"No," the Speaker continued, "we must abandon this city and these woods. We plan to go west, into the unknown lands there, hoping to find a new home for our people—or perhaps even return to Silvanesti, the most ancient elvenhome. Until a week ago, our plans were advancing well. It will take three days of forced marching for the Dragon Highlord to move his men into attack position, and spies will inform us when the army leaves Solace. We will have time to escape into the west. But then we learned of a third dragonarmy at Pax Tharkas, less than a day's journey from us. Unless that army is stopped, we are doomed."

"And you know a way to stop that army?" Tanis asked.

"Yes." The Speaker looked at his youngest son. "As you know, men from Gateway and Solace and surrounding communities are being held prisoner in the fortress of Pax Tharkas, working as slaves for the Dragon Highlord. Verminaard is clever. Lest his slaves revolt, he keeps the women and children of these men hostages, ransom for the men's behavior. It is our belief that, were these captives freed, the men would turn on their masters and destroy them. It was to have been Gilthanas's mission to free the hostages and lead the revolt. He would have taken the humans south into the mountains, drawing off this third army in pursuit, allowing us time to escape."

"And what of the humans then?" Riverwind asked harshly. "It seems to me you throw them to the dragonarmies as a desperate man throws hunks of meat to pursuing wolves."

MARGARET WEIS & TRACY HICKMAN

"Lord Verminaard will not keep them alive much longer, we fear. The ore is nearly gone. He is gleaning every last little bit, then the slaves' usefulness to him will end. There are valleys in the mountains, caves where the humans can live and fend off the dragonarmies. They can easily hold the mountain passes against them, especially now that winter is setting in. Admittedly, some may die, but that is a price that must be paid. If you had the choice, man of the Plains, would you rather die in slavery or die fighting?"

Riverwind, not answering, stared down at the map darkly.

"Gilthanas's mission failed," Tanis said, "and now you want us to try and lead the revolt?"

"Yes, Tanthalas," the Speaker replied. "Gilthanas knows a way into Pax Tharkas—the Sla-Mori. He can lead you into the fortress. You not only have a chance to free your own kind, but you offer the elves a chance to escape"—the Speaker's voice hardened—"a chance to live that many elves were not given when humans brought the Cataclysm down upon us!"

Riverwind glanced up, scowling. Even Sturm's expression darkened. The Speaker drew a deep breath, then sighed. "Please forgive me," he said. "I do not mean to flog you with whips from the past. We are not uncaring about the humans' plight. I send my son, Gilthanas, with you willingly, knowing that—if we part—we may never see each other again. I make this sacrifice, so that my people—and yours—may live."

"We must have time to consider," Tanis said, though he knew what his decision must be. The Speaker nodded and elven warriors cleared a path through the crowd, leading the companions to a grove of trees. Here, they left them alone.

Tanis's friends stood before him, their solemn faces masks of light and shadow beneath the stars. All this time, he thought, I have fought to keep us together. Now I see that we must separate. We cannot risk taking the Disks into Pax Tharkas, and Goldmoon will not leave them behind.

"I will go to Pax Tharkas," Tanis said softly. "But I believe it is time now that we separate, my friends. Before you speak, let me say this. I would send Tika, Goldmoon, Riverwind, Caramon and Raistlin, and you, Fizban, with the elves in hopes that you may carry the Disks to safety. The Disks are too precious to risk on a raid into Pax Tharkas."

"That may be, Half-Elf," Raistlin whispered from the depths of his cowl, "but it is not among the Qualinesti elves that Goldmoon will find the one she seeks."

"How do you know?" Tanis asked, startled.

"He doesn't know anything, Tanis," Sturm interrupted bitterly. "More talk—"

"Raistlin?" Tanis repeated, ignoring Sturm.

"You heard the knight!" the mage hissed. "I know nothing!"

Tanis sighed, letting it go, and glanced around. "You named me your leader—"

"Aye, we did, lad," said Flint suddenly. "But this decision is coming from your head, not your heart. Deep inside, you don't really believe we should split up."

"Well, I'm not staying with these elves," Tika said, folding her arms across her chest. "I'm going with you, Tanis. I plan to become a swordswoman, like Kitiara."

Tanis winced. Hearing Kitiara's name was like a physical blow.

"I will not hide with elves," Riverwind said, "especially if it means leaving my kind behind to fight for me."

"He and I are one," Goldmoon said, putting her hand on his arm. "Besides," she said more softly, "somehow I know that what the mage says is true—the leader is not among the elves. They want to flee the world, not fight for it."

"We're all going, Tanis," Flint said firmly.

The half-elf looked helplessly around at the group, then he smiled and shook his head. "You're right. I didn't truly believe we should separate. It's the sensible, logical thing to do, of course, which is why we won't do it."

"Now maybe we can get some sleep." Fizban yawned.

"Wait a minute, Old One," Tanis said sternly. "You are not one of us. You're definitely going with the elves."

"Am I?" the old mage asked softly as his eyes lost their vague, unfocused look. He stared at Tanis with such a penetrating—almost menacing—gaze that the half-elf involuntarily took a step back, suddenly sensing an almost palpable aura of power surrounding the old man. His voice was soft and intense. "I go where I choose in this world, and I choose to go with you, Tanis Half-Elven."

Raistlin glanced at Tanis as if to say, *Now you understand!* Tanis, irresolute, returned the glance. He regretted putting off discussing this with Raistlin, but wondered how they could confer now, knowing the old man would not leave.

"I speak you this, Raistlin," Tanis said suddenly, using Camptalk, a corrupted form of Common developed among the racially mixed mercenaries of Krynn. The twins had done a bit of mercenary work in their time, as had most of the companions, in order to eat. Tanis knew Raistlin would understand. He was fairly certain the old man wouldn't.

"We talk if want," Raistlin answered in the same language, "but little know I."

"You fear. Why?"

Raistlin's strange eyes stared far away as he answered slowly. "I know not, Tanis. But—you right. There power be, within Old One. I feel great power. I fear." His eyes gleamed. "And I hunger!" The mage sighed and seemed to return from wherever it was he had been. "But he right. Try to stop him? Very much danger."

"As if there wasn't enough already," Tanis said bitterly, switching back to Common. "We take our own in with us in the form of a doddering old magician."

"Others there are, as dangerous, perhaps," Raistlin said, with a meaningful look at his brother. The mage returned to Common. "I am weary. I must sleep. Are you staying, brother?"

"Yes," Caramon answered, exchanging glances with Sturm. "We're going to talk with Tanis."

Raistlin nodded and gave his arm to Fizban. The old mage and the young one left, the old mage lashing out at a tree with his staff, accusing it of trying to sneak up on him.

"As if one crazed mage wasn't bad enough," Flint muttered. "I'm going to bed."

One by one the others left until Tanis stood with Caramon and Sturm. Wearily, Tanis turned to face them. He had a feeling he knew what this was going to be about. Caramon's face was flushed and he stared at his feet. Sturm stroked his moustaches and regarded Tanis thoughtfully.

"Well?" Tanis asked.

"Gilthanas," Sturm answered.

Tanis frowned and scratched his beard. "That's my business, not yours," he said shortly.

"It is *our* business, Tanis," Sturm persisted, "if he's leading us into Pax Tharkas. We don't want to pry, but it's obvious there's a score to settle between you two. I've seen his eyes when he looks at you, Tanis, and, if I were you, I wouldn't go anywhere without a friend at my back."

Caramon looked at Tanis earnestly, his brow furrowed. "I know he's an elf and all," the big man said slowly. "But, like Sturm says, he gets a funny look in his eyes sometimes. Don't you know the way to this Sla-Mori? Can't we find it ourselves? I don't trust him. Neither do Sturm and Raist."

"Listen, Tanis," Sturm said, seeing the half-elf's face darken with anger. "If Gilthanas was in such danger in Solace as he claimed, why was he casually sitting in the Inn? And then there's his story about his warriors 'accidentally' running into a whole damn army! Tanis, don't shake your head so quickly. He may not be evil, just misguided. What if Verminaard's got some hold over him? Perhaps the Dragon Highlord convinced him he'd spare his people if—in return—he betrays us! Maybe that's why he was in Solace, waiting for us."

"That's ridiculous!" Tanis snapped. "How would he know we were coming?"

"We didn't exactly keep our journey from Xak Tsaroth to Solace secret," Sturm returned coldly. "We saw draconians all along the way and those that escaped Xak Tsaroth must have realized we came for the Disks. Verminaard probably knows our descriptions better than he knows his own mother."

"No! I don't believe it!" Tanis said angrily, glaring at Sturm and Caramon. "You two are wrong! I'll stake my life on it. I grew up with Gilthanas, I know him! Yes, there *is* a score to settle between us, but we have discussed it and the matter is closed. I'll believe he's turned traitor to his people the day I believe you or Caramon turn traitor. And no, I don't know the way to Pax Tharkas. I've never been there. And one more thing," Tanis shouted, now in a fury, "if there's people I don't trust in this group, it's that brother of yours and that old man!" He stared accusingly at Caramon.

The big man grew pale and lowered his eyes. He began to turn away. Tanis came to his senses, suddenly realizing what he had said. "I'm sorry, Caramon." He put his hand on the warrior's arm. "I didn't mean that. Raistlin's saved our lives more than once on this insane journey. It's just that I can't believe Gilthanas is a traitor!"

"We know, Tanis," Sturm said quietly. "And we trust your judgment. But—it's too dark a night to walk with your eyes closed, as my people say."

Tanis sighed and nodded. He put his other hand on Sturm's arm. The knight clasped him and the three men stood in silence, then they left the grove and walked back to the Hall of the Sky. They could still hear the Speaker talking with his warriors.

"What does Sla-Mori mean?" Caramon asked.

"Secret Way," Tanis answered.

Tanis woke with a start, his hand on the dagger at his belt. A dark shape crouched over him in the night, blotting out the stars overhead. Reaching up quickly, he grabbed hold of and yanked the person down across his body, putting his dagger to the exposed throat.

"Tanthalas!" There was a small scream at the sight of the steel flashing in the starlight.

"Laurana!" Tanis gasped.

Her body pressed against his. He could feel her trembling and, now that he was fully awake, he could see the long hair flowing loosely about her shoulders. She was dressed only in a flimsy nightdress. Her cloak had fallen off in the brief struggle.

Acting on impulse, Laurana had risen from her bed and slipped out into the night, throwing a cloak around her to protect her from the cold. Now she lay across Tanis's chest, too frightened to move. This was a side of Tanis she had never known existed. She realized suddenly that if she had been an enemy, she would be dead now—her throat slit.

"Laurana . . ." Tanis repeated, thrusting the dagger back into his belt with a shaking hand. He pushed her away and sat up, angry at himself for frightening her and angry at her for awakening something deep within him. For an instant, when she lay on top of him, he was acutely conscious only of the smell of her hair, the warmth of her slender body. Laurana had been a girl when he left. He returned to find a woman—a very beautiful, desirable woman

"What in the name of the Abyss are you doing here at this time of night?"

"Tanthalas," she said, choking, pulling her cape around her tightly. "I came to ask you to change your mind. Let your friends go to free the humans in Pax Tharkas. You must come with us! Don't throw your life away. My father is desperate. He doesn't believe this will work—I know he doesn't. But he hasn't any choice! He's already mourning Gilthanas as if he were dead. I'm going to lose my brother. I can't lose you, too!" She began to sob. Tanis glanced around hastily. There were almost certainly elven guards around. If the elves caught him in this compromising situation . . .

"Laurana," he said, gripping her shoulders and shaking

her. "You're not a child anymore. You've got to grow up and grow up fast. I wouldn't let my friends face danger without me! I know the risks we're taking; I'm not blind! But if we can free the humans from Verminaard and give you and your people time to escape, it's a chance we have to take! There comes a time, Laurana, when you've got to risk your life for something you believe in—something that means more than life itself. Do you understand?"

She looked up at him through a mass of golden hair. Her sobs stopped and she ceased to tremble. She stared at him very intently.

"Do you understand, Laurana?" he repeated.

"Yes, Tanthalas," she answered softly. "I understand."

"Good!" He sighed. "Now go back to bed. Quickly. You've put me in danger. If Gilthanas saw us like this—"

Laurana stood up and walked swiftly from the grove, flitting along the streets and buildings like the wind among the aspens. Sneaking past the guards to get back inside her father's dwelling was simple—she and Gilthanas had been doing it since childhood. Returning quietly to her room, she stood outside her father's and mother's door for a moment, listening. There was light inside. She could hear parchment rustling, smell an acrid odor. Her father was burning papers. She heard her mother's soft murmur, calling her father to bed. Laurana closed her eyes for a moment in silent agony, then her lips tightened in firm resolve, and she ran down the dark, chill hallway to her bedchamber.

Doubts. Ambush! A New Friend.

10

The elves woke the companions before dawn. Storm clouds lowered on the northern horizon, reaching like grasping fingers toward Qualinesti. Gilthanas arrived after breakfast, dressed in a tunic of blue cloth and a suit of chain mail.

"We have supplies," he said, gesturing toward the warriors who held packs in their hands. "We can also provide weapons or armament, if you have need."

"Tika needs armor and shield and sword," said Caramon.

"We will provide what we can," Gilthanas said, "though I doubt if we have a full set of armor small enough."

"How is Theros Ironfeld this morning?" Goldmoon asked.

"He rests comfortably, cleric of Mishakal." Gilthanas bowed respectfully to Goldmoon. "My people will, of course, take him with them when we leave. You may bid him farewell."

Elves soon returned with armor of every make and description for Tika and a lightweight shortsword, favored by the elven women. Tika's eyes glowed when she saw the helm and shield. Both were of elvish design, tooled and decorated with jewels.

Gilthanas took the helm and shield from the elf. "I have yet to thank you for saving my life in the Inn," he said to Tika.

"Accept these. They are my mother's ceremonial armor, dating back to the time of the Kinslayer Wars. These would have gone to my sister, but Laurana and I both believe you are the proper owner."

"How beautiful," Tika murmured, blushing. She accepted the helm, then looked at the rest of the armor in confusion. "I don't know what goes where," she confessed.

"I'll help!" Caramon offered eagerly.

"I'll handle this," Goldmoon said firmly. Picking up the armor, she led Tika into a grove of trees.

"What does she know about armor?" Caramon grumbled.

Riverwind looked at the warrior and smiled, the rare, infrequent smile that softened his stern face. "You forget," he said—"she is Chieftain's Daughter. It was her duty, in her father's absence, to lead the tribe to war. She knows a great deal about armor, warrior—and even more about the heart that beats beneath it."

Caramon flushed. Nervously, he picked up a pack of supplies and glanced inside. "What's this junk?" he asked.

"*Quith-pa*," said Gilthanas. "Iron rations, in your language. It will last us for many weeks, if need be."

"It looks like dried fruit!" Caramon said in disgust.

"That's what it is," Tanis replied, grinning.

Caramon groaned.

Dawn was just beginning to tinge the wispy storm clouds with a pale, chill light when Gilthanas led the party out of Qualinesti. Tanis kept his eyes straight ahead, refusing to look back. He wished that his final trip here could have been happier. He had not seen Laurana all morning and, though he felt relieved to have avoided a tearful farewell, he secretly wondered why she hadn't come to bid him good-bye.

The trail moved south, descending gradually but constantly. It had been thick and overgrown with brush, but the party of warriors Gilthanas led before had cleared it as they moved, so that walking was relatively easy. Caramon walked beside Tika, resplendent in her mismatched armor, instructing her on the use of her sword. Unfortunately, the teacher was having a bad time of it.

Goldmoon had slit Tika's red barmaid skirt up to her thighs for easier movement. Caramon found it rather difficult to concentrate on his lesson. Absorbed in his pupil, he did not notice that his brother had disappeared.

"Where's the young mage?" Gilthanas asked harshly.

"Maybe something's happened to him," Caramon said worriedly, cursing himself for forgetting his brother. The warrior drew his sword and started back along the trail.

"Nonsense!" Gilthanas stopped him. "What could have happened to him? There is no enemy for miles. He must have gone off somewhere—for some purpose."

"What are you saying?" Caramon asked, glowering.

"Maybe he left to—"

"To collect what I need for the making of my magic, elf," Raistlin whispered, emerging from the brush. "And to replenish the herbs that heal my cough."

"Raist!" Caramon nearly hugged him in his relief. "You shouldn't go off by yourself—it's dangerous."

"My spell components are secret," Raistlin whispered irritably, shoving his brother away. Leaning on the Staff of Magius, the mage rejoined Fizban in the line.

Gilthanas cast a sharp glance at Tanis, who shrugged and shook his head. As the group continued on, the trail became steeper and steeper, leading down from the aspenwoods to the pines of the lowlands. It joined up with a clear brook that soon became a raging stream as they traveled farther south.

When they stopped for a hasty lunch, Fizban came over and hunkered down beside Tanis. "Someone's following us," he said in a penetrating whisper.

"What?" Tanis asked, his head snapping up to stare at the old man incredulously.

"Yes, indeed," the old mage nodded solemnly. "I've seen it—darting in and out among the trees."

Sturm saw Tanis's look of concern. "What's the matter?"

"The Old One says someone's following us."

"Bah!" Gilthanas threw down his last bit of quith-pa in disgust and stood up. "That's insane. Let us go now. The Sla-Mori is still many miles and we must be there by sundown."

"I'll take rear guard," Sturm said to Tanis softly.

They walked through the ragged pines for several more hours. The sun slanted down in the sky, lengthening shadows across the trail, when the group came suddenly to a clearing.

"Hsst!" Tanis warned, falling back in alarm.

Caramon, instantly alert, drew his sword, motioning for Sturm and his brother with his free hand.

"What is it?" piped Tasslehoff. "I can't see!"

"Shhh!" Tanis glared at the kender, and Tas clapped his own hand over his own mouth to save Tanis the trouble.

The clearing was the site of a recent bloody fight. Bodies of men and hobgoblins lay scattered about in the obscene postures of brutal death. The companions looked about fearfully and listened for long minutes but could hear nothing above the roar of the water.

"No enemy for miles!" Sturm glared at Gilthanas and started to step out into the clearing.

"Wait!" Tanis said. "I thought I saw something move!"

"Maybe one of them's still alive," Sturm said coolly and walked forward. The rest followed more slowly. A low moaning sound came from beneath two hobgoblin bodies. The warriors walked toward the carnage, swords level.

"Caramon . . ." Tanis gestured.

The big warrior shoved the bodies to one side. Beneath was a moaning figure.

"Human," Caramon reported. "And covered with blood. Unconscious, I think."

The rest came up to look at the man on the ground. Goldmoon started to kneel down, but Caramon stopped her.

"No, lady," he said gently. "It would be senseless to heal him if we just have to kill him again. Remember—humans fought for the Dragon Highlord in Solace."

The group gathered round to examine the man. He wore chain mail that was of good quality, if rather tarnished. His clothes were rich, though the cloth had worn thin in places. He appeared to be in his late thirties. His hair was thick and black, his chin firm, and his features regular. The stranger opened his eyes and stared up at the companions blearily.

"Thank the gods of the Seekers!" he said hoarsely. "My friends—are they all dead?"

"Worry about yourself first," Sturm said sternly. "Tell us who your friends were—the humans or the hobgoblins?"

"The humans—fighters against the dragonmen." The man broke off, his eyes widening. "Gilthanas?"

"Eben," Gilthanas said in quiet surprise. "How did you survive the battle at the ravine?"

"How did you, for that matter?" The man named Eben tried to stagger to his feet. Caramon reached out a hand to help him when suddenly Eben pointed. "Look out! Drac—"

Caramon whipped around, letting Eben fall back with a groan. The others turned to see twelve draconians standing at the edge of the clearing, weapons drawn.

"All strangers in the land are to be taken to the Dragon Highlord for questioning," one called out. "We charge you to come with us peacefully."

"No one was supposed to know about this path to Sla-Mori," Sturm whispered to Tanis with a meaningful glance at Gilthanas. "According to the elf, that is!"

"We do not take orders from Lord Verminaard!" Tanis yelled, ignoring Sturm.

"You will, soon enough," the draconian said and waved its arm. The creatures surged forward to attack.

Fizban, standing near the edge of the woods, pulled something from his pouch and began to mumble a few words.

"Not Fireball!" Raistlin hissed, grabbing the old mage's arm. "You'll incinerate everyone out there!"

"Oh, really? I suppose you're right." The old mage sighed in disappointment, then brightened. "Wait, I'll think of something else."

"Just stay here, under cover!" Raistlin ordered. "I'm going to my brother."

"Now, what was that web spell?" The old man pondered.

Tika, her new sword drawn and ready, trembled with fear and excitement. One draconian rushed her and she swung a tremendous blow. The blade missed the draconian by a mile, Caramon's head by inches. Pulling Tika behind him, he knocked the draconian down with the flat of his sword. Before it could rise, he stepped on its throat, breaking its neck.

"Get behind me," he said to Tika, then glanced down at the sword she was still waving around wildly. "On second thought," Caramon amended nervously, "run over to those trees with the old man and Goldmoon. There's a good girl."

"I will not!" Tika said indignantly. "I'll show him," she muttered, her sweaty palms slipping on the hilt of the sword. Two more draconians charged Caramon, but his brother was beside him now—the two combining magic and steel to destroy their enemy. Tika knew she would only get in their way, and she feared Raistlin's anger more than she feared draconians. She looked around to see if anyone needed her help. Sturm and Tanis fought side by side. Gilthanas made an unlikely team with Flint, while Tasslehoff, his hoopak planted solidly in the ground, sent a deadly barrage of rocks whizzing onto the field. Goldmoon stood beneath the trees, Riverwind near her. The old magician had pulled out a spellbook and was flipping through its pages.

"Web . . . web . . . how did that go?" he mumbled.

"Aaarrrgghh!" A screech behind Tika nearly caused her to swallow her tongue. Whirling around, she dropped her sword in alarm as a draconian, laughing horribly, launched itself into the air straight at her. Panic-stricken, Tika gripped her shield in both hands and struck the draconian in its hideous, reptilian face. The impact nearly jarred the shield from her hands, but it knocked the creature onto its back, unconscious. Tika picked up her sword and, grimacing in disgust, stabbed the creature through the heart. Its body immediately turned to stone, encasing her sword. Tika yanked at it, but it remained stuck fast.

"Tika, to your left!" yelled Tasslehoff shrilly.

Tika stumbled around and saw another draconian. Swinging her shield, she blocked its sword thrust. Then, with a strength born of terror, she hit at the creature again and again with her shield, knowing only that she had to kill the thing. She kept bashing until she felt a hand on her arm. Whipping around, her blood-stained shield ready, she saw Caramon.

"It's all right!" the big warrior said soothingly. "It's all over, Tika. They're all dead. You did fine, just fine."

Tika blinked. For a moment she didn't recognize the warrior. Then, with a shudder, she lowered her shield.

"I wasn't very good with the sword," she said, starting to tremble in reaction to her fear and the memory of the horrible creature lunging at her.

Caramon saw her start to shake. He reached out and clasped her in his arms, stroking the sweat-damp red curls.

"You were braver than many men I've seen—experienced warriors," the big man said in a deep voice.

Tika looked up into Caramon's eyes. Her terror melted away, replaced by exultation. Tika flung her arms around his neck and kissed him with such violence her teeth bit into his lip. She tasted blood in her mouth.

Caramon, astonished, felt the tingle of pain, an odd contrast to the softness of her lips, and was overwhelmed with desire. He wanted this woman more than any other woman—and there had been many—in his life. He forgot where he was, who was around him. His brain and his blood were on fire. Crushing Tika to his chest, he held her and kissed her with bruising intensity.

The pain of his embrace was delicious to Tika. She longed for the pain to grow and envelop her, but at the same time, she felt suddenly cold and afraid. Remembering stories told by the other barmaids of the terrible, wonderful things that happened between men and women, she began to panic.

Caramon completely lost all sense of reality. He caught Tika up in his arms with a wild idea of carrying her into the woods, when he felt a cold, familiar hand on his shoulder.

The big man stared at his brother and regained his senses with a gasp. He gently set Tika on her feet. Dizzy and disoriented, she opened her eyes to see Raistlin standing beside his brother, regarding her with his strange, glittering stare.

Tika's face burned. She backed away, stumbled over the body of the draconian, then picked up her shield and ran.

Caramon swallowed, cleared his throat, and started to say something, but Raistlin simply glanced at him in disgust and walked back to rejoin Fizban. Caramon, trembling like a newborn colt, sighed shakily and walked over to where Sturm, Tanis, and Gilthanas stood, talking to Eben.

"No, I'm fine," the man assured them. "I just felt a little faint when I saw those creatures, that's all. You really have a cleric among you? That's wonderful, but don't waste her healing powers on me. Just a scratch. It's more their blood than mine. My party and I were tracking these draconians through the woods when we were attacked by at least forty hobgoblins."

"And you alone live to tell the tale," Gilthanas said.

"Yes," Eben replied, returning the elf's suspicious gaze. "I am an expert swordsman, as you know. I killed these"—he gestured to the bodies of six hobgoblins who lay around him—"then fell to the overwhelming numbers. The rest must have assumed I was dead and left me. But, enough of my heroics. You fellows are pretty good with swords yourselves. Where are you headed?"

"Some place called the Sla—" began Caramon, but Gilthanas cut him off.

"Our journey is secret," Gilthanas said. Then he added in a tentative voice. "We could use an expert swordsman."

"As long as you're fighting draconians, your fight is my fight," Eben said cheerfully. He pulled his pack out from under the body of a hobgoblin and slung it over his shoulder.

"My name's Eben Shatterstone. I come from Gateway. You've probably heard of my family," he said. "We had one of the most impressive mansions west of—"

"That's it!" cried Fizban. "I remembered!"

Suddenly the air was filled with strands of sticky, floating cobweb.

The sun set just as the group reached an open plain edged by tall mountain peaks. Rivaling the mountains for dominance of the land before it was the gigantic fortress known as Pax Tharkas, which guarded the pass between the mountains. The companions stared at it in awed silence.

Tika's eyes widened at the sight of the massive twin towers soaring into the sky. "I've never seen anything so big! Who built it? They must have been powerful men."

"It was not men," said Flint sadly. The dwarf's beard quivered as he looked at Pax Tharkas with a wistful expression. "It was elves and dwarves working together. Once, long ago, when times were peaceful."

"The dwarf speaks truly," Gilthanas said. "Long ago Kith-Kanan broke his father's heart and left the ancient home of Silvanesti. He and his people came to the beautiful woods given them by the Emperor of Ergoth following the scribing of the Swordsheath Scroll that ended the Kinslayer Wars. Elves have lived in Qualinesti for long centuries since Kith-Kanan's death. His greatest achievement, however, was the building of Pax Tharkas. Standing between elven and dwarven kingdoms, it was constructed by both in a spirit of

123

friendship since lost on Krynn. It grieves me to see it now, the bastion of a mighty war machine."

Even as Gilthanas spoke, the companions saw the huge gate that stood at the front of Pax Tharkas swing open. An army—long rows of draconians, hobgoblins, and goblins— marched out into the plains. The sound of braying horns echoed back from the mountaintops. Watching them from above was a great red dragon. The companions cowered among the scrub brush and trees. Though the dragon was too far away to see them, the dragonfear touched them even from this distance.

"They march on Qualinesti," Gilthanas said, his voice breaking. "We must get inside and free the prisoners. Then Verminaard will be forced to call the army back."

"You're going inside Pax Tharkas!" Eben gasped.

"Yes," Gilthanas answered reluctantly, apparently regretting he had said so much.

"Whew!" Eben blew out a deep breath. "You people have guts, I'll give you that. So—how do we get in there? Wait until the army leaves? There will probably be only a couple of guards at the front gate. We could handle them easily, couldn't we, big man?" He nudged Caramon.

"Sure," Caramon grinned.

"That is not the plan," Gilthanas said coldly. The elf pointed to a narrow vale leading into the mountains, just visible in the rapidly fading light. "There is our way. We will cross in the cover of darkness."

He stood up and started off. Tanis hurried forward to catch up with him. "What do you know of this Eben?" the half-elf asked in elven, glancing back to where the man was chatting with Tika.

Gilthanas shrugged. "He was with the band of humans who fought with us at the ravine. Those who survived were taken to Solace and died there. I suppose he could have escaped. I did, after all," Gilthanas said, glancing sideways at Tanis. "He comes from Gateway where his father and father before him were wealthy merchants. The others told me, when he was out of hearing, that his family lost their money and he has since earned his living by his sword."

"I figured as much," Tanis said. "His clothes are rich, but they've seen better days. You made the right decision, bringing him along."

"I dared not leave him behind," Gilthanas answered grimly. "One of us should keep an eye on him."

"Yes." Tanis fell silent.

"And on me, too, you're thinking," Gilthanas said in a tight voice. "I know what the others say—the knight especially. But, I swear to you, Tanis, I'm not a traitor! I want one thing!" The elf's eyes gleamed feverishly in the dying light. "I want to destroy this Verminaard. If you could have seen him as his dragon destroyed my people! I'd gladly sacrifice my life—" Gilthanas stopped abruptly.

"And our lives as well?" Tanis asked.

As Gilthanas turned to face him, his almond-shaped eyes regarding Tanis without emotion. "If you must know, Tanthalas, your life means that—" He snapped his fingers. "But the lives of my people are everything to me. That is all I care for now." He walked on ahead as Sturm caught up with them.

"Tanis," he said. "The old man was right. We are being followed."

SUSPICIONS GROW.
THE SLA-MORI.

11

The narrow trail climbed steeply up from the plains into a wooded valley in the foothills. Evening's shadows gathered close around them as they followed the stream up into the mountain. They had traveled only a short distance, however, when Gilthanas left the trail and disappeared into the brush. The companions stopped, looking at each other doubtfully.

"This is madness," Eben whispered to Tanis. "Trolls live in this valley—who do you think made that trail?" The dark-haired man took Tanis's arm with a cool familiarity the half-elf found disconcerting. "Admittedly, I'm the new kid in town, so to speak, and the gods know you don't have any reason to trust me, but how much do you know about this Gilthanas?"

"I know—" Tanis began, but Eben ignored him.

"There were some of us who didn't believe that draconian army stumbled onto us by accident, if you take my meaning. My boys and I had been hiding in the hills, fighting the dragonarmies ever since they hit Gateway. Last week, these elves showed up out of nowhere. They told us they were going to raid one of the Dragon Highlord's fortresses and would we like to come along and help? We said, sure, why not—anything to stick a bone in the Dragon High Man's craw.

"As we hiked, we began to get really nervous. There were

draconian tracks all over the place! But it didn't bother the elves. Gilthanas said the tracks were old. That night we made camp and posted a watch. It didn't do us a lot of good, just gave us about twenty seconds warning before the draconians hit. And"—Eben glanced around and moved even closer—"while we were trying to wake up, grab our weapons, and fight those foul creatures, I heard the elves calling out, as if someone was lost. And who do you suppose they were calling for?"

Eben regarded Tanis intently. The half-elf frowned and shook his head, irritated at the dramatics.

"Gilthanas!" Eben hissed. "He was gone! They shouted and shouted for him—their leader!" The man shrugged. "Whether he ever showed up or not, I don't know. I was captured. They took us to Solace, where I got away. Anyway, I'd think twice about following that elf. He may have had good reason to be gone when the draconians attacked, but—"

"I've known Gilthanas a long time," Tanis interrupted gruffly, more disturbed than he wanted to admit.

"Sure. Just thought you should know," Eben said, smiling sympathetically. He clapped Tanis on the back and dropped back to stand by Tika.

Tanis didn't have to look around to know Caramon and Sturm had heard every word. Neither said anything, however, and before Tanis could talk to them, Gilthanas appeared suddenly, slipping out from among the trees.

"It is not much farther," the elf said. "The brush thins up ahead and the walking is easier."

"I say we just go in the front gate," Eben said.

"I agree," Caramon said. The big man glanced at his brother who sat limply beneath a tree. Goldmoon was pale with fatigue. Even Tasslehoff's head hung wearily.

"We could camp here tonight and go in by the front gates at dawn," Sturm suggested.

"We stick to the original plan," Tanis said sharply. "We make camp once we reach the Sla-Mori."

Then Flint spoke up. "You can go ring the bell at the gate and ask Lord Verminaard to let you in if you want, Sturm Brightblade. I'm sure he'd oblige. C'mon, Tanis." The dwarf stumped off down the trail.

"At least," Tanis said to Sturm in a low voice, "maybe this will throw off our pursuer."

"Whoever or whatever it is," Sturm answered. "It's woods-crafty, I'll say that for it. Every time I caught a glimpse and started back for a closer look, it vanished. I thought about ambushing it, but there wasn't time."

The group emerged from the brush thankfully, arriving at the base of a gigantic granite cliff. Gilthanas walked along the cliff face for several hundred feet, his hand feeling for something on the rock. Suddenly he stopped.

"We are here," he whispered. Reaching into his tunic, he removed a small gem that began to glow a soft, muted yellow. Running his hand over the rock wall, the elf found what he was searching for, a small niche in the granite. He placed the gem in the niche and began reciting ancient words and tracing unseen symbols in the night air.

"Very impressive," whispered Fizban. "I didn't know he was one of us," he said to Raistlin.

"A dabbler, nothing more," the mage replied. Leaning wearily on his staff, he watched Gilthanas intently, however.

Suddenly and silently, a huge block of stone separated from the cliff face and began moving slowly to one side. The companions backed up as a blast of chill, dank air flowed from the gaping hole in the rock.

"What's in there? " Caramon asked suspiciously.

"I do not know what is in there now," Gilthanas replied. "I have never entered. I know of this place only through the lore of my people."

"All right," Caramon growled. "What *used* to be in there?"

Gilthanas paused, then said. "This was the burial chamber of Kith-Kanan."

"More spooks," Flint grumbled, peering into the darkness.

"Send the mage in first, so he can warn them we're coming."

"Throw the dwarf in," Raistlin returned. "They are accustomed to living in dark, dank caves."

"You speak of the mountain dwarves!" Flint said, his beard bristling. "It has been long years since the hill dwarves lived below ground in the kingdom of Thorbardin."

"Only because you were cast out!" Raistlin hissed.

"Stop it, both of you!" Tanis said in exasperation. "Raistlin, what do you sense about this place?"

"Evil. Great evil," the mage replied.

"But I sense great goodness, too," Fizban spoke unexpectedly. "The elves are not truly forgotten within, though evil things have come to rule in their stead."

"This is crazy!" Eben shouted. The noise echoed uncannily among the rocks and the others whirled, startled, staring at him in alarm. "I'm sorry," he said, dropping his voice. "But I can't believe you people are going in there! It doesn't take a magician to tell there's evil inside that hole. *I* can feel it! Go back around to the front," he urged. "Sure, there'll be one or two guards, but that's nothing compared to whatever lurks in that darkness beyond!"

"He's got a point, Tanis," Caramon said. "You can't fight the dead. We learned that in Darken Wood."

"This is the only way!" Gilthanas said angrily. "If you are such cowards—"

"There's a difference between caution and cowardice, Gilthanas," Tanis said, his voice steady and calm. The half-elf thought a moment. "We might be able to take on the guards at the front gate, but not before they could alert others. I say we enter and at least explore this way. Flint, you lead. Raistlin, we'll need your light."

"Shirak," spoke the mage softly, and the crystal on his staff began to glow. He and Flint plunged into the cave, followed closely by the rest. The tunnel they entered was obviously ancient, but whether it was natural or artifact was impossible to tell.

"What about our pursuer?" Sturm asked in a low voice. "Do we leave the entrance open?"

"A trap," Tanis agreed softly. "Leave it open just a crack, Gilthanas, enough so that whoever's tracking us knows we came in here and can follow, but not enough so that it looks like a trap."

Gilthanas drew forth the gem, placed it in a niche on the inner side of the entrance, and spoke a few words. The stone began to slide silently back into place. At the last moment, when it was about seven or eight inches from closing, Gilthanas swiftly removed the gemstone. The stone shuddered to a halt, and the knight, the elf, and the half-elf joined the companions in the entrance to the Sla-Mori.

"There is a great deal of dust," Raistlin reported, coughing— "but no tracks, at least in this part of the cave."

"About one hundred and twenty feet farther on, there's a crossroads," Flint added. "We found footprints there, but we could not make out what they were. They don't look like draconians or hobgoblins and they don't come this direction. The mage says the evil flows from the road to the right."

"We will camp here for the night," Tanis said, "near the entry. We'll post double watch—one by the door, one down the corridor. Sturm, you and Caramon first. Gilthanas and I, Eben and Riverwind, Flint and Tasslehoff."

"And me," said Tika stoutly, though she couldn't ever remember being so tired in her life. "I'll take my turn."

Tanis was glad the darkness hid his smile. "Very well," he said. "You watch with Flint and Tasslehoff."

"Good!" Tika replied. Opening her pack, she shook out a blanket and lay down, conscious all the while of Caramon's eyes on her. She noticed Eben watching her, too. She didn't mind that. She was accustomed to men staring at her admiringly and Eben was handsomer even than Caramon. Certainly he was wittier and more charming than the big warrior. Still, just the memory of Caramon's arms around her made her shiver with delightful fear. She firmly put the memory from her mind and tried to get comfortable. The chain mail was cold and it pinched her through her blouse. Yet she noticed the others didn't take theirs off. Besides, she was tired enough to sleep dressed in a full suit of plate armor. The last thing Tika remembered as she drifted off was telling herself she was thankful she wasn't alone with Caramon.

Goldmoon saw the warrior's eyes linger on Tika. Whispering something to Riverwind—who nodded, smiling—she left him and walked over to Caramon. Touching him on the arm, she drew him away from the others into the shadow of the corridor.

"Tanis tells me you have an older sister," she stated.

"Yes," Caramon answered, startled. "Kitiara. Though she's my half-sister."

Goldmoon smiled and laid her hand gently on Caramon's arm. "I'm going to talk to you like an older sister."

Caramon grinned. "Not like Kitiara, you won't, Lady of Que-shu. Kit taught me the meaning of every swear word I'd ever heard, plus a few I hadn't. She taught me to use a sword and fight with honor in the tournaments, but she also taught me how to kick a man in the groin when the judges weren't watching. No, lady, you're not much like my older sister."

Goldmoon's eyes opened wide, startled by this portrayal of a woman she guessed the half-elf loved. "But I thought she and Tanis, I mean they . . ."

Caramon winked. "They certainly did!" he said.

Goldmoon drew a deep breath. She hadn't meant the conversation to wander off, but it did lead to her subject. "In a way, that's what I wanted to speak to you about. Only this has to do with Tika."

"Tika?" Caramon flushed. "She's a big girl. Begging your pardon, I don't see that what we do is any of your concern."

"She is a *girl*, Caramon," Goldmoon said gently. "Don't you understand? Don't rush her. She desperately wants approval

MARGARET WEIS & TRACY HICKMAN

from you, and she might do anything to win it. But don't let her use that as a reason to do something she'll regret later. If you truly love her, time will prove it and enhance the moment's sweetness."

"I guess you know that, huh?" Caramon said, looking at Goldmoon.

"Yes," she said softly her eyes going to Riverwind. "We have waited long, and sometimes the pain is unbearable. But the laws of my people are strict. I don't suppose it would matter now," she spoke in a whisper, more to herself than Caramon, "since we are the only two left. But, in a way, that makes it even more important. When our vows are spoken, we will lie together as man and wife. Not until then."

"I understand. Thanks for telling me about Tika," Caramon said. He patted Goldmoon awkwardly on the shoulder and returned to his post.

The night passed quietly, with no sign of their pursuer. When the watches changed, Tanis discussed Eben's story with Gilthanas and received an unsatisfactory answer. Yes, what the man said was true. Gilthanas had been gone when the draconians attacked. He had been trying to convince the druids to help. He'd returned when he heard the sounds of battle and that's when he'd been struck on the head. He told Tanis all this in a low, bitter voice.

The companions woke when morning's pale light crept through the door. After a quick breakfast, they gathered their things and walked down the corridor into the Sla-Mori.

Arriving at the crossroads, they examined both directions, left and right. Riverwind knelt to study the tracks, then rose, his expression puzzled.

"They are human," he said, "but they are not human. There are animal tracks as well—probably rats. The dwarf was right. I see no sign of draconians or goblins. What is odd, however, is that the animal tracks end right here where the paths cross. They do not go into the right-hand corridor. The other strange tracks do not go to the left."

"Well, which way do *we* go?" Tanis asked.

"I say we don't go either way!" Eben stated. "The entrance is still open. Let's turn back."

"Turning back is no longer an option," Tanis said coldly. "I would give you leave to go yourself, only—"

"Only you don't trust me," Eben finished. "I don't blame you, Tanis Half-Elven. All right, I said I'd help and I meant it. Which way—left or right?"

"The evil comes from the right," Raistlin whispered.

"Gilthanas?" Tanis asked. "Do you have any idea where we are?"

"No, Tanthalas," the elf answered. "Legend says that there were many entrances from Sla-Mori into Pax Tharkas, all secret. Only the elven priests were allowed down here, to honor the dead. One way is as good as another."

"Or as bad," whispered Tasslehoff to Tika. She gulped and crept over to stand near Caramon.

"We'll go left," Tanis said—"since Raistlin feels uneasy about the right."

Walking by the light of the mage's staff, the companions followed the dusty, rock-strewn tunnel for several hundred feet, then reached an ancient stone wall rent by a huge hole through which only darkness was visible. Raistlin's small light showed faintly the distant walls of a great hall.

The warriors entered first, flanking the mage, who held his staff high. The gigantic hall must once have been splendid, but now it had fallen into such decay that its faded splendor seemed pathetic and horrible. Two rows of seven columns ran the length of the hall, though some lay shattered on the floor. Part of the far wall was caved in, evidence of the destructive force of the Cataclysm. At the very back of the room stood two double bronze doors.

As Raistlin advanced, the others spread out, swords drawn. Suddenly Caramon, in the front of the hall, gave a strangled cry. The mage hurried to shine his light where Caramon pointed with a trembling hand.

MARGARET WEIS & TRACY HICKMAN

Before them was a massive throne, ornately carved of granite. Two huge marble statues flanked the throne, their sightless eyes staring forward into the darkness. The throne they guarded was not empty. Upon it sat the skeletal remains of what had once been a male—of what race, none could say, death being the great equalizer. The figure was dressed in regal robes that, even though faded and decayed, still gave evidence of their richness. A cloak covered the gaunt shoulders. A crown gleamed on the fleshless skull. The bone hands, fingers lying gracefully in death, rested on a sheathed sword.

Gilthanas fell to his knees. "Kith-Kanan," he said in a whisper. "We stand in the Hall of the Ancients, his burial tomb. None have seen this sight since the elven clerics vanished in the Cataclysm."

Tanis stared at the throne until, slowly, overcome by feelings he did not understand, the half-elf sank to his knees. "Fealan thalos, Im murquanethi. Sai Kith-Kananoth Murtari Larion," he murmured in tribute to the greatest of the elven kings.

"What a beautiful sword," Tasslehoff said, his shrill voice breaking the reverent silence. Tanis glared at him sternly. "I'm not going to take it!" the kender protested, looking wounded. "I just mentioned it, as an item of interest."

Tanis rose to his feet. "Don't touch it," he said sternly to the kender, then went to explore other parts of the room.

As Tas walked closer to examine the sword, Raistlin went with him. The mage began to murmur, "Tsaran korilath ith hakon," and moved his thin hand swiftly above the sword in a prescribed pattern. The sword began to give off a faint red glow. Raistlin smiled and said softly, "It is enchanted."

Tas gasped. "Good enchantment? Or bad?"

"I have no way of knowing," the mage whispered. "But since it has lain undisturbed for so long, I certainly would not venture to touch it!"

He turned away, leaving Tas to wonder if he dared disobey Tanis and risk being turned into something icky.

While the kender was wrestling with temptation, the rest searched the walls for secret entrances. Flint helped by giving them learned and lengthy descriptions of dwarven-built hidden doorways. Gilthanas walked to the far end from Kith-Kanan's throne, where the two huge bronze double doors stood. One, bearing a relief map of Pax Tharkas, was slightly ajar. Calling for light, he and Raistlin studied the map.

Caramon gave the skeletal figure of the long dead king a final backward glance and joined Sturm and Flint in searching the walls for secret doors. Finally Flint called, "Tasslehoff, you worthless kender, this is your specialty. At least you're always bragging about how you found the door that had been lost for one hundred years which led to the great jewel of the something-or-other."

"It was in a place like this, too," Tas said, his interest in the sword forgotten. Skipping over to help, he came to a sudden stop.

"What's that?" he asked, cocking his head.

"What's what?" Flint said absently, slapping the walls.

"A scraping sound," the kender said, puzzled. "It's coming from those doors."

Tanis looked up, having learned, long ago, to respect Tasslehoff's hearing. He walked toward the doors where Gilthanas and Raistlin were intent upon the map. Suddenly Raistlin took a step backward. Foul-smelling air wafted into the room through the open door. Now everyone could hear the scraping sound and a soft, squishing noise.

"Shut the door!" Raistlin whispered urgently.

"Caramon!" Tanis cried. "Sturm!" The two were already running for the door, along with Eben. All of them leaned against it, but they were flung backward as the bronze doors flew open, banging against the walls with a hollow booming sound. A monster slithered into the hall.

"Help us, Mishakal!" Goldmoon breathed the goddess's name as she sank back against the wall. The thing entered the room swiftly despite its great bulk. The scraping sound they had heard was caused by its gigantic, bloated body sliding along the floor.

"A slug!" Tas said, running up to examine it with interest. "But look at the size of that thing! How do you suppose it got so big? I wonder what it eats—"

"Us, you ninny!" Flint shouted, grabbing the kender and flinging him to the ground just as the huge slug spat out a stream of saliva. Its eyes, perched atop slender, rotating stalks on top of its head, were not of much use, nor did it need them. The slug could find and devour rats in the darkness by sense of smell alone. Now it detected much larger prey, and it shot its paralyzing saliva in the general direction of the living flesh it craved.

The deadly liquid missed as the kender and the dwarf rolled out of the way. Sturm and Caramon charged in, slashing at the monster with their swords. Caramon's sword didn't even penetrate the thick, rubbery hide. Sturm's two-handed blade bit, causing the slug to rear back in pain. Tanis charged forward as the slug's head swiveled toward the knight.

"Tanthalas!"

The scream pierced Tanis's concentration and he halted, turning back to stare in amazement at the entrance to the hall.

"Laurana!"

At that moment, the slug, sensing the half-elf, spat the corrosive liquid at him. The saliva struck his sword, causing the metal to fizz and smoke, then dissolve in his hand. The burning liquid ran down his arm, searing his flesh. Tanis, screaming in agony, fell to his knees.

"Tanthalas!" Laurana cried again, running to him.

"Stop her!" Tanis gasped, doubled over in pain, clutching a hand and sword-arm suddenly blackened and useless.

The slug, sensing success, slithered forward, dragging its pulsating gray body through the door. Goldmoon cast a fearful glance at the huge monster, then ran to Tanis. Riverwind stood over them, protectively.

"Get away!" Tanis said through clenched teeth.

Goldmoon grasped his injured hand in her own, praying to

the goddess. Riverwind fit an arrow to his bow and shot at the slug. The arrow struck the creature in the neck, doing little damage, but distracting its attention from Tanis.

The half-elf saw Goldmoon's hand touch his, but he could feel nothing but pain. Then the pain eased and feeling returned to his hand. Smiling at Goldmoon, he marveled at her healing powers, even as he lifted his head to see what was happening.

The others were attacking the creature with renewed fury, attempting to distract it from Tanis, but they might as well have been plunging their weapons into a thick, rubbery wall.

Tanis rose to his feet shakily. His hand was healed, but his sword lay on the ground, a molten lump of metal. Weaponless except for his longbow, he fell back, pulling Goldmoon with him as the slug slid into the room.

Raistlin ran to Fizban's side. "Now is the time for the casting of the fireball, Old One," he panted.

"It is?" Fizban's face filled with delight. "Wonderful! How does it go?"

"Don't you remember?" Raistlin practically shrieked, dragging the mage behind a pillar as the slug spat another glob of burning saliva onto the floor.

"I used to . . . let me see." Fizban's brow furrowed in concentration. "Can't you do it?"

"I have not gained the power yet, Old One! That spell is still beyond my strength!" Raistlin closed his eyes and began to concentrate on those spells he did know.

"Fall back! Get out of here!" Tanis shouted, shielding Laurana and Goldmoon as best he could while he fumbled for his longbow and his arrows.

"It'll just come after us!" Sturm yelled, thrusting his blade home once again. But all he and Caramon accomplished was to enrage the monster further.

Suddenly Raistlin held up his hands. "*Kalith karan, tobaniskar!*" he cried, and flaming darts sprang from his fingers, striking the creature in the head. The slug reared in silent agony and shook its head, but returned to the hunt. Suddenly it lunged straight forward, sensing victims at the end of the room where Tanis sought to protect Goldmoon and Laurana. Maddened by pain, driven wild by the smell of blood, the slug attacked with unbelievable speed. Tanis's arrow bounced off the leathery hide and the monster dove for him, its mouth gaping open. The half-elf dropped the useless bow and staggered backward, nearly stumbling over the steps leading to the throne of Kith-Kanan.

"Behind the throne!" he yelled, preparing to hold the monster's attention while Goldmoon and Laurana ran for cover. His hand reached out, grabbing for a huge rock, anything to hurl at the creature!—when his fingers closed over the metal hilt of a sword.

Tanis nearly dropped the weapon in amazement. The metal was so cold it burned his hand. The blade gleamed brightly in the wavering light of the mage's staff. There wasn't time to question, however. Tanis drove the point into the slug's gaping maw just as the creature swooped in for the kill.

"Run!" Tanis yelled. Grasping Laurana's hand, he dragged her toward the hole. Pushing her through, he turned around, preparing to help keep the slug at bay while the others escaped. But the slug's appetite had died. Writhing in misery, it slowly turned and slithered back toward its lair. Clear, sticky liquid dribbled from its wounds.

The companions crowded into the tunnel, stopping for a moment to calm their hearts and breathe deeply. Raistlin, wheezing, leaned on his brother. Tanis glanced around. "Where's Tasslehoff?" he asked in frustration. Whirling around to go back into the hall, he nearly fell over the kender.

"I brought you the scabbard," Tas said, holding it up. "For the sword."

"Back down the tunnel," Tanis said firmly, stopping everyone's questions.

Reaching the crossroads and sinking down on the dusty floor to rest, Tanis turned to the elfmaid. "What in the name of the Abyss are you doing here, Laurana? Has something happened in Qualinost?"

"Nothing happened," Laurana said, shaking from the encounter with the slug. "I . . . I . . . just came."

"Then you're going right back!" Gilthanas yelled angrily, grabbing Laurana. She broke away from his grasp.

"I'm not either going back," she said petulantly. "I'm coming with you and Tanis and . . . the rest."

"Laurana, this is madness," Tanis snapped. "We're not going on an outing. This isn't a game. You saw what happened in there—we were nearly killed!"

"I know, Tanthalas," Laurana said pleadingly. Her voice quivered and broke. "You told me that there comes a time when you've got to risk your life for something you believe in. I'm the one who followed you."

"You could have been killed—" Gilthanas began.

"But I wasn't!" Laurana cried defiantly. "I have been trained as a warrior—all elven women are, in memory of the time when we fought beside our men to save our homeland."

"It's not serious training—" Tanis began angrily.

"I followed you, didn't I?" Laurana demanded, casting a glance at Sturm. "Skillfully?" she asked the knight.

"Yes," he admitted. "Still, that doesn't mean—"

Raistlin interrupted him. "We are losing time," the mage whispered. "And I for one do not want to spend any longer than I must in this dank and musty tunnel." He was wheezing, barely able to breathe. "The girl has made her decision. We can spare no one to return with her, nor do we dare trust her to leave on her own. She might be captured and reveal our plans. We must take her."

Tanis glared at the mage, hating him for his cold, unfeeling logic, and for being right. The half-elf stood up, yanking Laurana to her feet. He came very close to hating her, too, without quite understanding why, knowing simply that she was making a difficult task much harder.

"You are on your own," he told her quietly, as the rest stood up and gathered their things. "I can't hang around, protecting you. Neither can Gilthanas. You have behaved like a spoiled brat. I told you once before—you'd better grow up. Now, if you don't, you're going to die and probably get all the rest of us killed right along with you!"

"I'm sorry, Tanthalas," Laurana said, avoiding his angry gaze. "But I couldn't lose you, not again. I love you." Her lips tightened and she said softly, "I'll make you proud of me."

Tanis turned and walked away. Catching sight of Caramon's grinning face and hearing Tika giggle, he flushed. Ignoring them, he approached Sturm and Gilthanas. "It seems we must take the right-hand corridor after all, whether or not Raistlin's feelings about evil are correct." He buckled on his new sword belt and scabbard, noticing, as he did so, Raistlin's eyes lingering on the weapon.

"What is it now?" he asked irritably.

"The sword is enchanted," Raistlin said softly, coughing. "How did you get it?"

Tanis started. He stared at the blade, moving his hand as though it might turn into a snake. He frowned, trying to remember. "I was near the body of the elven king, searching for something to throw at the slug, when, suddenly, the sword was in my hand. It had been taken out of the sheath and—"Tanis paused, swallowing.

"Yes?" Raistlin pursued, his eyes glittering eagerly.

"*He* gave it to me,"Tanis said softly. "I remember, his hand touched mine. He pulled it from its sheath."

"Who?" asked Gilthanas. "None of us were near there."

"Kith-Kanan. . . ."

THE ROYAL GUARD.
THE CHAIN ROOM.

12

Perhaps it was just imagination, but the darkness seemed thicker as they walked down the other tunnel and the air grew colder. No one needed the dwarf to tell them that this was not normal in a cave, where the temperature supposedly stayed constant. They reached a branch in the tunnel, but no one felt inclined to go left, which might lead them back to the Hall of the Ancients—and the wounded slug.

"The elf almost got us killed by the slug," Eben said accusingly. "I wonder what's in store for us down here?"

No one answered. By now, everyone was experiencing the sense of growing evil Raistlin had warned of. Their footsteps slowed, and it was only through force of group will that they continued on. Laurana felt fear convulse her limbs and she clung to the wall for support. She longed for Tanis to comfort her and protect her, as he had done when they were younger and facing imaginary foes, but he walked at the head of the line with her brother. Each had his own fear to contend with. At that moment, Laurana decided that she would die before she asked for their help. It occurred to her, then, that she was really serious when she said she wanted to make Tanis proud of her. Shoving herself away from the side of the crumbling tunnel, she gritted her teeth and moved forward.

The tunnel came to an abrupt end. Crumbled stone and rubble lay beneath a hole in the rock wall. The sense of malevolent evil flowing from the darkness beyond the hole could almost be felt, wafting across the flesh like the touch of unseen fingers. The companions stopped, none of them—not even the nerveless kender—daring to enter.

"It's not that I'm afraid," Tas confided in a whisper to Flint. "Its just that I'd rather be somewhere else."

The silence became oppressive. Each could hear his own heart beat and the breathing of the others. The light jittered and wavered in the mage's shaking hand.

"Well, we can't stay here forever," Eben said hoarsely. "Let the elf go in. He's the one who brought us here!"

"I'll go," Gilthanas answered. "But I'll need light."

"None may touch the staff but I," Raistlin hissed. He paused, then added reluctantly, "I'll go with you."

"Raist—" Caramon began, but his brother stared at him coldly. "I'll go, too," the big man muttered.

"No," Tanis said. "You stay here and guard the others. Gilthanas, Raistlin, and I will go."

Gilthanas entered the hole in the wall, followed by the mage and Tanis, the half-elf assisting Raistlin. The light revealed a narrow chamber, vanishing into darkness beyond the staff's reach. On either side were rows of large stone doors, each held in place by huge iron hinges, spiked directly into the rock wall. Raistlin held the staff high, shining it down the shadowy chamber. Each knew that the evil was centered here.

"There's carving on the doors," Tanis murmured. The staff's light threw the stone figures into high relief.

Gilthanas stared at it. "The Royal Crest!" he said in a strangled voice.

"What does that mean?" Tanis asked, feeling the elf's fear infect him like a plague.

"These are the crypts of the Royal Guard," Gilthanas whispered. "They are pledged to continue their duties, even in death, and guard the king—so the legends speak."

"And so the legends come to life!" Raistlin breathed, gripping Tanis's arm. Tanis heard the sound of huge stone blocks shifting, of rusting iron hinges creaking. Turning his head, he saw each of the stone doors begin to swing wide! The hallway filled with a cold so severe that Tanis felt his fingers go numb. Things moved behind the stone doors.

"The Royal Guard! They made the tracks!" Raistlin whispered frantically. "Human and not human. There is no escape!" he said, grasping Tanis tighter. "Unlike the spectres of Darken Wood, these have but one thought—to destroy all who commit the sacrilege of disturbing the king's rest!"

"We've got to try!" Tanis said, unclenching the mage's biting fingers from his arm. He stumbled backward and reached the entryway, only to find it blocked by two figures.

"Get back!" Tanis gasped. "Run! Who, Fizban? No, you crazy old man! We've got to run! The dead guards—"

"Oh, calm down," the old man muttered. "Young people. Alarmists." He turned around and helped someone else enter. It was Goldmoon, her hair gleaming in the light.

"It's all right, Tanis," she called softly. "Look!" She drew aside her cape: the medallion she wore glowed blue. "Fizban said they would let us pass, Tanis, if they saw the medallion. And when he said that—it began to glow!"

"No!" Tanis started to order her back, but Fizban tapped him on the chest with a long, bony finger.

"You're a good man, Tanis Half-Elven," the old mage said softly, "but you worry too much. Now just relax and let us send these poor souls back to their sleep. Bring the others along, will you?"

Tanis, too startled for words, fell back as Goldmoon and Fizban walked past, Riverwind following. As Tanis watched, they walked slowly between the rows of gaping stone doors. Behind each stone door, movement ceased as she passed. Even at that distance, he could feel the sense of malevolent evil slip away.

As the others came to the crumbling entryway and he

helped them through, he answered their whispered questions with a shrug. Laurana didn't say a word to him as she entered; her hand was cold to the touch and he could see, to his astonishment, blood on her lip. Knowing she must have bitten it to keep from screaming, Tanis, remorseful, started to say something to her. But the elfmaid held her head high and refused to look at him.

The others ran after Goldmoon hurriedly, but Tasslehoff, pausing to peek into one of the crypts, saw a tall figure dressed in resplendent armor lying on a stone bier. Skeletal hands grasped the hilt of a longsword lying across the body. Tas looked up at the Royal Crest curiously, sounding out the words.

"Sothi Nuinqua Tsalarioth," said Tanis, coming up behind the kender.

"What does it mean?" Tas asked.

"Faithful beyond Death," Tanis said softly.

At the west end of the crypts, they found a set of bronze double doors. Goldmoon pushed it open easily and led them into a triangular passage that opened into a large hall. Inside this room, the only difficulty they faced was in trying to get the dwarf out of it. The hall was perfectly intact, the only room in the Sla-Mori they had encountered so far that had survived the Cataclysm without damage. And the reason for that, Flint explained to anyone who would listen, was the wonderful dwarven construction—particularly the twenty-three columns supporting the ceiling.

The only way out was two identical bronze doors at the far end of the chamber, leading west. Flint, tearing himself away from the columns, examined each and grumbled that he hadn't any idea what was behind them or where they led. After a brief discussion, Tanis decided to take the door to his right.

The door opened onto a clean, narrow passageway that led them, after about thirty feet, to another single bronze door. This door, however, was locked. Caramon pushed, tugged, pried—all to no avail.

"It's no use," the big man grunted. "It won't budge."

Flint watched Caramon for several minutes, then finally stumped forward. Examining the door, he snorted and shook his head. "It's a false door!"

"Looks real to me!" Caramon said, staring at the door suspiciously. "It's even got hinges!"

"Of course, it does," Flint snorted. "We don't build false doors to look false—even a gully dwarf knows that."

"So we're at a dead end!" Eben said grimly.

"Stand back," Raistlin whispered, carefully leaning his staff against a wall. He placed both hands on the door, touching it only with the tips of his fingers, then said, "Khetsaram pakliol!" There was a flare of orange light, but not from the door—it came from the wall!

"Move!" Raistlin grabbed his brother and jerked him back, just as the entire wall, bronze door and all, began to pivot.

"Quickly, before it shuts," Tanis said, and everyone hurried through the door, Caramon catching his brother as Raistlin staggered.

"Are you all right?" Caramon asked, as the wall slammed shut behind them.

"Yes, the weakness will pass," Raistlin whispered. "That is the first spell I have cast from the spellbook of Fistandantilus. The spell of opening worked, but I did not believe it would drain me like this."

The door led them into another passageway that ran straight west for about forty feet, took a sharp turn to the south, then east, then continued south again. Here the way was blocked by another single bronze door.

Raistlin shook his head. "I can only use the spell once. It is gone from my memory."

"A fireball would open the door," said Fizban. "I think I remember that spell now—"

"No, Old One," Tanis said hastily. "It would fry all of us in this narrow passage. Tas—"

Reaching the door, the kender pushed on it. "Drat, it's

open," he said, disappointed not to have to pick a lock. He peered inside. "Just another room."

They entered cautiously, Raistlin illuminating the chamber with the staff's light. The room was perfectly round, about one hundred feet in diameter. Directly across from them, to the south, stood a bronze door and in the center of the room—

"A crooked column," Tas said, giggling. "Look, Flint. The dwarves built a crooked column!"

"If they did, they had a good reason," the dwarf snapped, shoving the kender aside to examine the tall, thin column. It definitely slanted.

"Hmmmm," said Flint, puzzled. Then—"It isn't a column at all, you doorknob!" Flint exploded. "It's a great, huge chain! Look, you can see here it's hooked to an iron bracket on the floor."

"Then we are in the Chain Room!" Gilthanas said in excitement. "This is the famed defense mechanism of Pax Tharkas. We must be almost in the fortress."

The companions gathered around, staring at the monstrous chain in wonder. Each link was as long as Caramon was tall and as thick around as the trunk of an oak.

"What does the mechanism do?" asked Tasslehoff, longing to climb up the great chain. "Where does this lead?"

"The chain leads to the mechanism itself," Gilthanas answered. "As to how it works, you must ask the dwarf for I am unfamiliar with engineering. But if this chain is released from its moorings"—he pointed to the iron bracket in the floor—"massive blocks of granite drop down behind the gates of the fortress. Then no force on Krynn can open them."

Leaving the kender to peer up into the shadowy darkness, trying in vain to get a glimpse of the wondrous mechanism, Gilthanas joined the others in searching the room.

"Look at this!" he finally cried, pointing to a faint door-shaped line in the stones on the north wall. "A secret door! This must be the entrance!"

"There's the catch." Tasslehoff, turning from the chain, pointed to a chipped piece of stone at the bottom. "The dwarves slipped up," he said, grinning at Flint. "This is a false door that looks false."

"And therefore not to be trusted," Flint said flatly.

"Bah, dwarves have bad days like everyone else," Eben said, bending down to try the catch.

"Don't open it!" Raistlin said suddenly.

"Why not?" asked Sturm. "Because you want to alert someone before we find the way into Pax Tharkas?"

"If I had wanted to betray you, knight, I could have done so a thousand times before this!" Raistlin hissed, staring at the secret door. "I sense a power behind that door greater than any I have felt since—" He stopped, shuddering.

"Since when?" his brother prompted gently.

"The Towers of High Sorcery!" Raistlin whispered. "I warn you, do not open that door!"

"See where the south door leads," Tanis told the dwarf.

Flint stumped over to the bronze door on the south wall and shoved it open. "Near as I can tell, it leads down another passage exactly like all the others," he reported glumly

"The way to Pax Tharkas is through a secret door," Gilthanas repeated. Before anyone could stop him, he reached down and pulled out the chipped stone. The door shivered and began to swing silently inward.

"You will regret this!" Raistlin choked.

The door slid aside to reveal a large room, nearly filled with yellow, brick-like objects. Through a thick layer of dust, a faint yellowish color was visible.

"A treasure room!" Eben cried. "We've found the treasure of Kith-Kanan!"

"All in gold," Sturm said coldly. "Worthless, these days, since steel's the only thing of any value. . . ." His voice trailed off, his eyes widened in horror.

"What is it?" shouted Caramon, drawing his sword.

"I don't know!" Sturm said, more as a gasp than words.

"I do!" Raistlin breathed as the thing took shape before his eyes. "It is the spirit of a dark elf! I warned you not to open that door."

"Do something!" Eben said, stumbling backward.

"Put up your weapons, fools!" Raistlin said in a piercing whisper. "You cannot fight her! Her touch is death, and if she wails while we are within these walls, we are doomed. Her keening voice alone kills. Run, run all of you! Quickly! Through the south door!"

Even as they fell back, the darkness in the treasure room took shape, coalescing into the coldly beautiful, distorted features of a female drow—an evil elf of ages past, whose punishment for crimes unspeakable had been execution. Then the powerful elven magic-users chained her spirit, forcing her to guard forever the king's treasure. At the sight of these living beings, she stretched out her hands, craving the warmth of flesh, and opened her mouth to scream out her grief and her hatred of all living things.

The companions turned and fled, stumbling over each other in their haste to escape through the bronze door. Caramon fell over his brother, knocking the staff from Raistlin's hand. The staff clattered on the floor, its light still glowing, for only dragonfire can destroy the magic crystal. But now its light flared out over the floor, plunging the rest of the room into darkness.

Seeing her prey escaping, the spirit flitted into the Chain Room, her grasping hand brushing Eben's cheek. He screamed at the chilling, burning touch and collapsed. Sturm caught him and dragged him through the door just as Raistlin grabbed his staff and he and Caramon lunged through.

"Is that everyone?" Tanis asked, reluctant to close the door. Then he heard a low, moaning sound, so frightful that he felt his heart stop beating for a moment. Fear seized him. He couldn't breathe. The cry ceased, and his heart gave a great, painful leap. The spirit sucked in its breath to scream again.

"No time to look!" Raistlin gasped. "Shut the door, brother!"

Caramon threw all his weight on the bronze door. It slammed shut with a boom that echoed through the hall.

"That won't stop her!" Eben cried, panic-stricken.

"No," said Raistlin softly. "Her magic is powerful, more powerful than mine. I can cast a spell on the door, but it will weaken me greatly. I suggest you run while you can. If it fails, perhaps I can stall her."

"Riverwind, take the others on ahead," Tanis ordered. "Sturm and I'll stay with Raistlin and Caramon."

The others crept down the dark corridor, looking back to watch in horrible fascination. Raistlin ignored them and handed the staff to his brother. The light from the glowing crystal flashed out at the unfamiliar touch.

The mage put his hands on the door, pressing both palms flat against it. Closing his eyes, he forced himself to forget everything except the magic. "Kalis-an budrunin—" His concentration broke as he felt a terrible chill.

The dark elf! She had recognized his spell and was trying to break him! Images of his battle with another dark elf in the Towers of High Sorcery came back to his mind. He struggled to blot out the evil memory of the battle that wrecked his body and came close to destroying his mind, but he felt himself losing control. He had forgotten the words! The door trembled. The elf was coming through!

Then from somewhere inside the mage came a strength he had discovered within himself only twice before—in the Tower and on the altar of the black dragon in Xak Tsaroth. The familiar voice that he could hear clearly in his mind yet never identify, spoke to him, repeating the words of the spell. Raistlin shouted them aloud in a strong, clear voice that was not his own. "Kalis-an budrunin kara-emarath!"

From the other side of the door came a wail of disappointment, failure. The door held. The mage collapsed.

Caramon handed the staff to Eben as he picked up his brother in his arms and followed the others as they groped their way along the dark passage. Another secret door opened easily to Flint's hand, leading to a series of short, debris-filled tunnels. Trembling with fear, the companions wearily made their way past these obstacles. Finally they emerged into a large, open room filled from ceiling to floor with stacks of wooden crates. Riverwind lit a torch on the wall. The crates were nailed shut. Some bore the label SOLACE, some GATEWAY.

"This is it. We're inside the fortress." Gilthanas said, grimly victorious. "We stand in the cellar of Pax Tharkas."

"Thank the true gods!" Tanis sighed and sank onto the floor, the others slumping down beside him. It was then they noticed that Fizban and Tasslehoff were missing.

LOST. THE PLAN. BETRAYED!

13

Tasslehoff could never afterward clearly recall those last, few, panicked moments in the Chain Room. He remembered saying, "A dark elf? Where?" and standing on his tiptoes, trying desperately to see, when suddenly the glowing staff fell on the floor. He heard Tanis shouting, and—above that—a kind of a moaning sound that made the kender lose all sense of where he was or what he was doing. Then strong hands grabbed him around the waist, lifting him up into the air.

"Climb!" shouted a voice beneath him.

Tasslehoff stretched out his hands, felt the cool metal of the chain, and began to climb. He heard a door boom, far below, and the chilling wail of the dark elf again. It didn't sound deadly this time, more like a cry of rage and anger. Tas hoped this meant his friends had escaped.

"I wonder how I'll find them again," he asked himself softly, feeling discouraged for a moment. Then he heard Fizban muttering to himself and cheered up. He wasn't alone.

Thick, heavy darkness wrapped around the kender. Climbing by feel alone, he was growing extremely tired when he felt cool air brush his right cheek. He sensed, rather than saw, that he must be coming to the place where the chain and the mechanism linked up (Tas was rather proud of that pun). If only he could see! Then he remembered. He was, after all, with a magician.

"We could use a light," Tas called out.

"A fight? Where?" Fizban nearly lost his grip on the chain.

"Not fight! Light!" Tas said patiently, clinging to a link. "I think we're near the top of this thing and we really ought to have a look around."

"Oh, certainly. Let's see, light . . ." Tas heard the magician fumbling in his pouches. Apparently he found what he was searching for, because he soon gave a little crow of triumph, spoke a few words, and a small puffball of bluish-yellow flame appeared, hovering near the magician's hat.

The glowing puffball whizzed up, danced around Tasslehoff as if to inspect the kender, then returned to the proud magician. Tas was enchanted. He had all sorts of questions regarding the wonderful flaming puffball, but his arms were getting shaky and the old magician was nearly done in. He knew they had better find some way to get off this chain.

Looking up, he saw that they were, as he had guessed, at the top part of the fortress. The chain ran up over a huge wooden cogwheel mounted on an iron axle anchored in solid stone. The links of the chain fit over teeth big as tree trunks, then the chain stretched out across the wide shaft, disappearing into a tunnel to the kender's right.

"We can climb onto that gear and crawl along the chain into the tunnel," the kender said, pointing. "Can you send the light up here?"

"Light, to the wheel," Fizban instructed.

The light wavered in the air for a moment, then danced back and forth in a decidedly nay-saying manner.

Fizban frowned. "Light—to the wheel!" he repeated firmly.

The puffball flame darted around to hide behind the magician's hat. Fizban, making a wild grab for it, nearly fell, and flung both arms around the chain. The puffball light danced in the air behind him as if enjoying the game.

"Uh, I guess we've got enough light, after all," Tas said.

"No discipline in the younger generation," Fizban grumbled. "His father—now there was a puffball . . ." The old magician's voice died away as he began to climb again, the puffball flame hovering near the tip of his battered hat.

Tas soon reached the first tooth on the wheel. Discovering the teeth were rough hewn and easy to climb, Tas crawled from one to another until he reached the top. Fizban, his robes hiked up around his thighs, followed with amazing agility.

"Could you ask the light to shine in the tunnel?" Tas asked.

"Light—to the tunnel," Fizban ordered, his bony legs wrapped around a link in the chain.

The puffball appeared to consider the command. Slowly it skittered to the edge of the tunnel, and then stopped.

"Inside the tunnel!" the magician commanded.

The puffball flame refused.

"I think it's afraid of the dark," Fizban said apologetically.

"My goodness, how remarkable!" the kender said in astonishment. "Well," he thought for a moment, "if it will stay where it is, I think I can see enough to make my way across the chain. It looks like it's only about fifteen feet or so to the tunnel." With nothing below but several hundred feet of darkness and air, never mind the stone floor at the bottom, Tas thought.

"Someone should come up here and grease this thing," Fizban said, examining the axle critically. "That's all you get today, shoddy workmanship."

"I'm really rather glad they didn't," Tas said mildly, crawling forward onto the chain. About halfway across the gap, the kender considered what it would be like to fall from this height, tumbling down and down and down, then hitting the stone floor at the bottom. He wondered what it would feel like to splatter all over the floor. . . .

"Get a move on!" Fizban shouted, crawling out onto the chain after the kender.

Tas crawled forward quickly to the tunnel entrance where the puffball flame waited, then jumped off the chain onto the stone floor about five feet below him. The puffball flame darted in after him, and finally Fizban reached the tunnel entrance, too. At the last moment, he fell, but Tas caught hold of his robes and dragged the old man to safety.

They were sitting on the floor resting when suddenly the old man's head snapped up.

"My staff," he said.

"What about it?" Tas yawned, wondering what time it was.

The old man struggled to his feet. "Left it down below," he mumbled, heading for the chain.

"Wait! You can't go back!" Tasslehoff jumped up in alarm.

"Who says?" asked the old man petulantly, his beard bristling.

"I m-mean . . ." Tas stuttered, "it would be too dangerous. But I know you how feel—my hoopak's down there."

"Hmmmm," Fizban said, sitting back down disconsolately.

"Was it magic?" Tas asked after a moment.

"I was never quite certain," Fizban said wistfully.

"Well," said Tas practically, "maybe after we've finished the adventure we can go back and get it. Now let's try to find some place to rest."

He glanced around the tunnel. It was about seven feet from floor to ceiling. The huge chain ran along the top with numerous smaller chains attached, stretching across the tunnel floor into a vast dark pit beyond. Tas, staring down into it, could vaguely make out the shape of gigantic boulders.

"What time do you suppose it is?" Tas asked.

"Lunch time," said the old man. "And we might as well rest right here. It's as safe a place as any." He plopped back down. Pulling out a handful of quith-pa, he began to chew on it noisily. The puffball flame wandered over and settled on the brim of the magician's hat.

Tas sat down next to the mage and began to nibble on his own bit of dried fruit. Then he sniffed. There was suddenly a very peculiar smell, like someone burning old socks. Looking up, he sighed and tugged on the magician's robe.

"Uh, Fizban," he said. "Your hat's on fire."

"Flint," Tanis said sternly, "for the last time—I feel as badly as you do about losing Tas, but we cannot go back! He's with Fizban and, knowing those two, they'll both manage to get out of whatever predicament they're in."

"If they don't bring the whole fortress down around our ears," Sturm muttered.

The dwarf wiped his hand across his eyes, glared at Tanis, then whirled on his heel and stumped back to a corner where he hurled himself onto the floor, sulking.

Tanis sat back down. He knew how Flint felt. It seemed odd—there'd been so many times he could happily have strangled the kender, but now that he was gone, Tanis missed him—and for exactly the same reasons. There was an innate, unfailing cheerfulness about Tasslehoff that made him an invaluable companion. No danger ever frightened a kender and, therefore, Tas never gave up. He was never at a loss for something to do in an emergency. It might not always be the right thing, but at least he was ready to act. Tanis smiled sadly. I only hope this emergency doesn't prove to be his last, he thought.

The companions rested for an hour, eating quith-pa and drinking fresh water from a deep well they discovered. Raistlin regained consciousness but could eat nothing. He sipped water, then lay limply back. Caramon broke the news to him about Fizban hesitantly, fearing his brother might take the old mage's disappearance badly. But Raistlin simply shrugged, closed his eyes, and sank into a deep sleep.

After Tanis felt his strength return, he rose and walked toward Gilthanas, noting that the elf was intently studying a map. Passing Laurana, who sat alone, he smiled at her. She refused to acknowledge it. Tanis sighed. Already he regretted speaking harshly to her back in the Sla-Mori. He had to admit that she had handled herself remarkably well under terrifying circumstances. She had done what she was told to quickly and without question. Tanis supposed he would have to apologize, but first he needed to talk to Gilthanas.

"What's the plan?" he asked, sitting down on a crate.

"Yes, where are we?" Sturm asked. Soon almost everyone was crowded around the map except Raistlin who appeared to sleep, though Tanis thought he saw a slit of gold shining through the mage's supposedly closed eyelids.

Gilthanas spread his map flat.

"Here is the fortress of Pax Tharkas and the surrounding mine area," he said, then he pointed. "We are in the cellars here on the lowest level. Down this hallway, about fifty feet from here, are the rooms where the women are imprisoned. This is a guard room, across from the women, and this"—he tapped the map gently—"is the lair of one of the red dragons, the one Lord Verminaard called Ember. The dragon is so big, of course, that the lair extends up above ground level, communicating with Lord Verminaard's chambers on the first floor, up through the gallery on the second floor, and out into the open sky.

Gilthanas smiled bitterly. "On the first floor, behind Verminaard's chambers, is the prison where the children are kept. The Dragon Highlord is wise. He keeps the hostages separated, knowing that the women would never consider leaving without their children, and the men would not leave without their families. The children are guarded by a second red dragon in this room. The men—about three hundred of them—work in mines out in the mountain caves. There are several hundred gully dwarves working the mines as well."

"You seem to know a lot about Pax Tharkas," Eben said.

Gilthanas glanced up quickly. "What do you insinuate?"

"I'm not insinuating anything," Eben answered. "It's just that you know a lot about this place for never having been here! And wasn't it interesting that we kept running into creatures who damn near killed us back in the Sla-Mori."

"Eben," Tanis spoke very quietly, "we've had enough of your suspicions. I don't believe any of us is a traitor. As Raistlin said, the traitor could have betrayed any of us long before this. What's the point of coming this far?"

"To bring me and the Disks to Lord Verminaard," Goldmoon said softly. "He knows I am here, Tanis. He and I are linked by our faith."

"That's ridiculous!" Sturm snorted.

"No, it isn't," Goldmoon said. "Remember, there are two constellations missing. One was the Queen of Darkness. From what little I have been able to understand in the Disks of Mishakal, the Queen was also one of the ancient gods. The gods of good are matched by the gods of evil, with the gods of neutrality striving to keep the balance. Verminaard worships the Queen of Darkness as I worship Mishakal: that is what Mishakal meant when she said we were to restore the balance. The promise of good that I bring is the one thing he fears and he is exerting all his will to find me. The longer I stay here . . ." Her voice died.

"All the more reason to quit bickering," Tanis stated, switching his gaze to Eben.

The fighter shrugged. "Enough said. I'm with you."

"What is your plan, Gilthanas?" Tanis asked, noticing with irritation that Sturm and Caramon and Eben exchanged quick glances, three humans sticking together against the elves, he caught himself thinking. But perhaps I'm just as bad, believing in Gilthanas because he's an elf.

Gilthanas saw the exchange of glances, too. For a moment he stared at them with an intense, unblinking gaze, then began to speak in a measured tone, considering his words, as if reluctant to reveal any more than was absolutely necessary.

"Every evening, ten to twelve women are allowed to leave their cells and take food to the men in the mines. Thus the Highlord lets the men see that he is keeping his side of the bargain. The women are allowed to visit the children once a day for the same reason. My warriors and I planned to disguise ourselves as women, go out to the men in the mines, tell them of the plan to free the hostages, and alert them to be ready to

159

strike. Beyond that we had not thought, particularly in regard to freeing the children. Our spies indicated something strange about the dragon guarding the children, but we could not determine what."

"What sp—?" Caramon started to ask, caught Tanis's eye, and thought better of his question. Instead he asked, "When will we strike? And what about the dragon, Ember?"

"We strike tomorrow morning. Lord Verminaard and Ember will most certainly join the army tomorrow as it reaches the outskirts of Qualinesti. He has been preparing for this invasion a long time. I do not believe he will miss it."

The group discussed the plan for several minutes, adding to it, refining it, generally agreeing that it appeared viable. They gathered their things as Caramon woke his brother. Sturm and Eben pushed open the door leading to the hallway. It appeared empty, although they could hear faint sounds of harsh, drunken laughter from a room directly across from them. Draconians. Silently, the companions slipped into the dark and dingy corridor.

Tasslehoff stood in the middle of what he had named the Mechanism Room, staring around the tunnel lighted dimly by the puffball. The kender was beginning to feel discouraged. It was a feeling he didn't get often and likened to the time he'd eaten an entire green tomato pie acquired from a neighbor. To this day, discouragement and green tomato pie both made him want to throw up.

"There's got to be some way out of here," said the kender. "Surely they inspect the mechanism occasionally, or come up to admire it, or give tours, or something!"

He and Fizban had spent an hour walking up and down the tunnel, crawling in and out among the myriad chains. They found nothing. It was cold and barren and covered with dust.

"Speaking of light," said the old magician suddenly, though they hadn't been. "Look there."

Tasslehoff looked. A thin sliver of light was visible through a crack in the bottom of the wall, near the entrance to the narrow tunnel. They could hear voices, and the light grew brighter as if torches were being lit in a room below them.

"Maybe that's a way out," the old man said.

Running lightly down the tunnel, Tas knelt down and peered through the crack. "Come here!"

The two looked down into a large room, furnished with every possible luxury. All that was beautiful, graceful, delicate, or valuable in the lands under Verminaard's control had been brought to decorate the private chambers of the Dragon Highlord. An ornate throne stood at one end of the room. Rare and priceless silver mirrors hung on the walls, arranged so cunningly that no matter where a trembling captive turned, the only image he saw was the grotesque, horned helm of the Dragon Highlord glowering at him.

"That must be him!" Tas whispered to Fizban. "That must be Lord Verminaard!" The kender sucked in his breath in awe. "That must be his dragon—Ember. The one Gilthanas told us about, that killed all the elves in Solace."

Ember, or Pyros (his true name being a secret known only to draconians, or to other dragons—never to common mortals) was an ancient and enormous red dragon. Pyros had been given to Lord Verminaard ostensibly as a reward from the Queen of Darkness to her cleric. In reality, Pyros was sent to keep a watchful eye on Verminaard, who had developed a strange, paranoid fear regarding discovery of the true gods. All the Dragon Highlords on Krynn possessed dragons, however, though perhaps not as strong and intelligent. For Pyros had another, more important mission that was secret even to the Dragon Highlord himself, a mission assigned to him by the Queen of Darkness and known only to her and her evil dragons.

Pyros's mission was to search this part of Ansalon for one man, a man of many names. The Queen of Darkness called him Everman. The dragons called him Green Gemstone Man. His human name was Berem. And it was because of this unceasing search for the human, Berem, that Pyros was present in Verminaard's chamber this afternoon when he would have much preferred to be napping in his lair.

Pyros had received word that Fewmaster Toede was bringing in two prisoners for interrogation. There was always the possibility this Berem might be one of them. Therefore, the dragon was always present during interrogations, though he often appeared vastly bored. The only time interrogations became interesting—as far as Pyros was concerned—was when Verminaard ordered a prisoner to "feed the dragon."

Pyros was stretched out along one side of the enormous throne room, completely filling it. His huge wings were folded at his sides, his flanks heaved with every breath he took like some great gnomish engine. Dozing, he snorted and shifted slightly. A rare vase toppled to the floor with a crash. Verminaard looked up from his desk where he was studying a map of Qualinesti.

"Transform yourself before you wreck the place," he snarled.

Pyros opened one eye, regarded Verminaard coldly for a moment, then grudgingly rumbled a brief word of magic.

The gigantic red dragon began to shimmer like a mirage, the monstrous dragon shape condensing into the shape of a human male, slight of build with dark black hair, a thin face, and slanting red eyes. Dressed in crimson robes, Pyros the man walked to a desk near Verminaard's throne. Sitting down, he folded his hands and stared at Verminaard's broad, muscled back with undisguised loathing.

There was a scratch at the door.

"Enter," Verminaard commanded absently.

A draconian guard threw open the door, admitting Fewmaster Toede and his prisoners, then withdrew, swinging the great bronze and gold doors shut. Verminaard kept the Few-master waiting several long minutes while he continued to study his battle plan. Then, favoring Toede with a condescending gaze, he walked over and ascended the steps to his throne. It was elaborately carved to resemble the gaping jaws of a dragon.

Verminaard was an imposing figure. Tall and powerfully built, he wore dark night-blue dragonscale armor trimmed in gold. The hideous mask of a Dragon Highlord concealed his face. Moving with a grace remarkable in such a large man, he leaned back comfortably, his leather-encased hand absently caressing a black, gold-trimmed mace by his side.

Verminaard regarded Toede and his two captives irritably, knowing full well that Toede had dredged up these two in an effort to redeem himself from the disastrous loss of the cleric. When Verminaard discovered from his draconians that a woman matching the description of the cleric had been among those prisoners taken from Solace and that she had been allowed to escape, his fury was terrifying. Toede had nearly paid for his mistake with his life, but the hobgoblin was exceptionally skilled at whining and groveling. Knowing this, Verminaard had considered refusing to admit Toede at all today, but he had a strange, nagging sensation that all was not well in his realm.

It's that blasted cleric! Verminaard thought. He could sense her power coming nearer and nearer, making him nervous and uneasy. He intently studied the two prisoners Toede led into the room. Then, seeing that neither of them matched the descriptions of those who had raided Xak Tsaroth, Verminaard scowled behind the mask.

Pyros reacted differently to the sight of the prisoners. The transformed dragon half-rose to his feet while his thin hands clenched the ebony desktop with such ferocity he left the impressions of his fingers in the wood. Shaking with excitement, it took a great effort of will to force himself to sit back down, outwardly calm. Only his eyes, burning with a devouring flame, gave a hint of his inner elation as he stared at the prisoners.

One of the prisoners was a gully dwarf, Sestun, in fact. He was chained hand and foot (Toede was taking no chances) and could barely walk. Stumbling forward, he dropped to his knees before the Dragon Highlord, terror-stricken. The other prisoner—the one Pyros watched—was a human male, dressed in rags, who stood staring at the floor.

"Why have you bothered me with these wretches, Fewmaster?" Verminaard snarled.

Toede, reduced to a quivering mass, gulped and immediately launched into his speech. "This prisoner"—he hobgoblin kicked Sestun—"was the one who freed the slaves from Solace, and this prisoner"—he indicated the man, who lifted his head, a confused and puzzled expression on his face— "was found wandering around Gateway which, as you know, has been declared off limits to all nonmilitary personnel."

"So why bring them to me?" asked Lord Verminaard irritably. "Throw them into the mines with the rest of the rabble."

Toede stammered. "I thought the human m-m-might b-be a s-spy. . . ."

The Dragon Highlord studied the human intently. He was tall, about fifty human years old. His hair was white and his clean-shaven face brown and weathered, streaked with lines of age. He was dressed like a beggar, which is probably what he was, Verminaard thought in disgust. There was certainly nothing unusual about him, except for his eyes which were bright and young. His hands, too, were those of a man in his prime. Probably elven blood. . . .

"The man is feeble-minded," Verminaard said finally. "Look at him—gaping like a landed fish."

"I b-b-believe he's, uh, deaf and dumb, my lord," Toede said, sweating.

Verminaard wrinkled his nose. Not even the dragonhelm could keep away the foul odor of perspiring hobgoblin.

165

"So you have captured a gully dwarf and a spy who can neither hear nor speak," Verminaard said caustically. "Well done, Toede. Perhaps now you can go out and pick me a bouquet of flowers."

"If that is your lordship's pleasure," Toede replied solemnly, bowing.

Verminaard began to laugh beneath his helm, amused in spite of himself. Toede was such an entertaining little creature, a pity he couldn't be taught to bathe. Verminaard waved his hand. "Remove them—and yourself."

"What shall I do with the prisoners, my lord?"

"Have the gully dwarf feed Ember tonight. And take your spy to the mines. Keep a watch on him though—he looks deadly!" The Dragon Highlord laughed.

Pyros ground his teeth and cursed Verminaard for a fool.

Toede bowed again. "Come on, you," he snarled, yanking on the manacles, and the man stumbled after him. "You, too!" He prodded Sestun with his foot. It was useless. The gully dwarf, hearing he was to feed the dragon, had fainted. A draconian was called to remove him.

Verminaard left his throne and walked over to his desk. He gathered up his maps in a great roll. "Send the wyvern with dispatches," he ordered Pyros. "We fly tomorrow morning to destroy Qualinesti. Be ready when I call."

When the bronze and golden doors had closed behind the Dragon Highlord, Pyros, still in human form, rose from the desk and began to pace feverishly back and forth across the room. There came a scratching at the door.

"Lord Verminaard has gone to his chambers!" Pyros called out, irritated at the interruption.

The door opened a crack.

"It is you I wish to see, royal one," whispered a draconian.

"Enter," Pyros said. "But be swift."

"The traitor has been successful, royal one," the draconian said softly. "He was able to slip away only for a moment, lest they suspect. But he has brought the cleric—"

"To the Abyss with the cleric!" Pyros snarled. "This news is of interest only to Verminaard. Take it to him. No, wait." The dragon paused.

"As you instructed, I came to you first," the draconian said apologetically, preparing to make a hasty departure.

"Don't go," the dragon ordered, raising a hand. "This news is of value to me after all. Not the cleric. There is much more at stake. . . . I must meet with our treacherous friend. Bring him to me tonight, in my lair. Do not inform Lord Verminaard—not yet. He might meddle." Pyros was thinking rapidly now, his plans coming together. "Verminaard has Qualinesti to keep him occupied."

As the draconian bowed and left the throne room, Pyros began pacing once again, back and forth, back and forth, rubbing his hands together, smiling.

NIGHT OF THE DRAGONS

14

"Stop that, you bold man!" Caramon sim-
pered, slapping Eben's hand as the
fighter slyly slid his hand up Caramon's skirt.

The women in the room laughed so heartily at the antics
of the two warriors that Tanis glanced nervously at the cell
door, afraid of arousing the suspicion of the guards.

Maritta saw his worried gaze. "Don't worry about the
guards!" she said with a shrug. "There are only two down here
on this level and they're drunk half the time, especially now
that the army's moved out." She looked up from her sewing at
the women and shook her head. "It does my heart good to hear
them laugh, poor things," she said softly. "They've had little
enough to laugh about these past days."

Thirty-four women were crowded into one cell—Maritta
said there were sixty women living in another nearby—under
conditions so shocking that even the hardened campaigners
were appalled. Rude straw mats covered the floor. The women
had no possessions beyond a few clothes. They were allowed
outdoors for a brief exercise period each morning. The rest
of the time they were forced to sew draconian uniforms.
Though they had been imprisoned only a few weeks, their
faces were pale and wan, their bodies thin and gaunt from
the lack of nourishing food.

Tanis relaxed. Though he had known Maritta only a few hours, he already relied on her judgment. She was the one who had calmed the terrified women when the companions burst into their cell. She was the one who listened to their plan and agreed that it had possibilities.

"Our menfolk will go along with you," she told Tanis. "It's the Highseekers who'll give you trouble."

"The Council of Highseekers?" Tanis asked in astonishment. "They're here? Prisoners?"

Maritta nodded, frowning. "That was their payment for believing in that black cleric. But they won't want to leave, and why should they? They're not forced to work in the mines—the Dragon Highlord sees to that! But we're with you." She glanced around at the others, who nodded firmly. "On one condition— that you'll not put the children in danger."

"I can't guarantee that," Tanis said. "I don't mean to sound harsh, but we may have to fight a dragon to reach them and—"

"Fight a dragon? Flamestrike?" Maritta looked at him in amazement. "Pah! There's no need to fight the pitiful critter. In fact, were you to hurt her, you'd have half the children ready to tear you apart, they're that fond of her."

"Of a dragon?" Goldmoon asked. "What's she done, cast a spell on them?"

"No. I doubt Flamestrike could cast a spell on anything anymore." Maritta smiled sadly. "The poor critter's more than half-mad. Her own children were killed in some great war or other and now she's got it in her head that our children are *her* children. I don't know where his lordship dug her up, but it was a sorry thing to do and I hope he pays for it someday!" She snapped a thread viciously.

"T'won't be difficult to free the children," she added, seeing Tanis's worried look. "Flamestrike always sleeps late of a morning. We feed the children their breakfast, take them out for their exercise, and she never stirs. She'll never know they're gone till she wakes, poor thing."

The women, filled with hope for the first time, began modifying old clothes to fit the men. Things went smoothly until it came time to fit them.

"Shave!" Sturm roared in such fury that the women scurried away from the knight in alarm. Sturm had taken a dim view of the disguise idea, anyway, but had agreed to go along with it. It seemed the best way to cross the wide-open courtyard between the fortress and the mines. But, he announced, he would rather die a hundred deaths at the hands of the Dragon Highlord than shave his moustaches. He only calmed down when Tanis suggested covering his face with a scarf.

Just when that was settled, another crisis arose. Riverwind stated flatly that he would not dress up as a woman and no amount of arguing could convince him otherwise. Goldmoon finally took Tanis aside to explain that, in their tribe, any warrior who committed a cowardly act in battle was forced to wear women's clothes until he redeemed himself. Tanis was baffled by this one. But Maritta had wondered how they would manage to outfit the tall man anyway.

After much discussion, it was decided Riverwind would bundle up in a long cloak and walk hunched over, leaning on a staff like an old woman. Things went smoothly after this, for a time at least.

Laurana walked over to a corner of the room where Tanis was wrapping a scarf around his own face.

"Why don't you shave?" Laurana asked, staring at Tanis's beard. "Or do you truly enjoy flaunting your human side as Gilthanas says?"

"I don't flaunt it," Tanis replied evenly. "I just got tired of trying to deny it, that's all." He drew a deep breath. "Laurana, I'm sorry I spoke to you as I did back in the Sla-Mori. I had no right—"

"You had every right," Laurana interrupted. "What I did was the act of a lovesick little girl. I foolishly endangered your lives." Her voice faltered, then she regained control. "It will not happen again. I will prove I can be of value to the group."

Exactly how she meant to do this, she wasn't certain. Although she talked glibly about being skilled in fighting, she had never killed so much as a rabbit. She was so frightened now that she was forced to clasp her hands behind her back to keep Tanis from seeing how she trembled. She was afraid that if she let herself, she would give way to her weakness and seek comfort in his arms, so she left him and went over to help Gilthanas with his disguise.

Tanis told himself he was glad Laurana was showing some signs of maturity at last. He steadfastly refused to admit that his soul stood breathless whenever he looked into her large, luminous eyes.

The afternoon passed swiftly and soon it was evening and time for the women to take dinner to the mines. The companions waited for the guards in tense silence, laughter forgotten. There had, after all, been one last crisis. Raistlin, coughing until he was exhausted, said he was too weak to accompany them. When his brother offered to stay behind with him, Raistlin glared at him irritably and told him not to be a fool.

"You do not need me this night," the mage whispered. "Leave me alone. I must sleep."

"I don't like leaving him here—" Gilthanas began, but before he could continue, they heard the sound of clawed feet outside the cell, and another sound of pots rattling. The cell door swung open and two draconian guards, both smelling strongly of stale wine, stepped inside. One of them reeled a bit as it peered, bleary-eyed, at the women.

"Get moving," it said harshly.

As the "women" filed out, they saw six gully dwarves standing in the corridor, lugging large pots of some sort of nameless stew. Caramon sniffed hungrily, then wrinkled his nose in disgust. The draconians slammed the cell door shut behind them. Glancing back, Caramon saw his twin, shrouded in blankets, lying in a dark, shadowy corner.

Fizban clapped his hands. "Well done, my boy!" said the old magician in excitement as part of the wall in the Mechanism Room swung open.

"Thanks," Tas replied modestly. "Actually, finding the secret door was more difficult than opening it. I don't know how you managed. I thought I'd looked everywhere."

He started to crawl through the door, then stopped as a thought occurred to him. "Fizban, is there any way you can tell that light of yours to stay behind? At least until we see if anyone's in here? Otherwise, I'm going to make an awfully good target and we're not far from Verminaard's chambers."

"I'm afraid not." Fizban shook his head. "It doesn't like to be left alone in dark places."

Tasslehoff nodded—he had expected the answer. Well, there was no use worrying about it. If the milk's spilled, the cat will drink it, as his mother used to say. Fortunately, the narrow hallway he crawled into appeared empty. The flame hovered near his shoulder. He helped Fizban through, then explored his surroundings. They were in a small hallway that ended abruptly not forty feet away in a flight of stairs descending into darkness. Double bronze doors in the east wall provided the only other exit.

"Now," muttered Tas, "we're above the throne room. Those stairs probably lead down to it. I suppose there's a million draconians guarding it! So that's out." He put his ear to the door. "No sound. Let's look around." Pushing gently, he easily opened the double doors. Pausing to listen, Tas entered cautiously, followed closely by Fizban and the puffball flame.

"Some sort of art gallery," he said, glancing around a giant room where paintings, covered with dust and grime, hung on the walls. High slit windows in the walls gave Tas a glimpse of the stars and the tops of high mountains. With a good idea of where he was now, he drew a crude map in his head.

"If my calculations are correct, the throne room is to the west and the dragon's lair is to the west of that. At least that's where he went when Verminaard left this afternoon. The dragon must have some way to fly out of this building, so the lair should open up into the sky, which means a shaft of some sort, and maybe another crack where we can see what's going on."

So involved was Tas with his plans that he was not paying any attention to Fizban. The old magician was moving purposefully around the room, studying each painting as if searching for one in particular.

"Ah, here it is," Fizban murmured, then turned and whispered, "Tasslehoff!"

The kender lifted his head and saw the painting suddenly begin to glow with a soft light. "Look at that!" Tasslehoff said, entranced. "Why, it's a painting of dragons—red dragons like Ember, attacking Pax Tharkas and . . ."

The kender's voice died. Men—Knights of Solamnia—mounted on other dragons were fighting back! The dragons the Knights rode were beautiful dragons—gold and silver dragons—and the men carried bright weapons that gleamed with a shining radiance. Suddenly Tasslehoff understood! There were *good* dragons in the world, if they could be found, who would help fight the evil dragons, and there was—

"The Dragonlance!" he murmured.

The old magician nodded to himself. "Yes, little one," he whispered. "You understand. You see the answer. And you will remember. But not now. Not now." Reaching out, he ruffled the kender's hair with his gnarled hand.

"Dragons. What was I saying?" Tas couldn't remember. And what was he doing here anyhow, staring at a painting so covered with dust he couldn't make it out. The kender shook his head. Fizban must be rubbing off on him. "Oh, yes. The dragon's lair. If my calculations are correct, it's over here." He walked away.

The old magician shuffled along behind, smiling.

174

The companions' journey to the mines proved uneventful. They saw only a few draconian guards, and they appeared half-asleep with boredom. No one paid any attention to the women going by. They passed the glowing forge, continually fed by a scrambling mass of exhausted gully dwarves.

Hurrying past that dismal sight quickly, the companions entered the mines where draconian guards locked the men in huge cave rooms at night, then returned to keep an eye on the gully dwarves. Guard duty over the men was a waste of time, anyway, Verminaard figured—the humans weren't going anyplace.

And, for a while, it looked to Tanis as if this might prove horribly true. The men weren't going anyplace. They stared at Goldmoon, unconvinced, as she spoke. After all, she was a barbarian, her accent was strange, her dress even stranger. She told what seemed a children's tale of a dragon dying in a blue flame she herself survived. And all she had to show for it was a collection of shining platinum disks.

Hederick, the Solace Theocrat, was loud in his denunciation of the Que-shu woman as a witch and a charlatan and a blasphemer. He reminded them of the scene in the Inn, exhibiting his scarred hand as evidence. Not that the men paid a great deal of attention to Hederick. The Seeker gods, after all, had not kept the dragons from Solace.

Many of them, in fact, were interested in the prospect of escape. Nearly all bore some mark of ill-treatment—whip lashes, bruised faces. They were poorly fed, forced to live in conditions of filth and squalor, and everyone knew that when the iron beneath the hills was gone, their usefulness to Lord Verminaard would end. But the Highseekers—still the governing body, even in prison—opposed such a reckless plan.

Arguments started. The men shouted back and forth. Tanis hastily posted Caramon, Flint, Eben, Sturm, and Gilthanas at the doors, fearing the guards would hear the disturbance and return. The half-elf hadn't expected this—the arguing might last for days! Goldmoon sat despondently before the men, looking as though she might cry. She had been so imbued with her newfound convictions, and so eager to bring her knowledge to the world, that she was cast into despair when her beliefs were doubted.

"These humans are fools!" Laurana said softly, coming up to stand beside Tanis.

"No," replied Tanis, sighing. "If they were fools, it would be easier. We promise them nothing tangible and ask them to risk the only thing they have left—their lives. And for what? To flee into the hills, fighting a running battle all the way. At least here they are alive—for the time being."

"But how can life be worth anything, living like this?" Laurana asked.

"That's a very good question, young woman," said a feeble voice. They turned to see Maritta kneeling beside a man lying on a crude cot in a corner of the cell. Wasted with illness and deprivation, his age was indeterminable. He struggled to sit up, stretching out a thin, pale hand to Tanis and Laurana. His breath rattled in his chest. Maritta tried to hush him, but he stared at her irritably. "I know I'm dying, woman! It doesn't mean I have to be bored to death first. Bring that barbarian woman over to me."

Tanis looked at Maritta questioningly. She rose and came over, drawing him to one side. "He is Elistan," she said as if Tanis should know the name. When Tanis didn't respond, she clarified. "Elistan—one of the Highseekers from Haven. He was much loved and respected by the people, the only one who spoke out against this Lord Verminaard. But no one listened—not wanting to hear, of course."

"You speak of him in the past tense," Tanis said. "He isn't dead yet."

"No, but it won't be long." Maritta wiped away a tear. "I've seen the wasting sickness before. My own father died of it.

There's something inside of him, eating him alive. These last few days he has been half mad with the pain, but that's gone now. The end is very near."

"Maybe not." Tanis smiled. "Goldmoon is a cleric. She can heal him."

"Perhaps, perhaps not," Maritta said skeptically. "I wouldn't want to chance it. We shouldn't excite Elistan with false hope. Let him die in peace."

"Goldmoon," Tanis said as the Chieftain's Daughter came near. "This man wants to meet you." Ignoring Maritta, the half-elf led Goldmoon over to Elistan. Goldmoon's face, hard and cold with disappointment and frustration, softened as she saw the man's pitiful condition.

Elistan looked up at her. "Young woman," he said sternly, though his voice was weak, "you claim to bring word from ancient gods. If it truly was we humans who turned from them, not the gods who turned from us as we've always thought, then why have they waited so long to make their presence known?"

Goldmoon knelt down beside the dying man in silence, thinking how to phrase her answer. Finally, she said, "Imagine you are walking through a wood, carrying your most precious possession—a rare and beautiful gem. Suddenly you are attacked by a vicious beast. You drop the gem and run away. When you realize the gem is lost, you are afraid to go back into the woods and search for it. Then someone comes along with another gem. Deep in your heart, you know it is not as valuable as the one you lost, but you are still too frightened to go back to look for the other. Now, does this mean the gem has left the forest, or is it still lying there, shining brightly beneath the leaves, waiting for you to return?"

Elistan closed his eyes, sighing, his face filled with anguish. "Of course, the gem waits for our return. What fools we have been! I wish I had time to learn of your gods," he said, reaching out his hand.

Goldmoon caught her breath, her face drained until she was nearly as pale as the dying man on the cot. "You will be given time," she said softly, taking his hand in hers.

Tanis, absorbed in the drama before him, started in alarm when he felt a touch on his arm. He turned around, his hand on his sword, to find Sturm and Caramon standing behind him.

"What is it?" he asked swiftly. "The guards?"

"Not yet," Sturm said harshly. "But we can expect them any minute. Both Eben and Gilthanas are gone."

MARGARET WEIS & TRACY HICKMAN

Night deepened over Pax Tharkas.

Back in his lair, the red dragon, Pyros, had no room to pace, a habit he had fallen into in his human form. He barely had room to spread his wings in this chamber, though it was the largest in the fortress and had even been expanded to accommodate him. But the ground-floor chamber was so narrow, all the dragon could do was turn his great body around.

Forcing himself to relax, the dragon laid down upon the floor and waited, his eyes on the door. He didn't notice two heads peeking over the railing of a balcony on the third level far above him.

There was a scratch on the door. Pyros raised his head in eager anticipation, then dropped it again with a snarl as two goblins appeared, dragging between them a wretched specimen.

"Gully dwarf!" Pyros sneered, speaking Common to underlings. "Verminaard's taken leave of his senses if he thinks I'd eat gully dwarf. Toss him in a corner and get out!" he snarled at the goblins who hastened to do as instructed. Sestun cowered in the corner, whimpering.

"Shut up!" Pyros ordered irritably. "Perhaps I should just flame you and stop that blubbering—"

There came another sound at the door, a soft knocking the dragon recognized. His eyes burned red. "Enter!"

A figure came into the lair of the dragon. Dressed in a long cloak, a hood covered its face.

"I have come as you commanded, Ember," the figure said softly.

"Yes," Pyros replied, his talons scratching the floor. "Remove the hood. I would see the faces of those I deal with."

The man cast his hood back. Up above the dragon, on the third level, came a strangled, choking gasp. Pyros stared up at the darkened balcony. He considered flying up to investigate, but the figure interrupted his thought.

"I have only limited time, royal one. I must return before they suspect. And I should report to Lord Verminaard—"

"In due course," Pyros snapped irritably. "What are these fools that you accompany plotting?"

"They plan to free the slaves and lead them in revolt, forcing Verminaard to recall the army marching on Qualinesti."

"That's all?"

"Yes, royal one. Now I must warn the Dragon Highlord."

"Bah! What does that matter? It will be I who deal with the slaves if they revolt. Unless they have plans for me?"

"No, royal one. They fear you a great deal, as all must," the figure added. "They will wait until you and Lord Verminaard have flown to Qualinesti. Then they will free the children and escape into the mountains before you return."

"That seems to be a plan equal to their intelligence. Do not worry about Verminaard. I will see he learns of this when I am ready for him to learn of it. Much greater matters are brewing. Much greater. Now listen closely. A prisoner was brought in today by that imbecile Toede—" Pyros paused, his eyes glowing. His voice dropped to a hissing whisper. "It is *he*! The one we seek!"

The figure stared in astonishment. "Are you certain?"

"Of course!" Pyros snarled viciously. "I see this man in my dreams! He is here, within my grasp! When all of Krynn is searching for him, I have found him!"

"You will inform Her Dark Majesty?"

"No. I dare not trust a messenger. I must deliver this man in person, but I cannot leave now. Verminaard cannot deal with Qualinesti alone. Even if the war is just a ruse, we must keep up appearances, and the world will be better for the absence of elves anyway. I will take the Everman to the Queen when time permits."

"So why tell me?" the figure asked, an edge in his voice.

"Because you must keep him safe!" Pyros shifted his great bulk into a more comfortable position. His plans were coming together rapidly now. "It is a measure of Her Dark Majesty's power that the cleric of Mishakal and the man of the green gemstone arrive together within my reach! I will allow Verminaard the pleasure of dealing with the cleric and her friends tomorrow. In fact"—Pyros's eyes gleamed—"this may work out quite well! We can remove the Green Gemstone Man in the confusion and Verminaard will know nothing! When the slaves attack, you must find the Green Gemstone Man. Bring him back here and hide him in the lower chambers. When the humans have all been destroyed, and the army has wiped out Qualinesti, I will deliver him to my Dark Queen."

"I understand." The figure bowed again. "And my reward?"

"Will be all you deserve. Now leave me."

The man cast the hood up over his head and withdrew. Pyros folded his wings and, curling his great body around with the huge tail up over his snout, he lay staring into the darkness. The only sound that could be heard was Sestun's pitiful weeping.

"Are you all right?" Fizban asked Tasslehoff gently as they sat crouched by the balcony, afraid to move. It was pitch dark, Fizban having overturned a vase on the highly indignant puffball flame.

"Yes," Tas said dully. "I'm sorry I choked like that. I couldn't help myself. Even though I expected it—sort of—it's still hard to realize someone you know could betray you. Do you think the dragon heard me?"

180

"I couldn't say." Fizban sighed. "The question is, what do we do now?"

"I don't know," Tas said miserably. "I'm not supposed to be the one that thinks. I just come along for the fun. We can't warn Tanis and the others, because we don't know where they are. And if we start wandering around looking for them, we might get caught and only make things worse!" He put his chin in his hand. "You know," he said with unusual somberness, "I asked my father once why kenders were little, why we weren't big like humans and elves. I really wanted to be big," he said softly and for a moment he was quiet.

"What did your father say?" asked Fizban gently.

"He said kenders were small because we were meant to do small things. 'If you look at all the big things in the world closely,' he said, 'you'll see that they're really made up of small things all joined together.' That big dragon down there comes to nothing but tiny drops of blood, maybe. It's the small things that make the difference."

"Very wise, your father."

"Yes." Tas brushed his hand across his eyes. "I haven't seen him in a long time." The kender's pointed chin jutted forward, his lips tightened. His father, if he had seen him, would not have known this small, resolute person for his son.

"We'll leave the big things to the others," Tas announced finally. "They've got Tanis and Sturm and Goldmoon. They'll manage. We'll do the small thing, even if it doesn't seem very important. We're going to rescue Sestun."

QUESTIONS. NO ANSWERS.
FIZBAN'S HAT.

15

I heard something, Tanis, and I went to investigate," Eben said, his mouth set in a firm line. "I looked outside the cell door I was guarding and I saw a draconian crouched there, listening. I crept out and got it in a choke hold, then a second one jumped me. I knifed it, then took off after the first. I caught it and knocked it out, then decided I'd better get back here."

The companions had returned to the cells to find both Gilthanas and Eben waiting for them. Tanis had Maritta keep the women busy in a far corner while he questioned the two about their absence. Eben's story appeared true—Tanis had seen the bodies of the draconians as he returned to the prison—and Eben had certainly been in a fight. His clothes were torn, blood trickled from a cut on his cheek.

Tika got a relatively clean cloth from one of the women and began washing the cut. "He saved our lives, Tanis," she snapped. "I'd think you'd be grateful, instead of glaring at him as if he'd stabbed your best friend."

"No, Tika," Eben said gently. "Tanis has a right to ask. It did look suspicious, I admit. But I have nothing to hide." Catching hold of her hand, he kissed her fingertips. Tika flushed and dipped the cloth in water, raising it to his cheek again. Caramon, watching, scowled.

"What about you, Gilthanas?" the warrior asked abruptly. "Why did you leave?"

"Do not question me," the elf said sullenly. "You don't want to know."

"Know what?" Tanis said sternly. "Why did you leave?"

"Leave him alone!" Laurana cried, going to her brother's side.

Gilthanas's almond-eyes flashed as he glanced at them; his face was drawn and pale.

"This is important, Laurana," Tanis said. "Where did you go, Gilthanas?"

"Remember—I warned you." Gilthanas's eyes shifted to Raistlin. "I returned to see if our mage was really as exhausted as he said. He must not have been. He was gone."

Caramon stood up, his fists clenched, his face distorted with anger. Sturm grabbed hold of him and shoved him backwards as Riverwind stepped in front of Gilthanas.

"All have a right to speak and all have a right to respond in their own defense," the Plainsman said in his deep voice. "The elf has spoken. Let us hear from your brother."

"Why should I speak?" Raistlin whispered harshly, his voice soft and lethal with hatred. "None of you trusts me, so why should you believe me? I refuse to answer, and you may think as you choose. If you believe I am a traitor—kill me now! I will not stop you—" He began to cough.

"You'll have to kill me, too," Caramon said in a choked voice. He led his brother back to his bed.

Tanis felt sick.

"Double watches all night. No, not you, Eben. Sturm, you and Flint first, Riverwind and I'll take second." Tanis slumped down on the floor, his head on his arms. We've been betrayed, he thought. One of those three is a traitor and has been all along. The guards might come at any moment. Or perhaps Verminaard was more subtle, some trap to catch us all. . . .

Then Tanis saw it all with sickening clarity. Of course! Verminaard would use the revolt as an excuse to kill the hostages

184

and the cleric. He could always get more slaves, who would have a horrible example before their eyes of what happened to those who disobeyed him. This plan—Gilthanas's plan—played right into his hands!

We should abandon it, Tanis thought wildly, then he forced himself to calm down. No, the people were too excited. Following Elistan's miraculous healing and his announced determination to study these ancient gods, the people had hope. They believed that the gods had truly come back to them. But Tanis had seen the other Highseekers look at Elistan jealously. He knew that, though they made a show of supporting the new leader, given time they would try and subvert him. Perhaps, even now, they were moving among the people, spreading doubt.

If we backed out now, they'd never trust us again, Tanis thought. We must go ahead—no matter how great the risk. Besides, perhaps he was wrong. Maybe there was no traitor. Hoping, he fell into a fitful sleep.

The night passed in silence.

Dawn filtered through the gaping hole in the tower of the fortress. Tas blinked, then sat up, rubbing his eyes, wondering for a moment where he was. I'm in a big room, he thought, staring up at a high ceiling that had a hole cut in it to allow the dragon access to the outside. There are two other doors, besides the one Fizban and I came through last night.

Fizban! The dragon!

Tas groaned, remembering. He hadn't meant to fall asleep! He and Fizban had only been waiting until the dragon slept to rescue Sestun. Now it was morning! Perhaps it was too late! Fearfully the kender crept to the balcony and peered over the edge. No! He sighed in relief. The dragon was asleep. Sestun slept, too, worn out with fear.

Now was their chance! Tasslehoff crawled back to the mage. "Old One!" he whispered. "Wake up!" He shook him.

185

"What? Who? Fire?" The mage sat up, peering around blearily. "Where? Run for the exits!"

"No, not a fire." Tas sighed. "It's morning. Here's your hat—" He handed it to the magician who was groping around, searching for it. "What happened to the puffball light?"

"Humpf!" Fizban sniffed. "I sent it back. Kept me awake, shining in my eyes."

"We were supposed to stay awake, remember?" Tas said in exasperation. "Rescue Sestun from the dragon?"

"How were we going to do that?" Fizban asked eagerly.

"You were the one with the plan!"

"I was? Dear, dear." The old magician blinked. "Was it a good one?"

"You didn't tell me!" Tas nearly shouted, then he calmed down. "All you said was that we had to rescue Sestun before breakfast, because gully dwarf might start looking more appetizing to a dragon who hadn't eaten in twelve hours."

"Makes sense," Fizban conceded. "Are you sure I said it?"

"Look," said Tasslehoff patiently, "all we really need is a long rope to throw down to him. Can't you magic that up?"

"Rope!" Fizban glared at him. "As if I'd stoop so low! That is an insult to one of my skill. Help me stand."

Tas helped the mage stand. "I didn't mean to insult you," the kender said, "and I know there's nothing fancy about rope and you are very skilled. . . . It's just that—oh, all right!" Tas gestured toward the balcony. "Go ahead. I just hope we all survive," he muttered under his breath.

"I won't let you down, or Sestun either, for that matter," Fizban promised, beaming. The two peeked over the balcony. Everything was as before. Sestun lay in a corner. The dragon slept soundly. Fizban closed his eyes. Concentrating, he murmured eerie words, then stretched his thin hand through the railing of the balcony and began to make a lifting motion.

Tasslehoff, watching, felt his heart fly up in his throat. "Stop!" he gurgled. "You've got the wrong one!"

MARGARET WEIS & TRACY HICKMAN

186

Fizban's eyes flew open to see the red dragon, Pyros, slowly rising off the floor, his body still curled in sleep. "Oh, dear!" the magician gasped and, quickly saying different words, he reversed the spell, lowering the dragon to the ground. "Missed my aim," the mage said. "Now I'm zeroed in. Let's try again."

Tas heard the eerie words again. This time Sestun began to rise off the floor and, breath by breath, came level with the balcony. Fizban's face grew red with exertion.

"He's almost here! Keep going!" Tas said, hopping up and down in excitement. Guided by Fizban's hand, Sestun sailed peacefully over the balcony. He came to rest on the dusty floor, still asleep.

"Sestun!" Tas whispered, putting his hand over the gully dwarf's mouth so that he wouldn't yell. "Sestun! It's me, Tasslehoff. Wake up."

The gully dwarf opened his eyes. His first thought was that Verminaard had decided to feed him to a vicious kender instead of the dragon. Then the gully dwarf recognized his friend and went limp with relief.

"You're safe, but don't say a word," the kender warned. "The dragon can still hear us—" He was interrupted by a loud booming from below. The gully dwarf sat up in alarm.

"Shhh," said Tas, "probably just the door into the dragon's lair." He hurried back to the balcony where Fizban was peering through the railing. "What is it?"

"The Dragon Highlord," Fizban pointed to the second level where Verminaard stood on a ledge overlooking the dragon.

"Ember, awaken!" Verminaard yelled down at the sleeping dragon. "I have received reports of intruders! That cleric is here, inciting the slaves to rebellion!"

Pyros stirred and slowly opened his eyes, awakening from a disturbing dream in which he'd seen a gully dwarf fly. Shaking his giant head to clear away the sleep, he heard Verminaard ranting about clerics. He yawned. So the Dragon Highlord had found out the cleric was in the fortress. Pyros supposed he'd have to deal with this now, after all.

"Do not trouble yourself, my lord—" Pyros began, then stopped abruptly, staring at something very strange.

"Trouble myself!" Verminaard fumed. "Why I—" He stopped, too. The object at which both stared was drifting down through the air, gently as a feather.

Fizban's hat.

Tanis woke everyone in the darkest hour before dawn.

"Well," said Sturm, "do we go ahead?"

"We have no choice," Tanis said grimly, looking at the group. "If one of you has betrayed us, then he must live with the knowledge that he has brought about the deaths of innocents. Verminaard will kill not only us, but the hostages as well. I pray that there is no traitor, and so I'm going ahead with our plans."

No one said anything, but each glanced sideways at the others, suspicion gnawing at all of them.

When the women were awake, Tanis went over the plan again.

"My friends and I will sneak up to the children's room with Maritta, disguised as the women who usually bring the children breakfast. We'll lead them to the courtyard," Tanis said quietly. "You must go about your business as you do every morning. When you are allowed into the exercise area, get the children and start moving immediately toward the mines. Your menfolk will handle the guards there and you can escape safely into the mountains to the south. Do you understand?"

The women nodded silently as they heard the sound of the guards approaching.

"This is it," Tanis said softly. "Back to your work."

The women scattered. Tanis beckoned to Tika and Laurana. "If we have been betrayed, you will both be in great danger, since you'll be guarding the women—" he began.

"We'll all be in great danger," Laurana amended coldly. She hadn't slept all night. She knew that if she released the tight bands she had wrapped around her soul, fear would overwhelm her.

Tanis saw none of this inner turmoil. He thought she appeared unusually pale and exceptionally beautiful this morning. A long-time campaigner himself, his preoccupation made him forget the terrors of a first battle.

Clearing his throat, he said huskily, "Tika, take my advice. Keep your sword in your scabbard. You're less dangerous that way." Tika giggled and nodded nervously. "Go say goodbye to Caramon," Tanis told her.

Tika blushed crimson and, giving Tanis and Laurana a meaningful look, ran off.

Tanis gazed at Laurana steadily for a moment, and—for the first time—saw that her jaw muscles were clenched so tightly the tendons in her neck were stretched. He reached out to hold her, but she was stiff and cold as a draconian's corpse.

"You don't have to do this," Tanis said, releasing her. "This isn't your fight. Go to the mines with the other women."

Laurana shook her head, waiting to speak until she was certain her voice was under control. "Tika is not trained for fighting. I am. No matter if it was 'ceremonial.' " She smiled bitterly at Tanis's look of discomfiture. "I will do my part, Tanis." His human name came awkwardly to her lips. "Otherwise, you might think I am a traitor."

"Laurana, please believe me!" Tanis sighed. "I don't think Gilthanas is a traitor any more than you do! It's just, there are so many lives at stake, Laurana! Can't you realize?"

Feeling his hands on her arms shake, she looked up at him and saw the anguish and the fear in his own face, mirroring the fear she felt inside. Only his was not fear for himself, it was fear for others. She drew a deep breath. "I am sorry, Tanis," she said. "You are right. Look. The guards are here. It is time to go."

She turned and walked away without looking back. It didn't occur to her until it was too late that Tanis might have been silently asking for comfort himself.

Maritta and Goldmoon led the companions up a flight of narrow stairs to the first level. The draconian guards didn't accompany them, saying something about "special duty." Tanis asked Maritta if that was usual and she shook her head, her face worried. They had no choice but to go on. Six gully dwarves trailed after them, carrying heavy pots of what smelled like oatmeal. They paid little attention to the women until Caramon stumbled over his skirt climbing the stairs and fell to his knees, uttering a very unladylike oath. The gully dwarves' eyes opened wide.

"Don't even squeak!" Flint said, whirling around to face them, a knife flashing in his hand.

The gully dwarves cowered against the wall, shaking their heads frantically, the pots clattering.

The companions reached the top of the stairs and stopped.

"We cross this hall to the door—" Maritta pointed. "Oh, no!" She grasped Tanis's arm. "There's a guard at the door. It's never guarded!"

"Hush, it could be coincidence," Tanis said reassuringly, although he knew it wasn't. "Just keep on as we planned." Maritta nodded fearfully and walked across the hall.

"Guards!" Tanis turned to Sturm. "Be ready. Remember— quick and deadly. No noise!"

According to Gilthanas's map, the playroom was separated from the children's sleeping quarters by two rooms. The first was a storeroom which Maritta reported was lined with shelves containing toys and clothing and other items. A tunnel ran through this room to the second—the room that housed the dragon, Flamestrike.

"Poor thing," Maritta had said when discussing the plan with Tanis. "She is as much a prisoner as we are. The Dragon Highlord never allows her out. I think they're afraid she'll wander off. They've even built a tunnel through the storeroom, too small for her to fit through. Not that she wants to get out, but I think she might like to watch the children play."

Tanis regarded Maritta dubiously, wondering if they might encounter a dragon very different from the mad, feeble creature she described.

Beyond the dragon's lair was the room where the children slept. This was the room they would have to enter, to wake the children and lead them outdoors. The playroom connected directly with the courtyard through a huge door locked with a great oaken beam.

"More to keep the dragon in than us," Maritta stated.

It must be just about dawning, Tanis thought, as they emerged from the stairwell and turned toward the playroom. The torchlight cast their shadows ahead of them. Pax Tharkas was quiet, deathly quiet. Too quiet—for a fortress preparing for war. Four draconian guards stood huddled together talking at the doorway to the playroom. Their conversation broke off as they saw the women approach.

Goldmoon and Maritta walked in front, Goldmoon's hood was drawn back, her hair glimmering in the torchlight. Directly behind Goldmoon came Riverwind. Bent over a staff, the Plainsman was practically walking on his knees. Caramon and Raistlin followed, the mage staying close to his brother, then Eben and Gilthanas. All the traitors together, as Raistlin had sarcastically observed. Flint brought up the rear, turning occasionally to glower at the panic-stricken gully dwarves.

"You're early this morning," a draconian growled.

The women clustered like chickens in a half-circle around the guards and stood, waiting patiently to be allowed inside.

"It smells of thunder," Maritta said sharply. "I want the children to have their exercise before the storm hits. And what are you doing here? This door is never guarded. You'll frighten the children."

One of the draconians made some comment in their harsh language and two of the others grinned, showing rows of pointed teeth. The spokesman only snarled.

"Lord Verminaard's command. He and Ember are gone this morning to finish the elves. We're ordered to search you before you enter." The draconian's eyes fastened onto Gold-moon hungrily. "That's going to be a pleasure, I'd say."

"For you maybe," muttered another guard, staring at Sturm in disgust. "I've never seen an uglier female in my life than—ugh—" The creature slumped over, a dagger thrust deep into its ribs. The other three draconians died within seconds. Caramon wrapped his hands around the neck of one. Eben hit his in the stomach and Flint lobbed off its head with an axe as it fell. Tanis stabbed the leader through the heart with his sword. He started to let go of the weapon, expecting it to remain stuck in the creature's stony corpse. To his amazement, his new sword slid out of the stone carcass as easily as if it had been nothing more than goblin flesh.

He had no time to ponder this strange occurrence. The gully dwarves, catching sight of the flash of steel, dropped their pots and ran wildly down the corridor.

"Never mind them!" Tanis snapped at Flint. "Into the play-room. Hurry!" Stepping over the bodies, he flung the door open.

"If anyone finds these bodies, it'll be all over," Caramon said.

"It was over before we began!" Sturm muttered angrily. "We've been betrayed, so it's just a matter of time."

"Keep moving!" Tanis said sharply, shutting the door behind them.

"Be very quiet," Maritta whispered. "Flamestrike generally sleeps soundly. If she does waken, act like women. She'll never recognize you. She's blind in one eye."

The chill dawn light filtered in through tiny windows high above the floor, shining on a grim, cheerless play-room. A few well-used toys lay scattered about. There was no furniture. Caramon walked over to inspect the huge wooden beam barring the double doors that led to the court-yard outside.

"I can manage," he said. The big man appeared to lift the beam effortlessly, then set it against the wall and shoved on the door. "Not locked from the outside," he reported. "I guess they didn't expect us to get this far."

Or perhaps Lord Verminaard wants us out there, Tanis thought. He wondered if what the draconian said was true. Had the Dragon Highlord and the dragon really gone? Or were they—angrily he wrenched his mind back. It doesn't matter, he told himself. We have no choice. We must go on.

"Flint, stay here," he said. "If anyone comes, warn us first, then fight."

Flint nodded and took a position just inside the door leading to the corridor, first opening it a crack to see. The draconian bodies had turned to dust on the floor.

Maritta took a torch from the wall. Lighting it, she led the companions through a dark archway into the tunnel leading to the dragon's lair.

"Fizban! Your hat!" Tas risked whispering. Too late. The old magician made a grab for it but missed.

"Spies!" yelled Verminaard in a rage, pointing up to the balcony. "Capture them, Ember! I want them alive!"

Alive? the dragon repeated to himself. No, that could not be! Pyros recalled the strange sound he had heard last night and he knew without a doubt that these spies had overheard him talking about the Green Gemstone Man! Only a privileged few knew that dread secret, the great secret, the secret that would conquer the world for the Queen of Darkness. These spies must die, and the secret die with them.

Pyros spread his wings and launched himself into the air, using his powerful back legs to propel himself from the floor with tremendous speed.

This is it! thought Tasslehoff. Now we've done it. There's no escape this time.

Just as he resigned himself to being cooked by a dragon, he heard the magician shout a single word of command and a thick, unnatural darkness almost knocked the kender over.

"Run!" panted Fizban, grabbing the kender's hand and dragging Tas to his feet.

"Sestun—"

"I've got him! Run!"

Tasslehoff ran. They flew out the door and into the gallery, then he had no idea where he was going. He just kept hold of the old man and ran. Behind him he could hear the sound of the dragon whooshing up out of his lair and he heard the dragon's voice.

"So you are a magic-user, are you, spy?" Pyros shouted. "We can't have you running around in the dark. You might get lost. Let me light your way!"

Tasslehoff heard a great intake of breath into a giant body, then flames crackled and burned around him. The darkness vanished, driven away by the fire's flaring light, but, to his amazement, Tas wasn't touched by the flame. He looked at Fizban—hatless—running next to him. They were in the gallery still, heading for the double doors.

The kender twisted his head. Behind him loomed the dragon, more horrible than anything he had imagined, more terrifying than the black dragon in Xak Tsaroth. The dragon breathed on them again and once more Tas was enveloped by flame. The paintings on the walls blazed, furniture burned, curtains flared like torches, smoke filled the room. But none of it touched him and Sestun and Fizban. Tasslehoff looked at the mage in admiration, truly impressed.

"How long can you keep this up?" he shouted to Fizban as they wheeled around a corner, the double bronze doors in sight.

The old man's eyes were wide and staring. "I have no idea!" he gasped. "I didn't know I could do it at all!"

Another blast of flame exploded around them. This time, Tasslehoff felt the heat and glanced at Fizban in alarm. The mage nodded. "I'm losing it!" he cried.

"Hang on," Tasslehoff panted. "We're almost to the door! He can't get through it."

The three pushed through the bronze double doors that led from the gallery back into the hallway just as Fizban's magic spell wore off. Before them was the secret door, still open, that led to the Mechanism Room. Tasslehoff flung the bronze doors shut and stopped a moment to catch his breath.

But just as he was about to say, "We made it!" one of the dragon's huge clawed feet broke through the stone wall, right above the kender's head!

Sestun, giving a shriek, headed for the stairs.

"No!" Tasslehoff grabbed him. "That leads to Verminaard's quarters!"

"Back to the Mechanism Room!" Fizban cried. They dashed through the secret door just as the stone wall gave way with a tremendous crash. But they could not shut the door.

"I have a lot to learn about dragons, apparently," Tas muttered. "I wonder if there are any good books on the subject—"

"So I have run you rats into your hole and now you are trapped," boomed Pyros's voice from outside. "You have nowhere to go and stone walls do not stop me."

There was a terrible grinding and grating sound. The walls of the Mechanism Room trembled, then began to crack.

"It was a nice try," Tas said ruefully. "That last spell was a doozy. Almost worth getting killed by a dragon to see."

"Killed!" Fizban seemed to wake up. "By a dragon? I should say not! I've never been so insulted. There must be a way out—" His eyes began to gleam. "Down the chain!"

"The chain?" repeated Tas, thinking he must have misunderstood, what with the walls cracking around him and the dragon roaring and all.

"We'll crawl down the chain! Come on!" Cackling with delight, the old mage turned and ran down the tunnel.

Sestun looked dubiously at Tasslehoff, but just then the dragon's huge claw appeared through the wall. The kender and the gully dwarf turned and ran after the old magician.

By the time they reached the great wheel, Fizban had already crawled along the chain leading from the tunnel and reached the first tree-trunk tooth of the wheel itself. Tucking his robes up around his thighs, he dropped down from the tooth onto the first rung of the huge chain. The kender and gully dwarf swung onto the chain after him. Tas was just beginning to think they might get out of this alive after all, especially if the dark elf at the bottom of the chain had taken the day off, when Pyros burst suddenly into the shaft where the great chain hung.

Sections of the stone tunnel caved in around them, falling to the ground with a hollow booming thud. The walls shuddered, and the chain started to tremble. Above them hovered the dragon. He did not speak but simply stared at them with his red eyes. Then he drew in a huge breath that seemed to suck in the air of the whole valley. Tas started instinctively to close his eyes, then opened them wide. He'd never seen a dragon breathe fire and he wasn't going to miss seeing it now—especially as it would probably be his last chance.

Flames billowed out from the dragon's nose and mouth. The blast from the heat alone nearly knocked Tasslehoff off the chain. But, once again, the fire burned all around him and did not touch him. Fizban cackled with delight.

"Quite clever, old man," said the dragon angrily. "But I, too, am a magic-user and I feel you weakening. I hope your cleverness amuses you—all the way down!"

Flames flared out again, but this time the dragon's fire was not aimed at the trembling figures clinging to the chain. The flames struck the chain itself and the iron links began to glow red hot at the first touch of the dragonfire. Pyros breathed again and the links burned white hot. The dragon breathed a third time. The links melted. The massive chain gave a great shudder and broke, plunging into the darkness below.

Pyros watched it as it plummeted down. Then, satisfied that the spies would not live to tell their tale, he flew back to his lair where he could hear Verminaard shouting for him.

In the darkness left behind by the dragon, the great cog-wheel—free of the chain that had held it in place for centuries—gave a groan and began to turn.

MATAFLEUR. THE MAGIC SWORD. WHITE FEATHERS.

16

Light from Maritta's torch illuminated a large, barren windowless room. There was no furniture. The only objects in the chill, stone chamber were a huge basin of water, a bucket filled with what smelled like rotted meat, and a dragon.

Tanis caught his breath. He had thought the black dragon in Xak Tsaroth formidable. He was truly awed at the massive size of this red dragon. Her lair was enormous, probably over one hundred feet in diameter, and the dragon stretched the length of it, the tip of her long tail lying against the far wall. For a moment the companions stood stunned, with ghastly visions of the giant head rising up and searing them with the burning flame breathed by the red dragons, the flames that had destroyed Solace.

Maritta did not appear worried, however. She advanced steadily into the room and, after a moment's hesitation, the companions hurried after her. As they drew closer to the creature, they could see that Maritta had been right—the dragon was clearly in pitiful condition. The great head that lay on the cold stone floor was lined and wrinkled with age, the brilliant red skin grayish and mottled. She breathed noisily through her mouth, her jaws parted to reveal the once sword-sharp teeth, now yellowed and broken.

Long scars ran along her sides; her leathery wings were dry and cracked.

Now Tanis could understand Maritta's attitude. Clearly, the dragon had been ill-used, and he caught himself feeling pity, relaxing his guard. He realized how dangerous this was when the dragon—awakened by the torchlight—stirred in her sleep. Her talons were as sharp and her fire as destructive as any other red dragon in Krynn, Tanis reminded himself sharply.

The dragon's eyes opened, slits of glistening red in the torchlight. The companions halted, hands on their weapons.

"Is it time for breakfast already, Maritta?" Matafleur (Flamestrike being her name to common mortals) said in a sleepy, husky voice.

"Yes, we're just a bit early today, dearie," Maritta said soothingly. "But there's a storm brewing and I want the children to have their exercise before it breaks. Go back to sleep. I'll see they don't wake you on their way out."

"I don't mind." The dragon yawned and opened her eyes a bit farther. Now Tanis could see that one of them had a milky covering; she was blind in that eye.

"I hope we don't have to fight her, Tanis," Sturm whispered. "It'd be like fighting someone's grandmother."

Tanis forced his expression to harden. "She's a deadly grandmother, Sturm. Just remember that."

"The little ones had a restful night," the dragon murmured, apparently drifting off to sleep again. "See that they don't get wet if it does storm, Maritta. Especially little Erik. He had a cold last week." Her eyes closed.

Turning, Maritta beckoned the others on, putting her finger to her lips. Sturm and Tanis came last, their weapons and armor muffled by numerous cloaks and skirts. Tanis was about thirty feet from the dragon's head when the noise started.

At first he thought it was his imagination, that his nervousness was making him hear a buzzing sound in his head. But the sound grew louder and louder and Sturm turned, staring at him in alarm. The buzzing sound increased until it was like a thousand swarming locusts. Now the others were looking back, too—all of them staring at him! Tanis looked at his friends helplessly, an almost comic look of confusion on his face.

The dragon snorted and stirred in irritation, shaking her head as though the noise hurt her ears.

Suddenly Raistlin broke from the group and ran back to Tanis. "The sword!" he hissed. He grabbed the half-elf's cloak and threw it back to reveal the blade.

Tanis stared down at the sword in its antique scabbard. The mage was right. The blade hummed as if in the highest state of alarm. Now that Raistlin called his attention to it, the half-elf could actually feel the vibrations.

"Magic," the mage said softly, studying it with interest.

"Can you stop it?" yelled Tanis over the weird noise.

"No," said Raistlin. "I remember now. This is Wyrmslayer, the famed magical sword of Kith-Kanan. It is reacting to the presence of the dragon."

"This is an abysmal time to remember!" Tanis said in fury.

"Or a very convenient time," snarled Sturm.

The dragon slowly raised her head, her eyes blinking, a thin stream of smoke drifting from a nostril. She focused her bleary red eyes on Tanis, pain and irritation in her gaze.

"Who have you brought, Maritta?" Matafleur's voice was filled with menace. "I hear a sound I have not heard in centuries, I smell the foul smell of steel! These are not the women! These are warriors!"

"Don't hurt her!" Maritta wailed.

"I may not have any choice!" Tanis said viciously, drawing Wyrmslayer from its sheath. "Riverwind and Goldmoon, get Maritta out of here!" The blade began to shine with a brilliant white light as the buzzing grew louder and angrier. Matafleur shrank back. The light of the sword pierced her good eye painfully; the terrible sound went through her head like a spear. Whimpering, she huddled away from Tanis.

"Run, get the children!" Tanis yelled, realizing that they didn't need to fight—at least not yet. Holding the shining sword high in the air, he moved forward cautiously, driving the pitiful dragon back against the wall.

Maritta, after one fearful glance at Tanis, led Goldmoon to the children's room. About one hundred children were wide-eyed with alarm over the strange sounds outside their chamber. Their faces relaxed at the sight of Maritta and Goldmoon and a few of the littler ones actually giggled when Caramon came rushing in, his skirts flapping around his armored legs. But at the sight of warriors and their drawn weapons, the children sobered immediately.

"What is it, Maritta?" asked the oldest girl. "What's happening? Is it fighting again?"

"We hope there'll be no fighting, dear one," Maritta said softly. "But I'll not lie to you—it may come to that. Now I want you to gather your things, particularly your warm cloaks, and come with us. The older of you carry the wee ones, as you do when we go outdoors for exercise."

Sturm expected confusion and wailing and demands for explanations. But the children quickly did as they were told, wrapping themselves in warm clothing and helping to dress the younger ones. They were quiet and calm, if a bit pale. These were children of war, Sturm remembered.

"I want you to move very swiftly through the dragon's lair and out into the playroom. When we get there, the big man"—Sturm gestured to Caramon—"will lead you out into the courtyard. Your mothers are waiting for you there. When you get outside, look immediately for your mother and go to her. Does everyone understand?" He glanced dubiously at the smaller children, but the girl at the front of the line nodded.

"We understand, sir," she said.

"All right," Sturm turned. "Caramon?"

The warrior, flushing in embarrassment as one hundred pairs of eyes turned to look at him, led the way back into the dragon's lair. Goldmoon scooped up a toddler in her arms, Maritta picked up another one. The older boys and girls carried little ones on their backs. They hurried out the door in orderly fashion, without saying a word until they saw Tanis, the gleaming sword, and the terrified dragon.

"Hey, you! Don't hurt our dragon!" one little boy yelled. Leaving his place in line, the child ran up to Tanis, his fists raised, his face twisted into a snarl.

"Dougl!" cried the oldest girl, shocked. "Get back in line this instant!" But some of the children were crying now.

Tanis, the sword still raised—knowing that this was the only thing keeping the dragon at bay—shouted, "Get them out of here!"

"Children, please!" Chieftain's Daughter, her voice stern and commanding, brought order to the chaos. "Tanis will not hurt the dragon if he does not have to. He is a gentle man. You must leave now. Your mothers need you."

There was an edge of fear in Goldmoon's voice, a feeling of urgency that influenced even the youngest child. They got back into line quickly.

"Good-bye, Flamestrike," several of the children called out, wistfully, waving their hands as they followed Caramon. Dougl gave Tanis one final threatening glance, then he returned to line, wiping his eyes with grubby fists.

"No!" shrieked Matafleur in a heartbroken voice. "No! Don't fight my children. Please! It is me you want! Fight me! Don't harm my children!"

Tanis realized the dragon was back in her past, reliving whatever terrible event had deprived her of her children.

Sturm stayed near Tanis. "She's going to kill you when the children are out of danger, you know."

"Yes," said Tanis grimly. Already the dragon's eyes—even the bad eye, were flaring red. Saliva dripped from the great, gaping mouth, and her talons scratched the floor.

"Not my children!" she said with rage.

"I'm with you—" Sturm began, drawing his sword.

"Leave us, knight," Raistlin whispered softly from the shadows. "Your weapon is useless. *I* will stay with Tanis."

The half-elf glanced at the mage in astonishment. Raistlin's strange, golden eyes met his, knowing what he was thinking: do I trust him? Raistlin gave him no help, almost as if he were goading him to refusal.

"Get out," Tanis said to Sturm.

"What?" he yelled. "Are you crazy? You're trusting this—"

"Get out!" Tanis repeated. At that moment, he heard Flint yelling loudly. "Go, Sturm, they need you out there!"

The knight stood a moment, irresolute, but he could not in honor ignore a direct order from one he considered his commander. Casting a baleful glance at Raistlin, Sturm turned on his heel and entered the tunnel.

"There is little magic I can work against a red dragon," Raistlin whispered swiftly.

"Can you buy us time?" Tanis asked.

Raistlin smiled the smile of one who knows death is so near it is past fearing. "I can," he whispered. "Move back near the tunnel. When you hear me start to speak, run."

Tanis began backing up, still holding the sword high. But the dragon no longer feared its magic. She knew only that her children were gone and she must kill those responsible. She lunged directly at the warrior with the sword as he began to run toward the tunnel. Then darkness descended upon her, a darkness so deep Matafleur thought for a horrible moment she had lost the sight of the other eye. She heard whispered words of magic and knew the robed human had cast a spell.

"I'll burn them!" she howled, sniffing the smell of steel through the tunnel. "They will not escape!" But just as she sucked in a great breath, she heard another sound—the sound of her children. "No," she realized in frustration. "I dare not. My children! I might harm my children. . . ." Her head drooped down on the cold stone floor.

Tanis and Raistlin ran down the tunnel, the half-elf dragging the weakened mage with him. Behind them they heard a pitiful, heartbroken moan.

"Not my children! Please, fight me! Don't hurt my children!"

Tanis emerged from the tunnel into the playroom, blinking in the bright light as Caramon swung the huge doors open to the rising sun. The children raced out the door into the courtyard. Through the door, Tanis could see Tika and Laurana, standing with their swords drawn, looking their way anxiously. A draconian lay crumbling on the floor of the playroom, Flint's battle-axe stuck in its back.

"Outside, all of you!" Tanis shouted. Flint, retrieving his battle-axe, joined the half-elf as the last to leave the playroom. As they did so, they heard a terrifying roar, the roar of a dragon, but a very different dragon than the pitiful Matafleur. Pyros had discovered the spies. The stone walls began to tremble—the dragon was rising from his lair.

"Ember!" Tanis swore bitterly. "He hasn't gone!"

The dwarf shook his head. "I'll bet my beard," he said gloomily, "that Tasslehoff's involved."

The broken chain plummeted to the stone floor of the Chain Room in the Sla-Mori, three little figures falling with it.

Tasslehoff, clinging uselessly to the chain, tumbled through the darkness and thought, this is how it feels to die. It was an interesting sensation and he was sorry he couldn't experience it longer. Above him, he could hear Sestun shrieking in terror. Below, he heard the old mage muttering to himself, probably trying one last spell. Then Fizban raised his voice: "Pveatherf—" The word was cut off with a scream. There was the sound of a bone-crushing thud as the old magician crashed to the floor. Tasslehoff grieved, even though he knew he was next. The stone floor was approaching. Within a very few seconds he too would be dead. . . .

Then it was snowing.

At least that was what the kender thought. Then he realized with a shock that he was surrounded by millions and millions of feathers—like an explosion of chickens! He sank into a deep, vast pile of white feathers, Sestun tumbling in after him.

"Poor Fizban," Tas said, blinking tears from his eyes as he floundered in an ocean of white chicken feathers. "His last spell must have been *featherfall* like Raistlin uses. Wouldn't you know it? He just got the feathers."

Above him, the cogwheel turned faster and faster, the freed chain rushing through it as if rejoicing in its release from bondage.

Outdoors in the courtyard chaos reigned.

"Over here!" Tanis yelled, bursting out of the door, knowing they were doomed but refusing to give in. The companions gathered around him, weapons drawn, looking at him anxiously. "Run to the mines! Run for shelter! Verminaard and the red dragon didn't leave. It is a trap. They'll be on us any moment."

The others, their faces grim, nodded. All of them knew it was hopeless—they must cover about two hundred yards of flat, wide-open surface to reach safety.

They tried to herd the women and children along as swiftly as possible, but not very successfully. All the mothers and children needed to be sorted out. Then Tanis, looking over at the mines, swore aloud in added frustration.

The men of the mines, seeing their families free, quickly overpowered the guards and began running toward the courtyard! That wasn't the plan! What was Elistan thinking about? Within moments there would be eight hundred frantic people milling around out in the open without a scrap of shelter! He had to get them to head back south to the mountains.

"Where's Eben?" he called to Sturm.

"Last I saw him, he was running for the mines. I couldn't figure out why—"

The knight and half-elf gasped in sudden realization.

"Of course," said Tanis softly, his voice lost in the commotion. "It all fits."

As Eben ran for the mines, his one thought was to obey Pyros's command. Somehow, in the midst of this furor, he had to find the Green Gemstone Man. He knew what Verminaard and Pyros were going to do to these poor wretches. Eben felt a moment's pity—he was not, after all, cruel and vicious. He had simply seen, long ago, which side was bound to win, and he determined, for once, to be on a winning side.

When his family's fortune was wiped out, Eben was left with only one thing to sell—himself. He was intelligent, handy with a sword, and as loyal as money could buy. It was on a journey to the north, looking for possible buyers, that Eben met Verminaard. Eben had been impressed with Verminaard's power and had wormed his way into the evil cleric's favor. But more importantly, he had managed to make himself useful to Pyros. The dragon found Eben charming, intelligent, resourceful, and—after a few tests—trustworthy.

Eben was sent home to Gateway just before the dragon-armies struck. He conveniently "escaped" and started his resistance group. Stumbling upon Gilthanas's party of elves the first time they tried to sneak into Pax Tharkas was a stroke of luck that further improved Eben's relationship with both Pyros and Verminaard. When the cleric actually fell into Eben's hands, he couldn't believe his luck. It must go to show how much the Dark Queen favored him, he supposed.

He prayed that the Dark Queen continue to favor him. Finding the Green Gemstone Man in this confusion was going to take divine intervention. Hundreds of men were milling about uncertainly. Eben saw a chance to do Verminaard another favor. "Tanis wants you men to meet in the courtyard," he cried. "Join your families."

"No! That isn't the plan!" Elistan cried, trying to stop them. But he was too late. The men, seeing their families free, surged forward. Several hundred gully dwarves added to

207

the confusion, rushing gleefully out of the mines to join the fun, thinking, perhaps, it was a holiday.

Eben scanned the crowd anxiously for the Green Gemstone Man, then decided to look inside the prison cells. Sure enough, he found the man sitting alone, staring vaguely around the empty cell. Eben swiftly knelt beside him, racking his brain to come up with the man's name. It was something odd, old-fashioned. . . .

"Berem," Eben said after a moment. "Berem?"

The man looked up, interest lighting his face for the first time in many weeks. He was not, as Toede had assumed, deaf and dumb. He was, instead, a man obsessed, totally absorbed in his own secret quest. He was human, however, and the sound of a human voice speaking his name was inordinately comforting.

"Berem," said Eben again, licking his lips nervously. Now that he had him, he wasn't sure what to do with him. He knew the first thing those poor wretches outside would do when the dragon struck would be to head for the safety of the mines. He had to get Berem out of here before Tanis caught them. But where? He could take the man inside Pax Tharkas as Pyros had ordered, but Eben didn't like that idea. Verminaard would certainly find them and, his suspicions aroused, would ask questions Eben couldn't answer.

No, there was only one place Eben could take him and be safe—outside the walls of Pax Tharkas. They could lie low in the wilderness until the confusion died, then sneak back inside the fortress at night. His decision made, Eben took Berem's arm and helped the man rise to his feet.

"There's going to be fighting," he said. "I'm going to take you away, keep you safe until it is over. I am your friend. Do you understand?"

The man regarded him with a look of penetrating wisdom and intelligence. It was not the ageless look of the elves but of a human who has lived in torment for countless years. Berem gave a small sigh and nodded.

Verminaard strode from his chamber in a fury, yanking at his leather, armored gloves. A draconian trotted behind, carrying the Highlord's mace, Nightbringer. Other draconians milled around, acting on the orders Verminaard gave as he stepped into the corridor, returning to Pyros's lair.

"No, you fools, don't recall the army! This will take but a moment of my time. Qualinesti will be in flames by nightfall. Ember!" he shouted, throwing open the doors that led to the dragon's lair. He stepped out onto the ledge. Peering upward toward the balcony he could see smoke and flame and, in the distance, hear the dragon's roar.

"Ember!" There was no answer. "How long does it take to capture a handful of spies?" he demanded furiously. Turning, he nearly fell over a draconian captain.

"Will you be using the dragon saddle, my lord?"

"No, there isn't time. Besides, I use that only for combat and there will be no one to fight out there, simply a few hundred slaves to burn."

"But the slaves have overcome the guards at the mine and are rejoining their families in the courtyard."

"How strong are your forces?"

"Not nearly strong enough, my lord," the draconian captain said, its eyes glinting. The captain had never thought it wise to deplete the garrison. "We are forty or fifty, perhaps, to over three hundred men and an equal number of women. The women will undoubtedly fight alongside the men, your lordship, and if they ever get organized and escape into the mountains—"

"Bah! Ember!" Verminaard called. He heard, in another part of the fortress, a heavy, metallic thud. Then he heard another sound, the great wheel—unused in centuries—creaking with protest at being forced into labor. Verminaard was wondering what these odd sounds portended, when Pyros flew down into his lair.

The Dragon Highlord ran to the ledge as Pyros dropped past him. Verminaard climbed swiftly and skillfully onto the dragon's back. Though separated by mutual distrust, the two fought well together. Their hatred for the petty races they strove to conquer, combined with their desire for power, joined them in a bond much stronger than either cared to admit.

"Fly!" Verminaard roared, and Pyros rose into the air.

"It is useless, my friend," Tanis said quietly to Sturm laying his hand on the knight's shoulder as Sturm frantically called for order. "You're only wasting your breath. Save it for fighting."

"There'll be no fighting." Sturm coughed, hoarse from shouting. "We'll die, trapped like rats. Why won't these fools listen?"

He and Tanis stood at the northern end of the courtyard about twenty feet from the front gates of Pax Tharkas. Looking south, they could see the mountains and hope. Behind them were the great gates of the fortress that would, at any moment, open to admit the vast draconian army, and within these walls, somewhere, were Verminaard and the red dragon.

In vain, Elistan sought to calm the people and urge them to move southward. But the men insisted on finding their womenfolk, the women on finding their children. A few families, together again, were starting to move south, but too late and too slowly.

Then, like a blood-red, flaming comet, Pyros soared from the fortress of Pax Tharkas, his wings sleek, held close to his sides. His huge tail trailed behind him. His taloned forefeet were curled close to his body as he gained speed in the air. Upon his back rode the Dragon Highlord, the gilded horns of the hideous dragonmask glinting in the morning sun. Verminaard held onto the dragon's spiny mane with both hands as they flared into the sunlit sky, bringing night's shadows to the courtyard below.

The dragonfear spread over the people. Unable to scream or run, they could only cower before the fearful apparition, arms around each other, knowing death was inevitable.

At Verminaard's command, Pyros settled on one of the fortress towers. Verminaard stared out from behind the horned dragonmask, silent, furious.

Tanis, watching in helpless frustration, felt Sturm grip his arm. "Look!" The knight pointed north, toward the gates.

Tanis reluctantly lowered his gaze from the Dragon Highlord and saw two figures running toward the gates of the fortress. "Eben!" he cried in disbelief. "But who's that with him?"

"He won't escape!" Sturm shouted. Before Tanis could stop him, the knight ran after the two. As Tanis followed, he saw a flash of red out of the corner of his eye—Raistlin and his twin.

"I, too, have a score to settle with this man," the mage hissed. The three caught up with Sturm just as the knight gripped Eben by the collar and hurled him to the ground.

"Traitor!" Sturm yelled loudly. "Though I die this day, I'll send you to the Abyss first!" He drew his sword and jerked Eben's head back. Suddenly Eben's companion whirled around, came back, and caught hold of Sturm's sword-arm.

Sturm gasped. His hand loosened its grip on Eben as the knight stared, amazed at the sight before him.

The man's shirt had been torn open in his wild flight from the mines. Impaled in the man's flesh, in the center of his chest, was a brilliant green jewel! Sunlight flashed on the gem that was as big around as a man's fist, causing it to gleam with a bright and terrible light—an unholy light.

"I have never seen nor heard of magic like this!" Raistlin whispered in awe as he and the others stopped, stunned, beside Sturm.

Seeing their wide eyes focused on his body, Berem instinctively pulled his shirt over his chest. Then, loosening his hold on Sturm's arm, he turned and ran for the gates. Eben scrambled to his feet and stumbled after him.

Sturm leaped forward, but Tanis stopped him.

"No," he said. "It's too late. We have others to think of."

"Tanis, look!" Caramon shouted, pointing above the huge gates.

A section of the stone wall of the fortress above the massive front gates began to open, forming a huge, widening crack. Slowly at first, then with increasing speed, the massive granite boulders began to fall from the crack, smashing to the ground with such force that the flagstone cracked and great clouds of dust rose into the air. Above the roar could be dimly heard the sound of the massive chains releasing the mechanism.

The boulders began to fall just as Eben and Berem arrived at the gates. Eben shrieked in terror, instinctively and pitifully raised his arm to shield his head. The man next to him glanced up and—it seemed—gave a small sigh. Then both were buried under tons of cascading rock as the ancient defense mechanism sealed shut the gates of Pax Tharkas.

"This is your final act of defiance!" Verminaard roared. His speech had been interrupted by the fall of the rocks, an act that only enraged him more. "I offered you a chance to work to further the glory of my Queen. I cared for you and your families. But you are stubborn and foolish. You will pay with your lives!" The Dragon Highlord raised Nightbringer high in the air. "I will destroy the men. I will destroy the women! I will destroy the children!"

At a touch of the Dragon Highlord's hand, Pyros spread his huge wings and leaped high into the air. The dragon drew in a deep breath, preparing to swoop down upon the mass of people who wailed in terror in the wide-open courtyard and incinerate them with his fiery breath.

But the dragon's deadly dive was stopped.

Sweeping up into the sky from the pile of rubble made when she crashed out of the fortress, Matafleur flew straight at Pyros.

The ancient dragon had sunk deeper into her madness. Once more she relived the nightmare of losing her children. She could see the knights upon the silver and golden dragons, the wicked dragonlances gleaming in the sunshine. In vain she pleaded with her children not to join the hopeless fight, in vain she sought to convince them the war was at an end. They were young and would not listen. They flew off, leaving her weeping in her lair. As she watched in her mind's eye the bloody, final battle, as she saw her children die upon the dragonlances, she heard Verminaard's voice.

"I will destroy the children!"

And, as she had done so many centuries before, Matafleur flew out to defend them.

Pyros, stunned by the unexpected attack, swerved just in time to avoid the broken, yet still lethal teeth of the old dragon aiming for his unprotected flanks. Matafleur hit him a glancing blow, tearing painfully into one of the heavy muscles that drove the giant wings. Rolling in the air, Pyros lashed out at the passing Matafleur with a wicked, taloned forefoot, tearing a gash in the female dragon's soft underbelly.

In her madness, Matafleur did not even feel the pain, but the force of the larger and younger male dragon's blow knocked her backwards in the air.

The rollover maneuver had been an instinctive defensive action on the part of the male dragon. He had been able to gain both altitude and time to plan his attack. He had, however, forgotten his rider. Verminaard—riding without the dragon saddle he used in battle—lost his grip on the dragon's neck and fell to the courtyard below. It was not a long drop and he landed uninjured, only bruised and momentarily shaken.

Most of the people around him fled in terror when they saw him rise to his feet, but—glancing around swiftly—he noticed that there were four, near the northern end of the courtyard, who did not flee. He turned to face those four.

The appearance of Matafleur and her sudden attack on Pyros jolted the captive people out of their state of panic. This, combined with the fall of Verminaard into their midst, like the fall of some horrifying god, accomplished what Elistan and the others had not. The people were shaken out of their fear, sense returned, and they began fleeing south, toward the safety of the mountains. At this sight, the draconian captain sent his forces pouring into the crowd. He detailed another messenger, a wyvern, to fly from the fortress to recall the army.

The draconians surged into the refugees, but, if they hoped to cause a panic, they failed. The people had suffered enough. They had allowed their freedom to be taken away once, in return for the promise of peace and safety. Now they understood that there could be no peace as long as these monsters roamed Krynn. The people of Solace and Gateway—men, women, and children—fought back using every pitiful weapon they could grab, rocks, stones, their own bare hands, teeth, and nails.

The companions became separated in the crowd. Laurana was cut off from everyone. Gilthanas had tried to stay near her, but he was carried off in the mob. The elfmaiden, more frightened than she believed possible and longing to hide, fell back against the wall of the fortress, her sword in her hand. As she watched the raging battle in horror, a man fell to the ground in front her, clutching his stomach, his fingers red with his own blood. His eyes fixed in death, seeming to stare at her, as his blood formed a pool at her feet. Laurana stared at the blood in horrid fascination, then she heard a sound in front of her. Shaking, she looked up—directly into the hideous, reptilian face of the man's killer.

The draconian, seeing an apparently terror-stricken elven female before him, figured on an easy kill. Licking its bloodstained sword with its long tongue, the creature jumped over the body of his victim and lunged for Laurana.

Clutching her sword, her throat aching with terror, Laurana reacted out of sheer defensive instinct. She stabbed blindly, jabbing upward. The draconian was caught totally off guard. Laurana plunged her weapon into the draconian's body, feeling the sharp elven blade penetrate both armor and flesh, hearing bone splinter and the creature's last gurgling scream. It turned to stone, yanking the sword from her hand. But Laurana, thinking with a cold detachment that amazed her, knew from hearing the warriors talk that if she waited a moment, the stone body would turn to dust, releasing her weapon.

The sounds of battle raged around her, the screams, the death cries, the thuds and groans, the clash of steel—but she heard none of it.

She waited calmly until she saw the body crumble. Then she reached down and, sifting the dust aside with her hand, she grasped the hilt of her sword and lifted it into the air. Sunlight flashed on the blood-stained blade, her enemy lay dead at her feet. She looked around but could not see Tanis. She could not see any of the others. For all she knew, they might be dead. For all she knew, she might herself be dead within the next moment.

Laurana lifted her eyes to the sun-drenched blue sky. The world she might soon be leaving seemed newly made— every object, every stone, every leaf stood out in painful clarity. A warm fragrant southern breeze sprang up, driving back the storm clouds that hung over her homeland to the north. Laurana's spirit, released from its prison of fear, soared higher than the clouds, and her sword flashed in the morning sun.

THE DRAGON HIGHLORD.
MATAFLEUR'S CHILDREN.

17

Verminaard studied the four men as they approached him. These were not slaves, he realized. Then he recognized them as the ones who traveled with the golden-haired cleric. These, then, were the ones who had defeated Onyx in Xak Tsaroth, escaped the slave caravan, and broken into Pax Tharkas. He felt as if he knew them—the knight from that broken land of past glories; a half-elf trying to pass himself off as human; a deformed, sickly magician; and the mage's twin— a human giant whose brain was probably as thick as his arms.

It will be an interesting fight, he thought. He almost welcomed hand-to-hand combat—it had been a long time. He was growing bored with commanding armies from the back of a dragon. Thinking of Ember, he glanced into the sky, wondering if he might be able to summon aid.

But it appeared that the red dragon was having his own problems. Matafleur had been fighting battles when Pyros was still in the egg; what she lacked in strength, she made up for in guile and cunning. The air crackled with flames, dragon blood dropped down like red rain.

Shrugging, Verminaard looked back at the four approaching him warily. He could hear the magic-user reminding his companions that Verminaard was a cleric of the Queen of

Darkness and—as such—could call upon her aid. Verminaard knew from his spies that this magic-user, though young, was imbued with a strange power and considered very dangerous.

The four did not speak. There was no need for talk among these men, nor was there need for talk between enemies. Respect, grudging as it may be, was apparent on both sides. As for the battle rage, that was unnecessary. This would be fought coolly. The major victor would be death.

And so the four came forward, spreading to outflank him since he had nothing to set his back against. Crouching low, Verminaard swung Nightbringer in an arc, keeping them back, forming his plans. He must even the odds quickly. Gripping Nightbringer in his right hand, the evil cleric sprang forward from his crouched stance with all the strength in his powerful legs. His sudden move took his opponents by surprise. He did not raise his mace. All he needed now was his deadly touch. Landing on his feet in front of Raistlin, he reached out and grasped the magic-user by the shoulder, whispering a swift prayer to his Dark Queen.

Raistlin screamed. His body pierced by unseen, unholy weapons, he sank to the ground in agony. Caramon gave a great, bellowing roar and sprang at Verminaard, but the cleric was prepared. He swung the mace, Nightbringer, and struck the warrior a glancing blow. "Midnight," Verminaard whispered, and Caramon's bellow changed to a shout of panic as the spellbound mace blinded him.

"I can't see! Tanis, help me!" the big warrior cried, stumbling about. Verminaard, laughing grimly, struck him a solid blow to the head. Caramon went down like a felled ox.

Out of the corner of his eye, Verminaard saw the half-elf leap for him, a two-handed sword of ancient elvish design in his hands. Verminaard whirled, blocking Tanis's sword with Nightbringer's massive, oaken handle. For a moment, the two combatants were locked together, but Verminaard's greater strength won out and he hurled Tanis to the ground.

The Solamnic knight raised his sword in salute—a costly mistake. It gave Verminaard time to remove a small iron needle from a hidden pocket. Raising it, he called once more upon the Queen of Darkness to defend her cleric. Sturm, striding forward, suddenly felt his body grow heavier and heavier until he could walk no more.

Tanis, lying on the ground, felt an unseen hand press down on him. He couldn't move. He couldn't turn his head. His tongue was too thick to speak. He could hear Raistlin's screams choke off in pain. He could hear Verminaard laugh and shout a hymn of praise to the Dark Queen. Tanis could only watch in despair as the Dragon Highlord, mace raised, walked toward Sturm, preparing to end the knight's life.

"*Baravais, Kharas!*" Verminaard said in Solamnic. He lifted the mace in a gruesome mockery of the knight's salute, then aimed for the knight's head, knowing that this death would be the most torturous possible for a knight—dying at the mercy of the enemy.

Suddenly a hand caught Verminaard's wrist. In astonishment, he stared at the hand, the hand of a female. He felt a power to match his own, a holiness to match his unholiness. At her touch, Verminaard's concentration wavered, his prayers to his Dark Queen faltered.

And then it was that the Dark Queen herself looked up to find a radiant god, dressed in white and shining armor, appear on the horizon of her plans. She was not ready to fight this god, she had not expected his return, and so she fled to rethink her options and restructure her battle, seeing—for the first time—the possibility of defeat. The Queen of Darkness withdrew and left her cleric to his fate.

Sturm felt the spell leave his body, his muscles his own to command once more. He saw Verminaard turn his fury on Goldmoon, striking at her savagely. The knight lunged forward, seeing Tanis rise, the elven sword flashing in the sunlight.

Both men ran toward Goldmoon, but Riverwind was there before them. Thrusting her out of the way, the Plainsman received on his sword arm the blow of the cleric's mace that had been intended to crush Goldmoon's head. Riverwind heard the cleric shout "Midnight!" and his vision was obscured by the same unholy darkness that had overtaken Caramon.

But the Que-shu warrior, expecting this, did not panic. Riverwind could still hear his enemy. Resolutely ignoring the pain of his injury, he transferred the sword to his left hand and stabbed in the direction of his enemy's harsh breathing. The blade, turned aside by the Dragon Highlord's powerful armor, was jarred from Riverwind's hand. Riverwind fumbled for his dagger, though he knew it was hopeless, that death was certain.

At that moment, Verminaard realized he was alone, bereft of spiritual help. He felt the cold, skeletal hand of despair clutch at him and he called to his Dark Queen. But she had turned away, absorbed in her own struggle.

Verminaard began to sweat beneath the dragonmask. He cursed it as the helm seemed to stifle him; he couldn't catch his breath. Too late he realized its unsuitableness for hand-to-hand combat—the mask blocked his peripheral vision. He saw the tall Plainsman, blind and wounded, before him—he could kill him at his leisure. But there were two other fighters near. The knight and the half-elf had been freed of the unholy spell he had cast on them and they were coming closer. He could hear them. Catching a glimpse of movement, he turned quickly and saw the half-elf running toward him, the elvish blade glistening. But where was the knight? Verminaard turned and backed up, swinging his mace to keep them at bay, while with his free hand, he struggled to rip the dragonhelm from his head.

Too late. Just as Verminaard's hand closed over the visor, the magic blade of Kith-Kanan pierced his armor and slid into his back. The Dragon Highlord screamed and whirled in rage, only to see the Solamnic knight appear in his blood-dimmed vision.

The ancient blade of Sturm's fathers plunged into his bowels. Verminaard fell to his knees. Still he struggled to remove the helm—he couldn't breathe, he couldn't see. He felt another sword thrust, then darkness overtook him.

High overhead, a dying Matafleur—weakened by loss of blood and many wounds—heard the voices of her children crying to her. She was confused and disoriented: Pyros seemed to be attacking from every direction at once. Then the big red dragon was before her, against the wall of the mountain. Matafleur saw her chance. She would save her children.

Pyros breathed a great blast of flame directly into the face of the ancient red dragon. He watched in satisfaction as the head withered, the eyes melted.

But Matafleur ignored the flames that seared her eyes, forever ending her vision, and flew straight at Pyros.

The big male dragon, his mind clouded by fury and pain and thinking he had finished his enemy, was taken by surprise. Even as he breathed again his deadly fire, he realized with horror the position he was in—he had allowed Matafleur to maneuver him between herself and the sheer face of the mountain. He had nowhere to go, no room to turn.

Matafleur soared into him with all the force of her once-powerful body, striking him like a spear hurled by the gods. Both dragons slammed against the mountain. The peak trembled and split apart as the face of the mountain exploded in flames.

In later years when the Death of Flamestrike was legend, there were those who claimed to have heard a dragon's voice fade away like smoke on an autumn wind, whispering:

"My children . . . "

THE WEDDING

The last day of autumn dawned clear and bright. The air was warm— touched by the fragrant wind from the south, which had blown steadily ever since the refugees fled Pax Tharkas, taking with them only what they could scrounge from the fortress as they fled the wrath of the dragonarmies.

It had taken long days for the draconian army to scale the walls of Pax Tharkas, its gates blocked by boulders, its towers defended by gully dwarves. Led by Sestun, the gully dwarves stood on top of the walls throwing rocks, dead rats, and occasionally each other down on the frustrated draconians. This allowed the refugees time to escape into the mountains where, although they skirmished with small forces of draconians, they were not seriously threatened.

Flint volunteered to lead a party of men through the mountains, searching for a place where the people could spend the winter. These mountains were familiar to Flint since the hill dwarves' homeland was not far to the south. Flint's party discovered a valley nestled between vast, craggy peaks whose treacherous passes were choked with snow in the winter. The passes could be easily held against the might of the dragonarmies and there were caves where they could hide from the fury of the dragons.

Following a dangerous path, the refugees fled into the mountains and entered the valley. An avalanche soon blocked the route behind them and destroyed all trace of their passing. It would be months before the draconians discovered them.

The valley, far below the mountain peaks, was warm and sheltered from the harsh winter winds and snows. The woods were filled with game. Clear streams flowed from the mountains. The people mourned their dead, rejoiced in their deliverance, built shelters, and celebrated a wedding.

On the last day of autumn, as the sun set behind the mountains, kindling their snow-capped peaks with flame the color of dying dragons, Riverwind and Goldmoon were married.

When the two came to Elistan to ask him to preside over their exchange of vows, he had been deeply honored and had asked them to explain the ways of their people to him. Both of them replied steadily that their people were dead. The Que-shu were gone, their ways were no more.

"This will be our ceremony," Riverwind said. "The beginning of something new, not the continuation of that which has passed away."

"Though we will honor the memory of our people in our hearts," Goldmoon added softly, "we must look forward, not behind. We will honor the past by taking from it the good and the sorrowful that have made us what we are. But the past shall rule us no longer."

Elistan, therefore, studied the Disks of Mishakal to find what the ancient gods taught about marriage. He asked Goldmoon and Riverwind to write their own vows, searching their hearts for the true meaning of their love—for these vows would be spoken before the gods and last beyond death.

One custom of the Que-shu the couple kept. This was that the bridegift and the groomgift could not be purchased. This symbol of love must be made by the hand of the beloved. The gifts would be exchanged with the saying of the vows.

As the sun's rays spread across the sky, Elistan took his place on the top of a gentle rise. The people gathered in silence at the foot of the hill. From the east came Tika and Laurana, bearing torches. Behind them walked Goldmoon, Chieftain's Daughter. Her hair fell down around her shoulders in streams of molten gold, mingled with silver. Her head was crowned with autumn leaves. She wore the simple fringed doeskin tunic she had worn through their adventures. The medallion of Mishakal glittered at her throat. She carried her bridegift wrapped in a cloth as fine as cobweb, for the beloved one's eyes must be the first to see it.

Tika walked before her in solemn, misty-eyed wonder, the young girl's heart filled with dreams of her own, beginning to think that this great mystery shared by men and women might not be the terrifying experience she had feared, but something sweet and beautiful.

Laurana, next to Tika, held her torch high, brightening the day's dying light. The people murmured at Goldmoon's beauty; they fell silent when Laurana passed. Goldmoon was human, her beauty the beauty of the trees and mountains and skies. Laurana's beauty was elvish, otherworldly, mysterious.

The two women brought the bride to Elistan, then they turned, looking to the west, waiting for the groom.

A blaze of torches lit Riverwind's way. Tanis and Sturm, their solemn faces wistful and gentle, led. Riverwind came behind, towering over the others, his face stern as always. But a radiant joy, brighter than the torches, lit his eyes. His black hair was crowned with autumn leaves, his groomgift covered by one of Tasslehoff's handkerchiefs. Behind him walked Flint and the kender. Caramon and Raistlin came last, the mage bearing the lighted-crystal Staff of Magius instead of a torch.

The men brought the groom to Elistan, then stepped back to join the women. Tika found herself standing next to Caramon. Reaching out timidly, she touched his hand. Smiling down at her gently, he clasped her little hand in his big one.

As Elistan looked at Riverwind and Goldmoon, he thought of the terrible grief and fear and danger they had faced, the harshness of their lives. Did their future hold anything different? For a moment he was overcome and could not speak. The two, seeing Elistan's emotion and, perhaps, understanding his sorrow, reached out to him reassuringly. Elistan drew them close to him, whispering words for them alone.

"It was your love and your faith in each other that brought hope to the world. Each of you was willing to sacrifice your life for this promise of hope, each has saved the life of the other. The sun shines now, but already its rays are dimming and night is ahead. It is the same for you, my friends. You will walk through much darkness before morning. But your love will be as a torch to light the way."

Elistan then stepped back and began to speak to all assembled. His voice, husky to begin with, grew stronger and stronger as he felt the peace of the gods surround him and confirm their blessings on this couple.

"The left hand is the hand of the heart," he said, placing Goldmoon's left hand in Riverwind's left hand and holding his own left hand over them. "We join left hands that the love in the hearts of this man and this woman may combine to form something greater as two streams join together to form a mighty river. The river flows through the land, branching off into tributaries, exploring new ways, yet ever drawn to the eternal sea. Receive their love, Paladine—greatest of the gods; bless it and grant them peace at least in the hearts, if there is no peace in this shattered land."

In the blessed silence, husbands and wives put their arms around each other. Friends drew close, children quieted and crept near their parents. Hearts filled with mourning were comforted. Peace was granted.

226

"Pledge your vows, one to another," Elistan said, "and exchange the gifts of your hands and hearts."

Goldmoon looked into Riverwind's eyes and began to speak softly.

Wars have settled on the North
and dragons ride the skies,
"Now is the time for wisdom,"
say the wise and the nearly wise.
"Here in the heart of battle,
the time to be brave is at hand.
Now most things are larger than
the promise of woman to man."

But you and I, through burning plains,
through darkness of the earth,
affirm this world, its people,
the heavens that gave them birth,
the breath that passes between us,
this altar where we stand,
and all those things made larger by
the promise of woman to man.

Then Riverwind spoke:

Now in the belly of winter,
when ground and sky are gray,
here in the heart of sleeping snow,
now is the time to say
yes to the sprouting vallenwood
in the green countryside,
for these things are far larger than
a man's word to his bride.

Through these promises we keep,
forged in the yawning night,

proved in the presence of heroes
and the prospect of spring light,
the children will see moons and stars
where now the dragons ride,
and humble things made large by
a man's word to his bride.

When the vows were spoken, they exchanged gifts. Goldmoon shyly handed her present to Riverwind. He unwrapped it with hands that trembled. It was a ring plaited of her own hair, bound with bands of silver and of gold as fine as the hair they surrounded. Goldmoon had given Flint her mother's jewelry; the dwarf's old hands had not lost their touch.

In the wreckage of Solace, Riverwind had found a vallenwood branch spared by the dragon's fire and had carried it in his pack. Now that branch made Riverwind's gift to Goldmoon—a ring, perfectly smooth and plain. When polished, the wood of the tree was a rich gold color, marked by streaks and whorls of softest brown. Goldmoon, holding it, remembered the first night she had seen the great vallenwoods, the night they had stumbled—weary and frightened—into Solace, bearing the blue crystal staff. She began to cry softly and wiped her eyes with Tas's handkerchief.

"Bless the gifts, Paladine," Elistan said, "these symbols of love and sacrifice. Grant that during times of deepest darkness, these two may look upon these gifts and see their path lighted by love. Great and shining god, god of human and elf, god of kender and dwarf, give your blessing to these, your children. May the love they plant in their hearts today be nourished by their souls and grow into a tree of life, providing shelter and protection to all who seek refuge beneath its spreading boughs. With the joining of hands, the exchanging of vows, the giving of gifts, you two, Riverwind, grandson of Wanderer, and Goldmoon, Chieftain's Daughter—become one—in your hearts, in the sight of men, in the eyes of the gods."

Riverwind took his ring from Goldmoon and placed it upon her slender finger. Goldmoon took her ring from Riverwind. He knelt before her—as would have been the custom of the Que-shu. But Goldmoon shook her head.

"Rise, warrior," she said, smiling through her tears.

"Is that a command?" he asked softly.

"It is the last command of Chieftain's Daughter," she whispered.

Riverwind stood up. Goldmoon placed the golden ring on his finger. Then Riverwind took her in his arms. She put her arms around him. Their lips met, their bodies melded together, their spirits joined. The people gave a great shout and torches flared. The sun sank behind the mountains, leaving the sky bathed in a pearl-like hue of purples and soft reds, which soon deepened into the sapphire of night.

The bride and groom were carried down the hill by the cheering throng and feasting and merriment began. Huge tables, carved from the pine trees of the forest, were set up on the grass. The children, freed at last from the awe of the ceremony, ran and shouted, playing at dragon slaying. Tonight care and worry were far from their minds. Men broached the huge casks of ale and wine they had salvaged in Pax Tharkas and began drinking salutes to the bride and groom. Women brought in huge plates of food—game and fruits and vegetables gathered in the forest and taken from the stores in Pax Tharkas.

"Get out of my way, don't crowd me," Caramon grumbled as he sat down at the table. The companions, laughing, moved over to give the big man room. Maritta and two other women came forward and placed a huge platter of deer meat before the big warrior.

"Real food," sighed the warrior.

"Hey," roared Flint, stabbing at a piece of sizzling meat on Caramon's plate with his fork, "you gonna eat that?"

Caramon promptly and silently—without missing a bite—emptied a flagon of ale over the dwarf's head.

Tanis and Sturm sat side by side, talking quietly. Tanis's eyes strayed to Laurana occasionally. She sat at a different table talking animatedly with Elistan. Tanis, thinking how lovely she looked tonight, realized how changed she was from the willful, lovesick girl who had followed him from Qualinesti. He told himself he liked the change in her. But he caught himself wondering just what she and Elistan found so interesting.

Sturm touched his arm. Tanis started. He had lost track of the conversation. Flushing, he began to apologize when he saw the look on Sturm's face.

"What is it?" Tanis said in alarm, half-rising.

"Hush, don't move!" Sturm ordered. "Just look—over there—sitting off to himself."

Tanis looked where Sturm gestured, puzzled, then he saw the man—sitting alone, hunched over his food, eating it absently as if he didn't really taste it. Whenever anyone approached, the man shrank back, eyeing him nervously until he passed. Suddenly, perhaps sensing Tanis's eyes on him, he raised his head and stared directly at them. The half-elf gasped and dropped his fork.

"But that's impossible!" he said in a strangled voice. "We saw him die! With Eben! No one could have survived—"

"Then I was right," Sturm said grimly. "You recognize him, too. I thought I was going mad. Let's go talk to him."

But when they looked again, he was gone. Swiftly, they searched the crowd, but it was impossible to find him now.

As the silver moon and the red rose in the sky, the married couples formed a ring around the bride and groom and began singing wedding songs. Unmarried couples danced in pairs outside the circle while the children leaped and shouted and reveled in staying up past their bedtime. Bonfires burned brightly, voices and music filled the night air, the silver moon and the red rose to light the sky. Goldmoon and Riverwind stood, their arms around each other, their eyes shining brighter than the moons or the blazing fire.

Tanis lingered on the outskirts, watching his friends. Laurana and Gilthanas performed an ancient elvish dance of grace and beauty, singing together a hymn of joy. Sturm and Elistan fell into conversation about their plans to travel south in search of the legendary seaport city of Tarsis the Beautiful, where they hoped to find ships to carry the people from this war-torn land. Tika, tired of watching Caramon eat, teased Flint until the dwarf finally agreed to dance with her, blushing bright red beneath his beard.

Where was Raistlin? Tanis wondered. The half-elf recalled seeing him at the banquet. The mage ate little and drank his herbal mixture. He had seemed unusually pale and quiet. Tanis decided to go in search of him. The company of the dark-souled, cynical mage seemed more suited to him tonight than music and laughter.

Tanis wandered into the moonlit darkness, knowing somehow he was headed in the right direction. He found Raistlin sitting on the stump of an old tree whose lightning-shattered, blackened remains lay scattered over the ground. The half-elf sat down next to the silent mage.

A small shadow settled among the trees behind the half-elf. Finally, Tas would hear what these two discussed!

Raistlin's strange eyes stared into the southlands, barely visible between a gap in the tall mountains. The wind still blew from the south, but it was beginning to veer again. The temperature was falling. Tanis felt Raistlin's frail body shiver. Looking at him in the moonlight, Tanis was startled to see the mage's resemblance to his half-sister, Kitiara. It was a fleeting impression and gone almost as soon as it came, but it brought the woman to Tanis's mind, adding to his feelings of unrest and disquiet. He restlessly tossed a piece of bark back and forth, from hand to hand.

"What do you see to the south?" Tanis asked abruptly.

Raistlin glanced at him. "What do I ever see with these eyes of mine, Half-Elf?" the mage whispered bitterly. "I see death, death and destruction. I see war." He gestured up above. "The constellations have not returned. The Queen of Darkness is not defeated."

"We may not have won the war," Tanis began, "but surely we have won a major battle—"

Raistlin coughed and shook his head sadly.

"Do you see no hope?"

"Hope is the denial of reality. It is the carrot dangled before the draft horse to keep him plodding along in a vain attempt to reach it."

"Are you saying we should just give up?" Tanis asked, irritably tossing the bark away.

"I'm saying we should remove the carrot and walk forward with our eyes open," Raistlin answered. Coughing, he drew his robes more closely around him. "How will you fight the dragons, Tanis? For there will be more! More than you can imagine! And where now is Huma? Where now is the Dragonlance? No, Half-Elf. Do not talk to me of hope."

Tanis did not answer, nor did the mage speak again. Both sat silently, one continuing to stare south, the other glancing up into the great voids in the glittering, starlit sky.

Tasslehoff sank back into the soft grass beneath the pine trees. "No hope!" the kender repeated bleakly, sorry he had followed the half-elf. "I don't believe it," he said, but his eyes went to Tanis, staring at the stars. Tanis believes it, the kender realized, and the thought filled him with dread.

Ever since the death of the old magician, an unnoticed change had come over the kender. Tasslehoff began to consider that this adventure was in earnest, that it had a purpose for which people gave their lives. He wondered why he was involved and thought perhaps he had given the answer to Fizban—the small things he was meant to do were important, somehow, in the big scheme of things.

But until now it had never occurred to the kender that all this might be for nothing, that it might not make any difference, that they might suffer and lose people they loved like Fizban, and the dragons would still win in the end.

"Still," the kender said softly, "we have to keep trying and hoping. That's what's important, the trying and the hoping. Maybe that's most important of all."

Something floated gently down from the sky, brushing past the kender's nose. Tas reached out and caught it in his hand.

It was a small, white chicken feather.

The "Song of Huma" was the last, and many consider the greatest, work of the elven bard, Quivalen Soth. Only fragments of the work remained following the Cataclysm. It is said that those who study it diligently will find hints to the future of the turning world.

SONG OF HUMA

Out of the village, out of the thatched and clutching shires,
Out of the grave and furrow, furrow and grave,
Where his sword first tried
The last cruel dances of childhood, and awoke to the shires
Forever retreating, his greatness a marshfire,
The banked flight of the Kingfisher always above him,
Now Huma walked upon Roses,
In the level Light of the Rose.
And troubled by Dragons, he turned to the end of the land,
To the fringe of all sense and senses,
To the Wilderness, where Paladine bade him to turn,
And there in the loud tunnel of knives
He grew in unblemished violence, in yearning,
Stunned into himself by a deafening gauntlet of voices.

It was there and then that the White Stag found him,
At the end of a journey planned from the shores of
Creation,
And all time staggered at the forest edge
Where Huma, haunted and starving,
Drew his bow, thanking the gods for their bounty
and keeping,
Then saw, in the ranged wood,
In the first silence, the dazed heart's symbol,
The rack of antlers resplendent.
He lowered the bow and the world resumed.

235

Then Huma followed the Stag, its tangle of antlers receding
As a memory of young light, as the talons of birds ascending.
The Mountains crouched before them. Nothing would
change now,
The three moons stopped in the sky,
And the long night tumbled in shadows.

It was morning when they reached the grove,
The lap of the mountain, where the Stag departed,
Nor did Huma follow, knowing the end of this journey
Was nothing but green and the promise of green
that endured
In the eyes of the woman before him.
And holy the days he drew near her, holy the air
That carried his words of endearment, his forgotten songs,
And the rapt moons knelt on the Great Mountain.
Still, she eluded him, bright and retreating as marshfire,
Nameless and lovely, more lovely because she was nameless,
As they learned that the world, the dazzling shelves
of the air,
The Wilderness itself
Were plain and diminished things to the heart's thicket.
At the end of the days, she told him her secret.

For she was not of woman, nor was she mortal,
But the daughter and heiress from a line of Dragons.
For Huma the sky turned indifferent, cluttered by moons,
The brief life of the grass mocked him, mocked his fathers,
And the thorned light bristled on the gliding Mountain.
But nameless she tendered a hope not in her keeping,
That Paladine only might answer, that through his
enduring wisdom
She might step from forever, and there in her silver arms
The promise of the grove might rise and flourish.
For that wisdom Huma prayed, and the Stag returned,
And east, through the desolate fields, through ash,

Through cinders and blood, the harvest of dragons,
Traveled Huma, cradled by dreams of the Silver Dragon,
The Stag perpetual, a signal before him.

At last the eventual harbor, a temple so far to the east
That it lay where the east was ending.
There Paladine appeared
In a pool of stars and glory, announcing
That of all choices, one most terrible had fallen to Huma.
For Paladine knew that the heart is a nest of yearnings,
That we can travel forever toward light, becoming
What we can never be.
For the bride of Huma could step into the devouring sun,
Together they would return to the thatched shires
And leave behind the secret of the Lance, the world
Unpeopled in darkness, wed to the dragons.
Or Huma could take on the Dragonlance, cleansing
all Krynn
Of death and invasion, of the green paths of his love.

The hardest of choices, and Huma remembered
How the Wilderness cloistered and baptized his first
thoughts
Beneath the sheltering sun, and now
As the black moon wheeled and pivoted, drawing the air
And the substance from Krynn, from the things of Krynn,
From the grove, from the Mountain, from the abandoned
shires,
He would sleep, he would send it all away,
For the choosing was all of the pain, and the choices
Were heat on the hand when the arm has been severed.
But she came to him, weeping and luminous,
In a landscape of dreams, where he saw
The world collapse and renew on the glint of the Lance.
In her farewell lay collapse and renewal.
Through his doomed veins the horizon burst.

He took up the Dragonlance, he took up the story,
The pale heat rushed through his rising arm
And the sun and the three moons, waiting for wonders,
Hung in the sky together.
To the West Huma rode, to the High Clerist's Tower
On the back of the Silver Dragon,
And the path of their flight crossed over a desolate country
Where the dead walked only, mouthing the names
of dragons.
And the men in the Tower, surrounded and riddled
by dragons,
By the cries of the dying, the roar in the ravenous air,
Awaited the unspeakable silence,
Awaited far worse, in fear that the crash of the senses
Would end in a moment of nothing
Where the mind lies down with its losses and darkness.

But the winding of Huma's horn in the distance
Danced on the battlements. All of Solamnia lifted
Its face to the eastern sky, and the dragons
Wheeled to the highest air, believing
Some terrible change had come.
From out of their tumult of wings, out of the chaos
of dragons,
Out of the heart of nothing, the Mother of Night,
Aswirl in a blankness of colors,
Swooped to the East, into the stare of the sun
And the sky collapsed into silver and blankness.
On the ground Huma lay, at his side a woman,
Her silver skin broken, the promise of green
Released from the gifts of her eyes. She whispered her name
As the Queen of Darkness banked in the sky above Huma.
She descended, the Mother of Night,
And from the loft of the battlements, men saw shadows
Boil on the colorless dive of her wings:
A hovel of thatch and rushes, the heart of a Wilderness,

MARGARET WEIS & TRACY HICKMAN

A lost silver light spattered in terrible crimson,
And then from the center of shadows
Came a depth in which darkness itself was aglimmer,
Denying all air, all light, all shadows.
And thrusting his lance into emptiness,
Huma fell to the sweetness of death, into abiding sunlight.
Through the Lance, through the dear might and
brotherhood
Of those who must walk to the end of the breath
and the senses,
He banished the dragons back to the core of nothing,
And the long lands blossomed in balance and music.

Stunned in new freedom, stunned by the brightness
and colors,
By the harped blessing of the holy winds,
The Knights carried Huma, they carried the Dragonlance
To the grove in the lap of the Mountain.
When they returned to the grove in pilgrimage, in homage,
The Lance, the armor, the Dragonbane himself
Had vanished to the day's eye.
But the night of the full moons red and silver
Shines down on the hills, on the forms of a man
and a woman
Shimmering steel and silver, silver and steel,
Above the village, over the thatched and nurturing shires.

About the Authors

Margaret Weis is the author of fourteen DRAGONLANCE novels, the four-volume galactic fantasy Star of the Guardian, co-author with Don Perrin of *The Doom Brigade, Draconian Measures, Knights of the Black Earth, Robot Blues, Hung Out,* and *Brothers in Arms.* She currently lives in a converted barn in southern Wisconsin.

Tracy Hickman started at TSR, Inc. as a game designer, where he helped conceive of the world that became the DRAGONLANCE campaign setting. He has written, in collaboration with Margaret Weis, many DRAGONLANCE novels, the Darksword series, and the Death Gate Cycle. He and his wife Laura are currently at work on a new fantasy series. He lives in Utah with his wife, two daughters, and two sons.

The story continues in

The Nightmare Lands
By Margaret Weis & Tracy Hickman

Available October 2003